MINECRAFT™

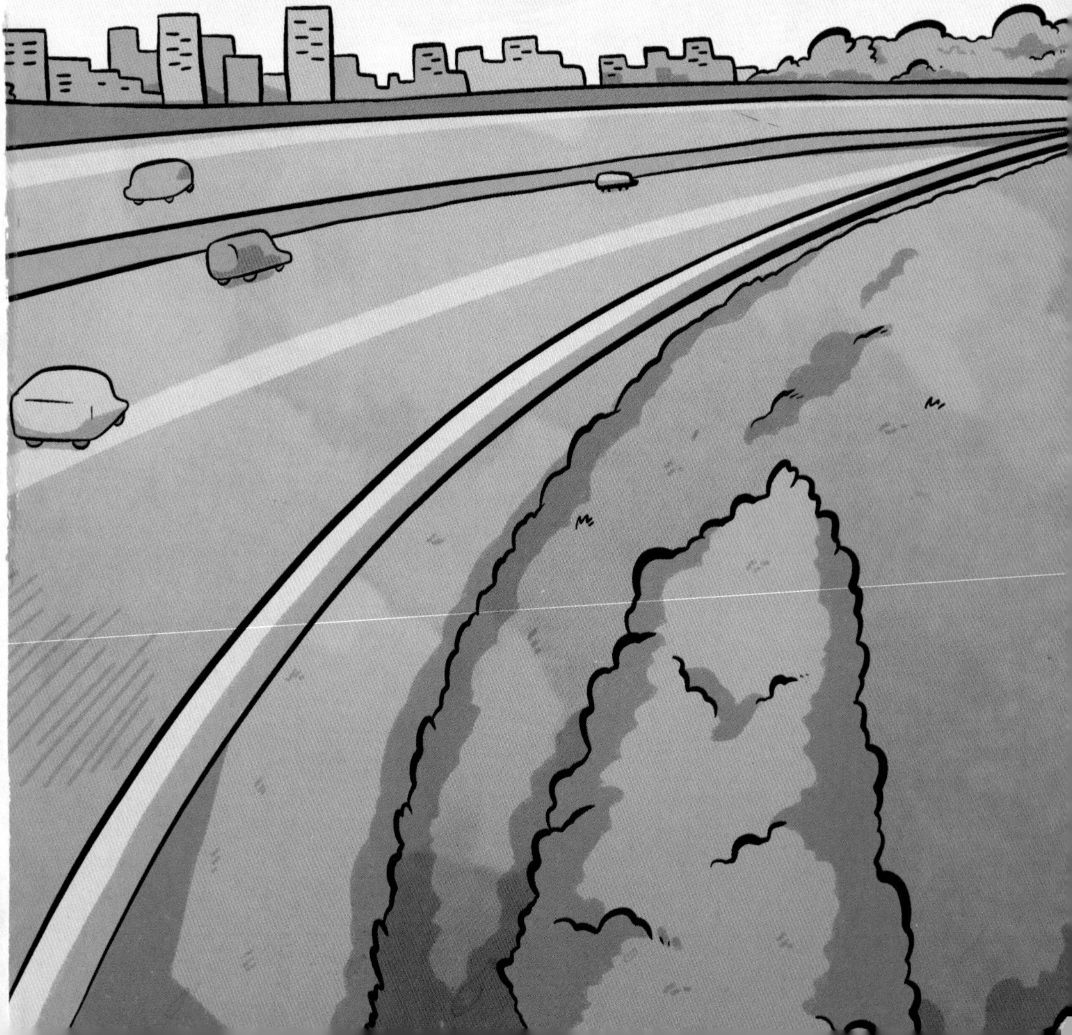

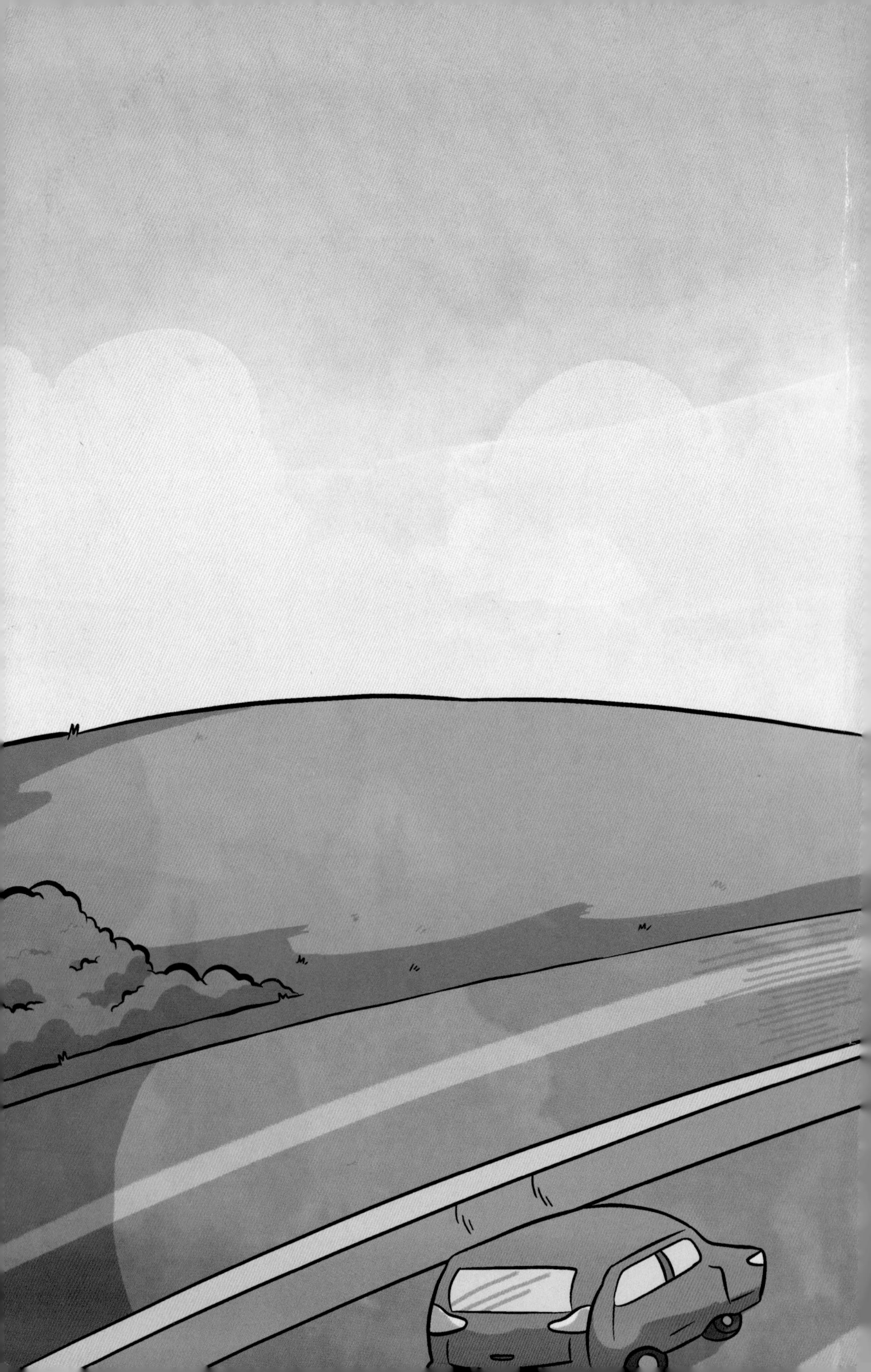

MINECRAFT™

WRITTEN BY
SFÉ R. MONSTER

ILLUSTRATED BY
SARAH GRALEY

COLOR ASSISTANCE BY
STEF PURENINS

LETTERED BY
JOHN J. HILL

MOJANG STUDIOS

DARK HORSE BOOKS

PRESIDENT & PUBLISHER
MIKE RICHARDSON

EDITOR
SHANTEL LaROCQUE

ASSOCIATE EDITOR
BRETT ISRAEL

ASSISTANT EDITOR
SANJAY DHARAWAT

DESIGNER
KEITH WOOD

DIGITAL ART TECHNICIAN
SAMANTHA HUMMER

SPECIAL THANKS TO
**ALEX WILTSHIRE, KELSEY HOWARD,
AND SHERIN KWAN.**

Published by Dark Horse Books
A division of Dark Horse Comics LLC
10956 SE Main Street
Milwaukie, OR 97222

MINECRAFT.NET
DARKHORSE.COM

To find a comics shop in your area, visit ComicShopLocator.com.

First edition: October 2021
Ebook ISBN 978-1-50672-581-9
Trade paperback ISBN 978-1-50672-580-2

10 9 8 7 6 5 4 3 2 1

Printed in China

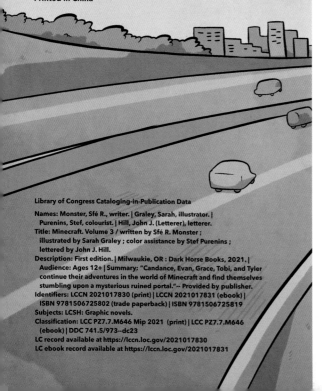

Neil Hankerson
Executive Vice President

Tom Weddle
Chief Financial Officer

Dale LaFountain
Chief Information Officer

Tim Wiesch
Vice President of Licensing

Matt Parkinson
Vice President of Marketing

Vanessa Todd-Holmes
Vice President of Production and Scheduling

Mark Bernardi
Vice President of Book Trade and Digital Sales

Ken Lizzi
General Counsel

Dave Marshall
Editor in Chief

Davey Estrada
Editorial Director

Chris Warner
Senior Books Editor

Cary Grazzini
Director of Specialty Projects

Lia Ribacchi
Art Director

Matt Dryer
Director of Digital Art and Prepress

Michael Gombos
Senior Director of Licensed Publications

Kari Yadro
Director of Custom Programs

Kari Torson
Director of International Licensing

Sean Brice
Director of Trade Sales

Randy Lahrman
Director of Product Sales

MINECRAFT™

Minecraft™ © 2021 Mojang AB. All Rights Reserved.
Minecraft, the MINECRAFT logo and the MOJANG
STUDIOS logo are trademarks of the Microsoft
group of companies. Dark Horse Books® and the
Dark Horse logo are registered trademarks of Dark
Horse Comics LLC. All rights reserved. No portion of
this publication may be reproduced or transmitted,
in any form or by any means, without the express
written permission of Dark Horse Comics, Inc. Names,
characters, places, and incidents featured in this
publication either are the product of the author's
imagination or are used fictitiously. Any resemblance
to actual persons (living or dead), events, institutions,
or locales, without satiric intent, is coincidental.

Library of Congress Cataloging-in-Publication Data

Names: Monster, Sfé R., writer. | Graley, Sarah, illustrator. |
    Purenins, Stef, colourist. | Hill, John J. (Letterer), letterer.
Title: Minecraft. Volume 3 / written by Sfé R. Monster ;
    illustrated by Sarah Graley ; color assistance by Stef Purenins ;
    lettered by John J. Hill.
Description: First edition. | Milwaukie, OR : Dark Horse Books, 2021. |
    Audience: Ages 12+ | Summary: "Candance, Evan, Grace, Tobi, and Tyler
    continue their adventures in the world of Minecraft and find themselves
    stumbling upon a mysterious ruined portal."-- Provided by publisher.
Identifiers: LCCN 2021017830 (print) | LCCN 2021017831 (ebook) |
    ISBN 9781506725802 (trade paperback) | ISBN 9781506725819
Subjects: LCSH: Graphic novels.
Classification: LCC PZ7.7.M646 Mip 2021 (print) | LCC PZ7.7.M646
    (ebook) | DDC 741.5/973--dc23
LC record available at https://lccn.loc.gov/2021017830
LC ebook record available at https://lccn.loc.gov/2021017831

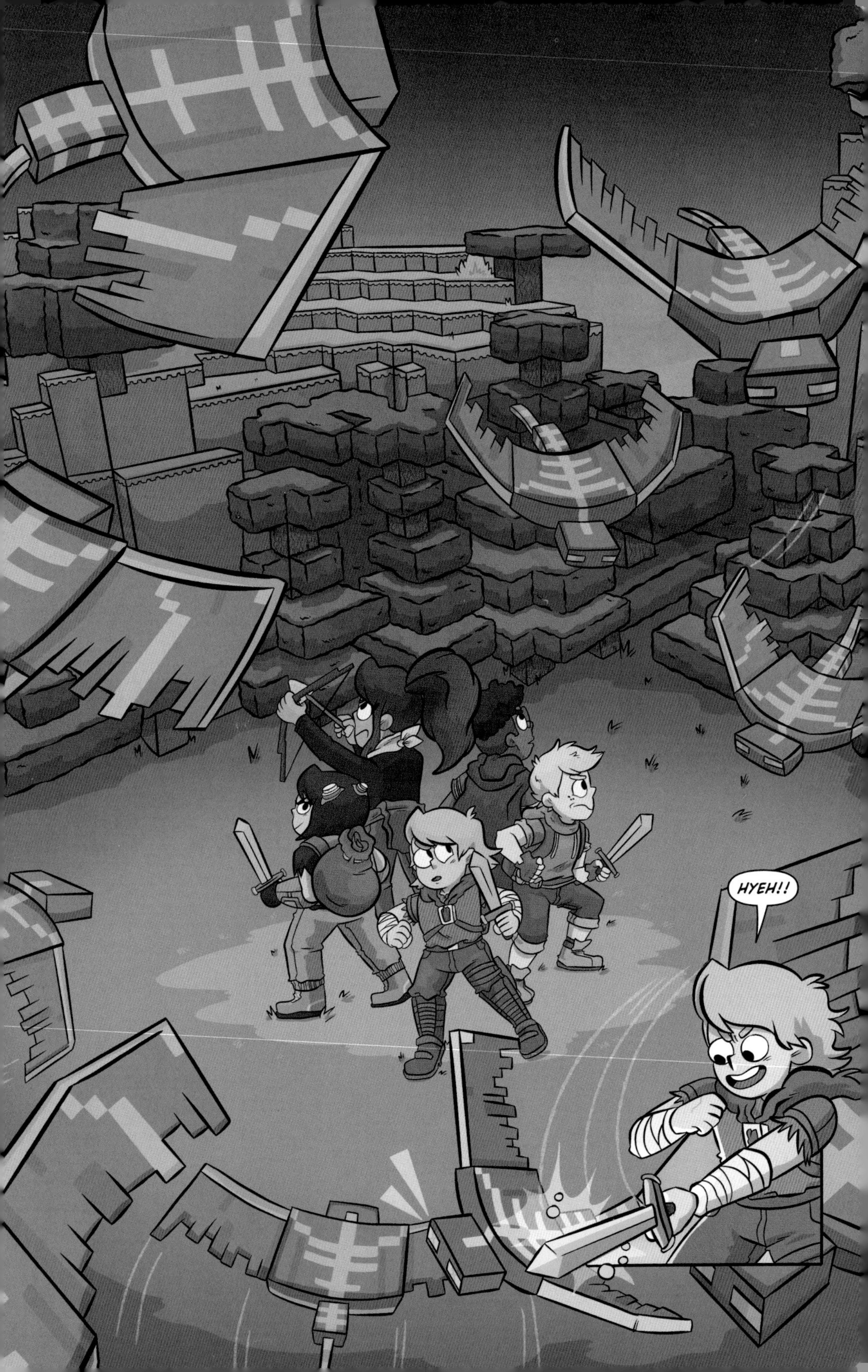
HYEH!!

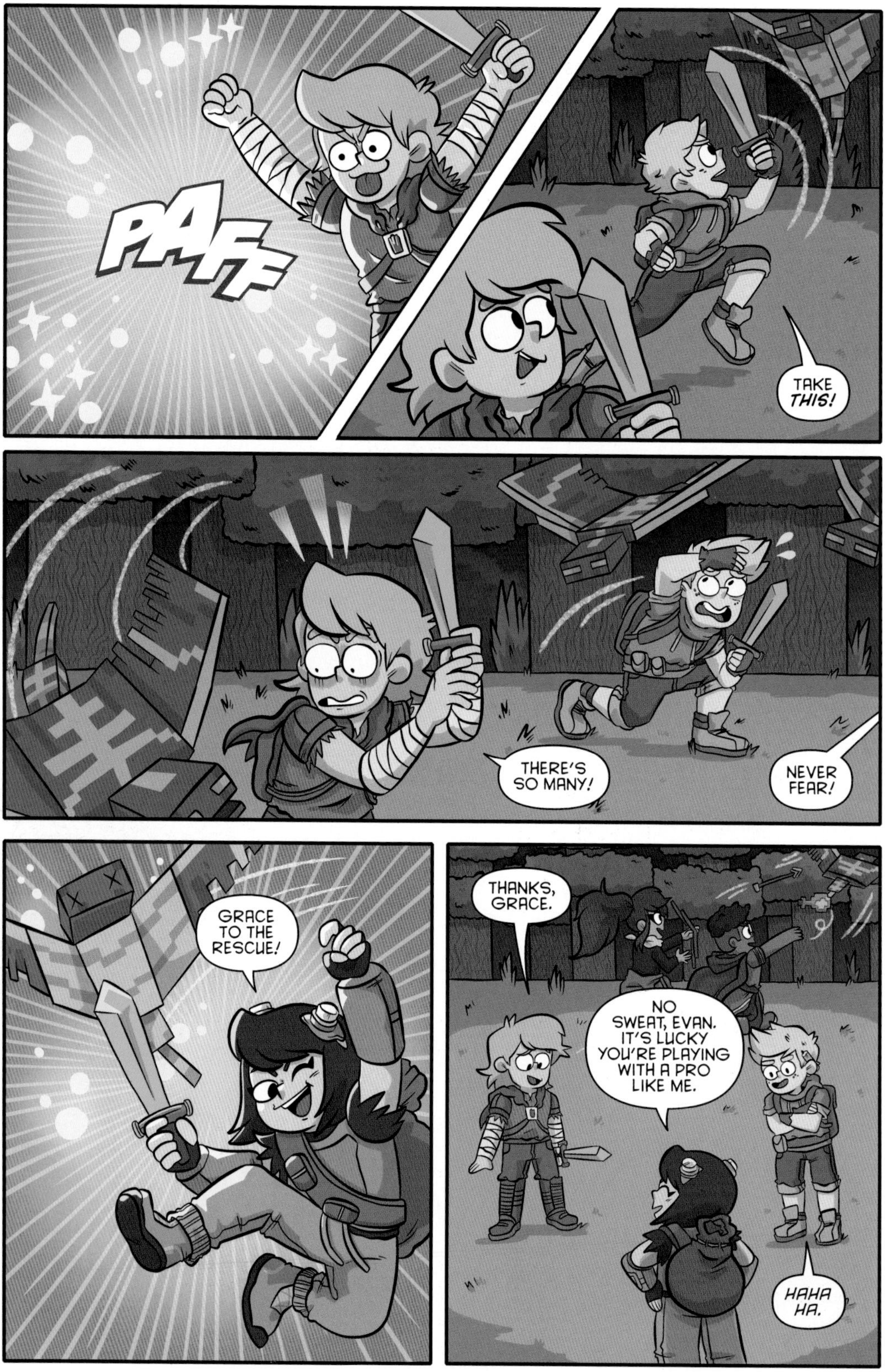
PAFF
TAKE THIS!
THERE'S SO MANY!
NEVER FEAR!
GRACE TO THE RESCUE!
THANKS, GRACE.
NO SWEAT, EVAN. IT'S LUCKY YOU'RE PLAYING WITH A PRO LIKE ME.
HAHA HA.

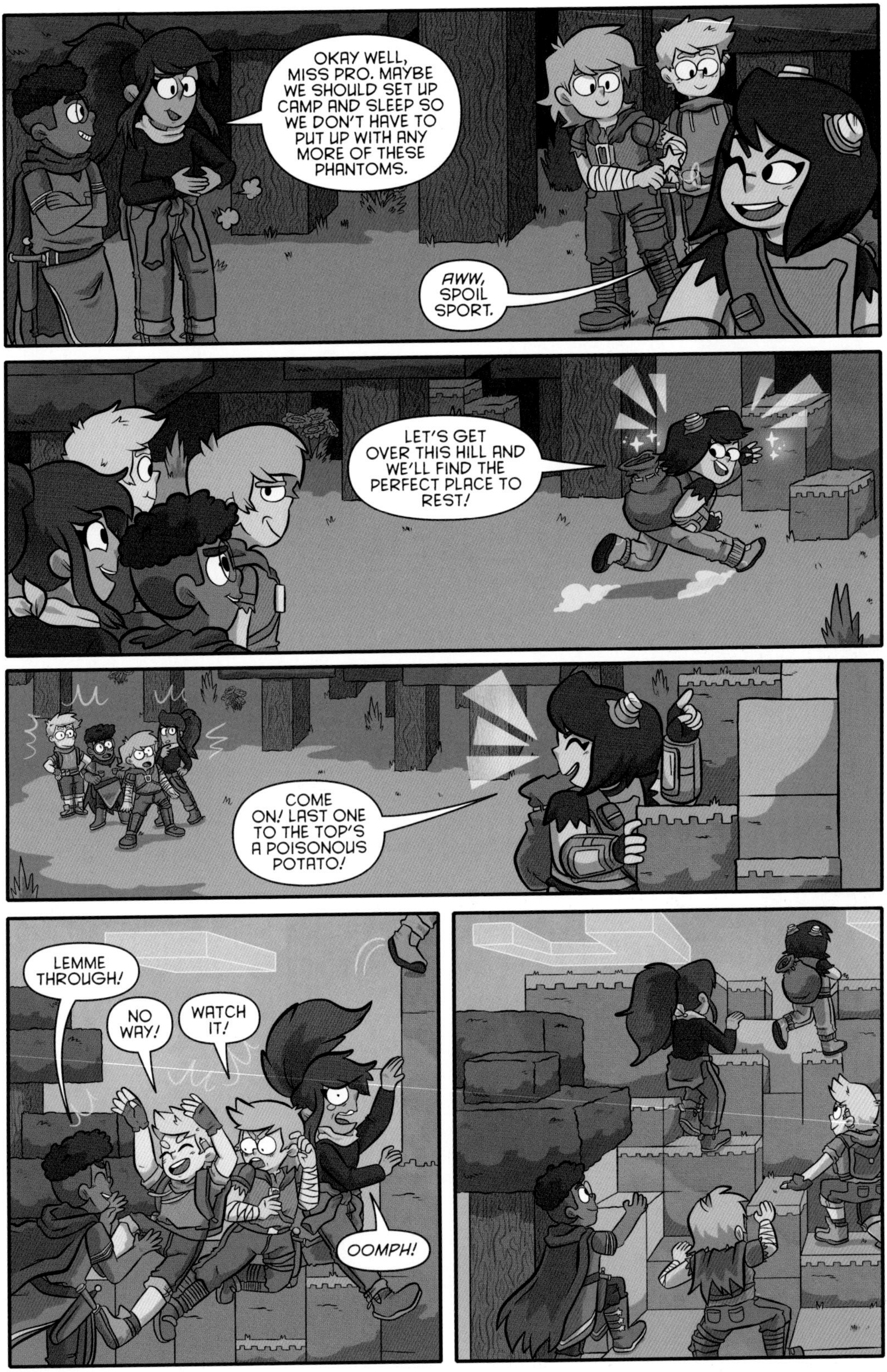
OKAY WELL, MISS PRO. MAYBE WE SHOULD SET UP CAMP AND SLEEP SO WE DON'T HAVE TO PUT UP WITH ANY MORE OF THESE PHANTOMS.
AWW, SPOIL SPORT.
LET'S GET OVER THIS HILL AND WE'LL FIND THE PERFECT PLACE TO REST!
COME ON! LAST ONE TO THE TOP'S A POISONOUS POTATO!
LEMME THROUGH!
NO WAY!
WATCH IT!
OOMPH!

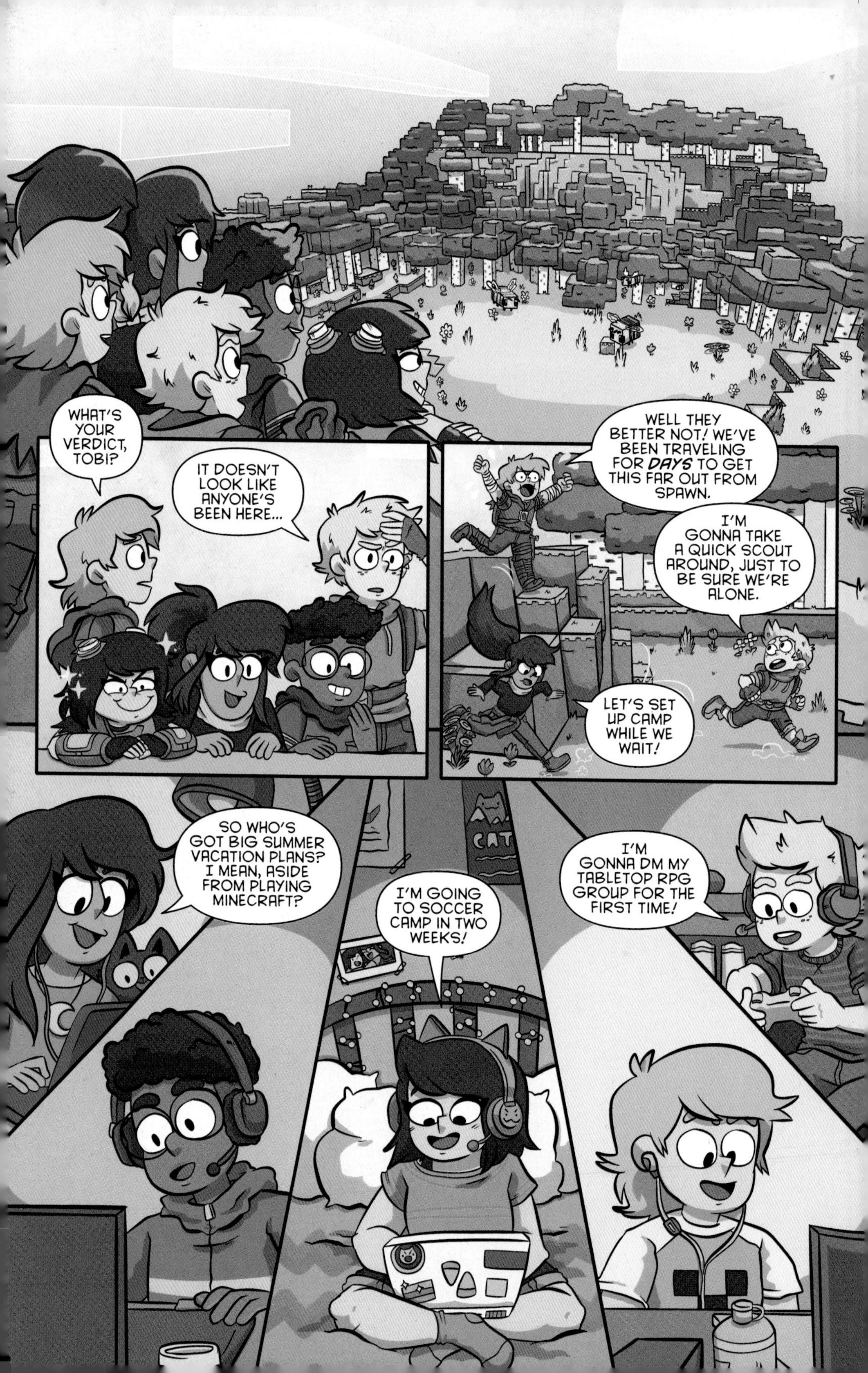
WHAT'S YOUR VERDICT, TOBI?
IT DOESN'T LOOK LIKE ANYONE'S BEEN HERE...
WELL THEY BETTER NOT! WE'VE BEEN TRAVELING FOR DAYS TO GET THIS FAR OUT FROM SPAWN.
I'M GONNA TAKE A QUICK SCOUT AROUND, JUST TO BE SURE WE'RE ALONE.
LET'S SET UP CAMP WHILE WE WAIT!
SO WHO'S GOT BIG SUMMER VACATION PLANS? I MEAN, ASIDE FROM PLAYING MINECRAFT?
I'M GOING TO SOCCER CAMP IN TWO WEEKS!
I'M GONNA DM MY TABLETOP RPG GROUP FOR THE FIRST TIME!

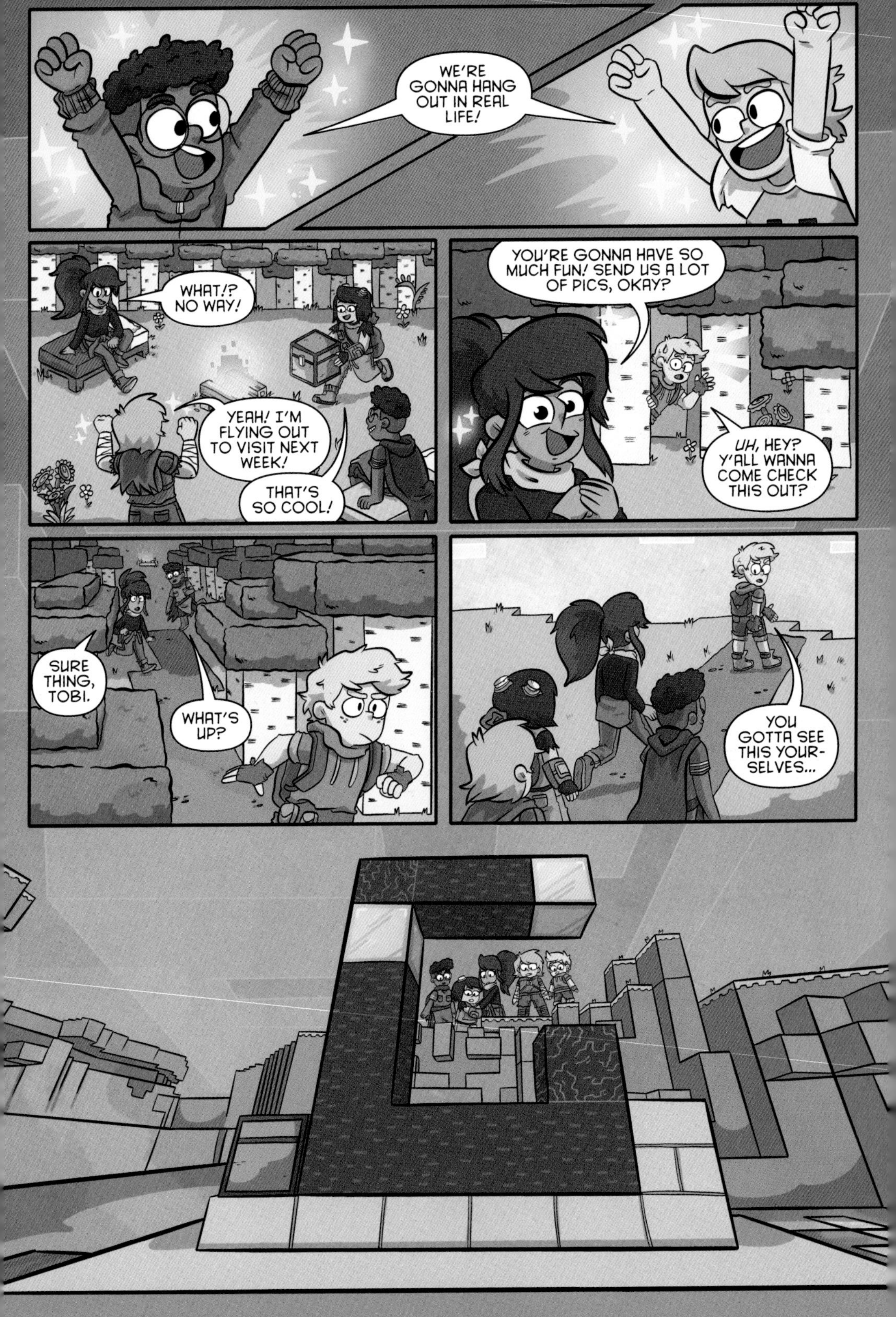
WE'RE GONNA HANG OUT IN REAL LIFE!
WHAT!? NO WAY!
YEAH! I'M FLYING OUT TO VISIT NEXT WEEK!
THAT'S SO COOL!
YOU'RE GONNA HAVE SO MUCH FUN! SEND US A LOT OF PICS, OKAY?
UH, HEY? Y'ALL WANNA COME CHECK THIS OUT?
SURE THING, TOBI.
WHAT'S UP?
YOU GOTTA SEE THIS YOUR-SELVES...

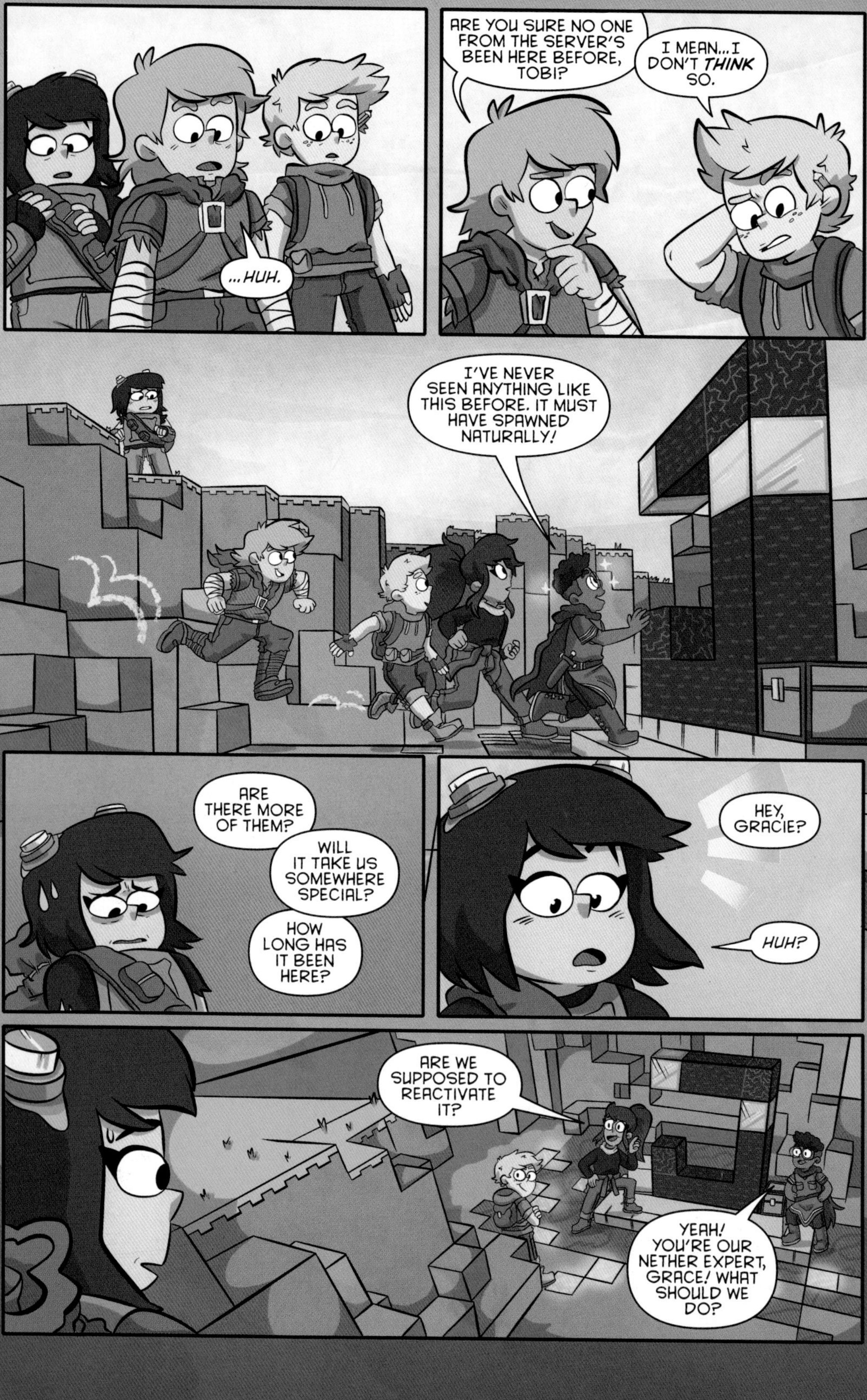
...HUH.
ARE YOU SURE NO ONE FROM THE SERVER'S BEEN HERE BEFORE, TOBI?
I MEAN...I DON'T *THINK* SO.
I'VE NEVER SEEN ANYTHING LIKE THIS BEFORE. IT MUST HAVE SPAWNED NATURALLY!
ARE THERE MORE OF THEM?
WILL IT TAKE US SOMEWHERE SPECIAL?
HOW LONG HAS IT BEEN HERE?
HEY, GRACIE?
HUH?
ARE WE SUPPOSED TO REACTIVATE IT?
YEAH! YOU'RE OUR NETHER EXPERT, GRACE! WHAT SHOULD WE DO?

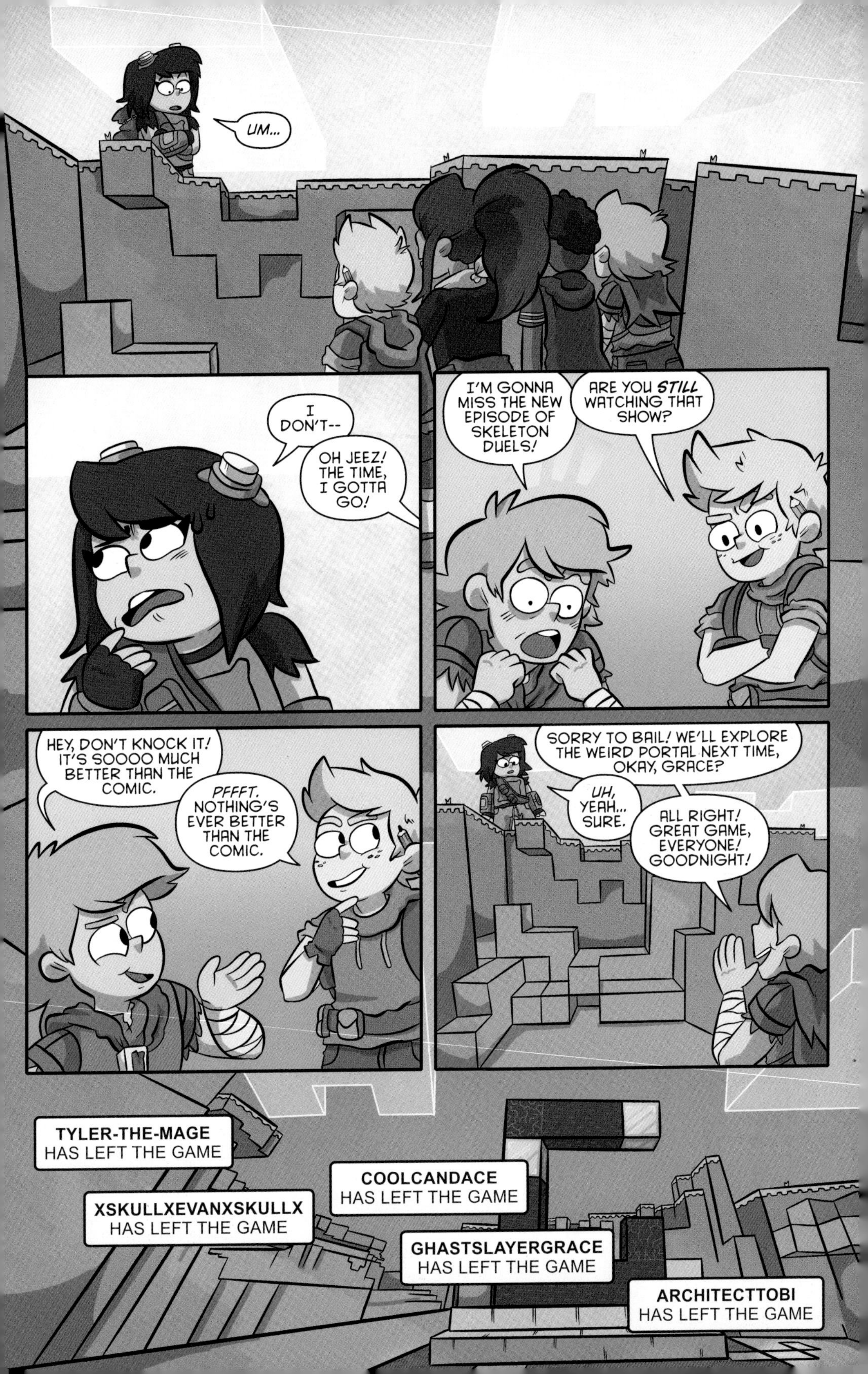
UM...
I DON'T--
OH JEEZ! THE TIME, I GOTTA GO!
I'M GONNA MISS THE NEW EPISODE OF SKELETON DUELS!
ARE YOU STILL WATCHING THAT SHOW?
HEY, DON'T KNOCK IT! IT'S SOOOO MUCH BETTER THAN THE COMIC.
PFFFT. NOTHING'S EVER BETTER THAN THE COMIC.
SORRY TO BAIL! WE'LL EXPLORE THE WEIRD PORTAL NEXT TIME, OKAY, GRACE?
UH, YEAH... SURE.
ALL RIGHT! GREAT GAME, EVERYONE! GOODNIGHT!
TYLER-THE-MAGE HAS LEFT THE GAME
XSKULLXEVANXSKULLX HAS LEFT THE GAME
COOLCANDACE HAS LEFT THE GAME
GHASTSLAYERGRACE HAS LEFT THE GAME
ARCHITECTTOBI HAS LEFT THE GAME

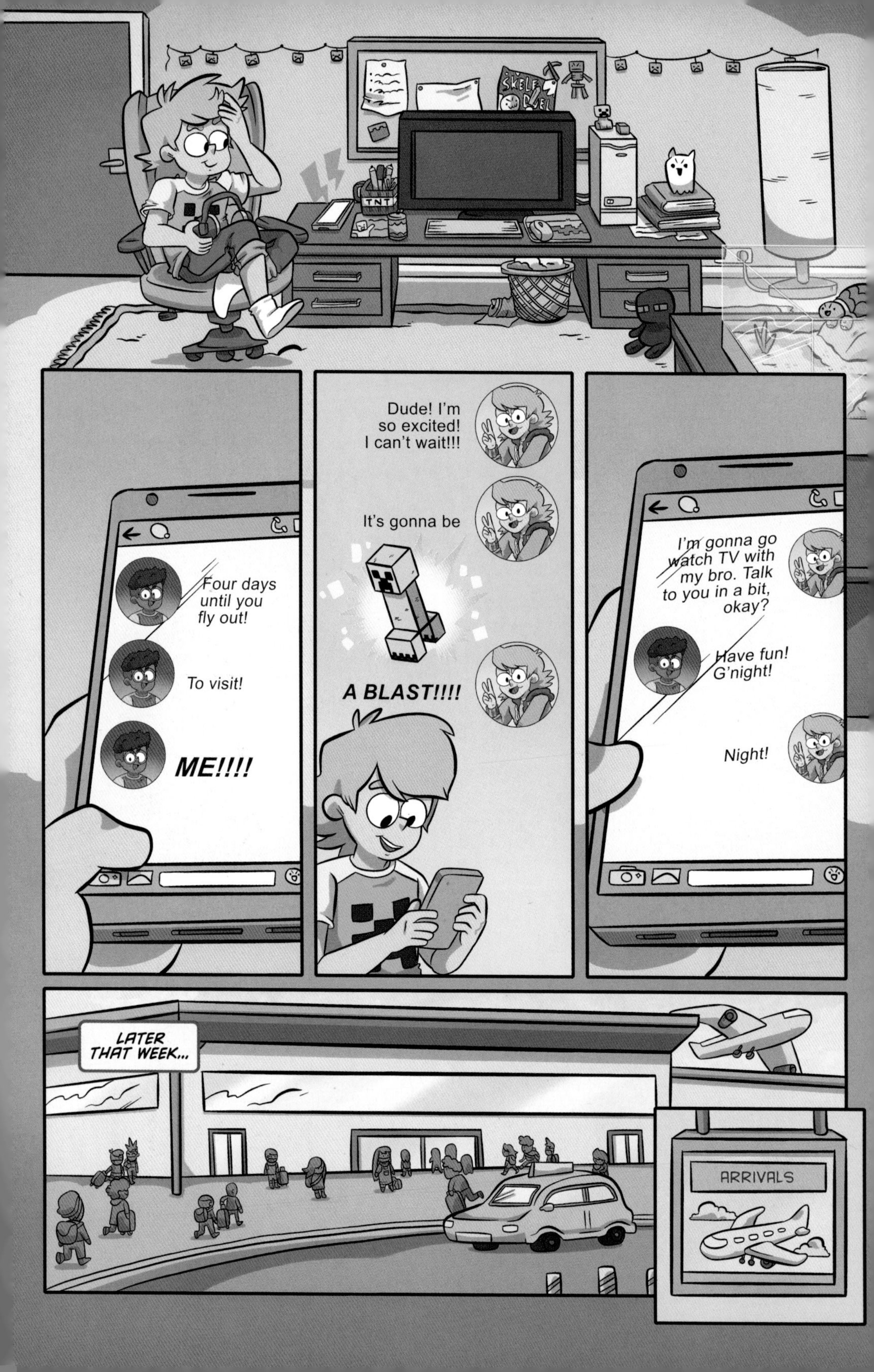

TNT
Four days until you fly out!
To visit!
ME!!!!
Dude! I'm so excited! I can't wait!!!
It's gonna be
A BLAST!!!!
I'm gonna go watch TV with my bro. Talk to you in a bit, okay?
Have fun! G'night!
Night!
LATER THAT WEEK...
ARRIVALS

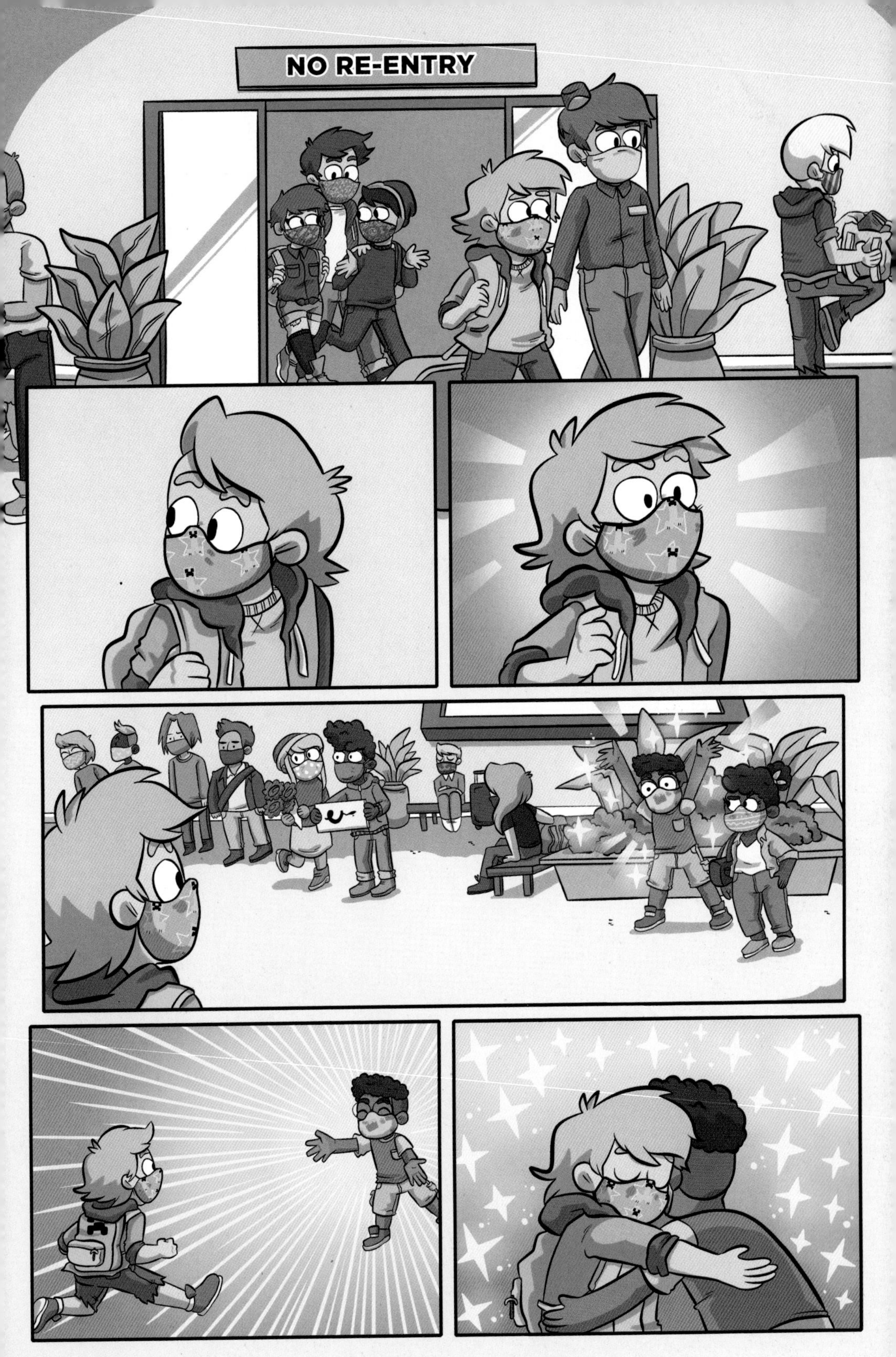
NO RE-ENTRY

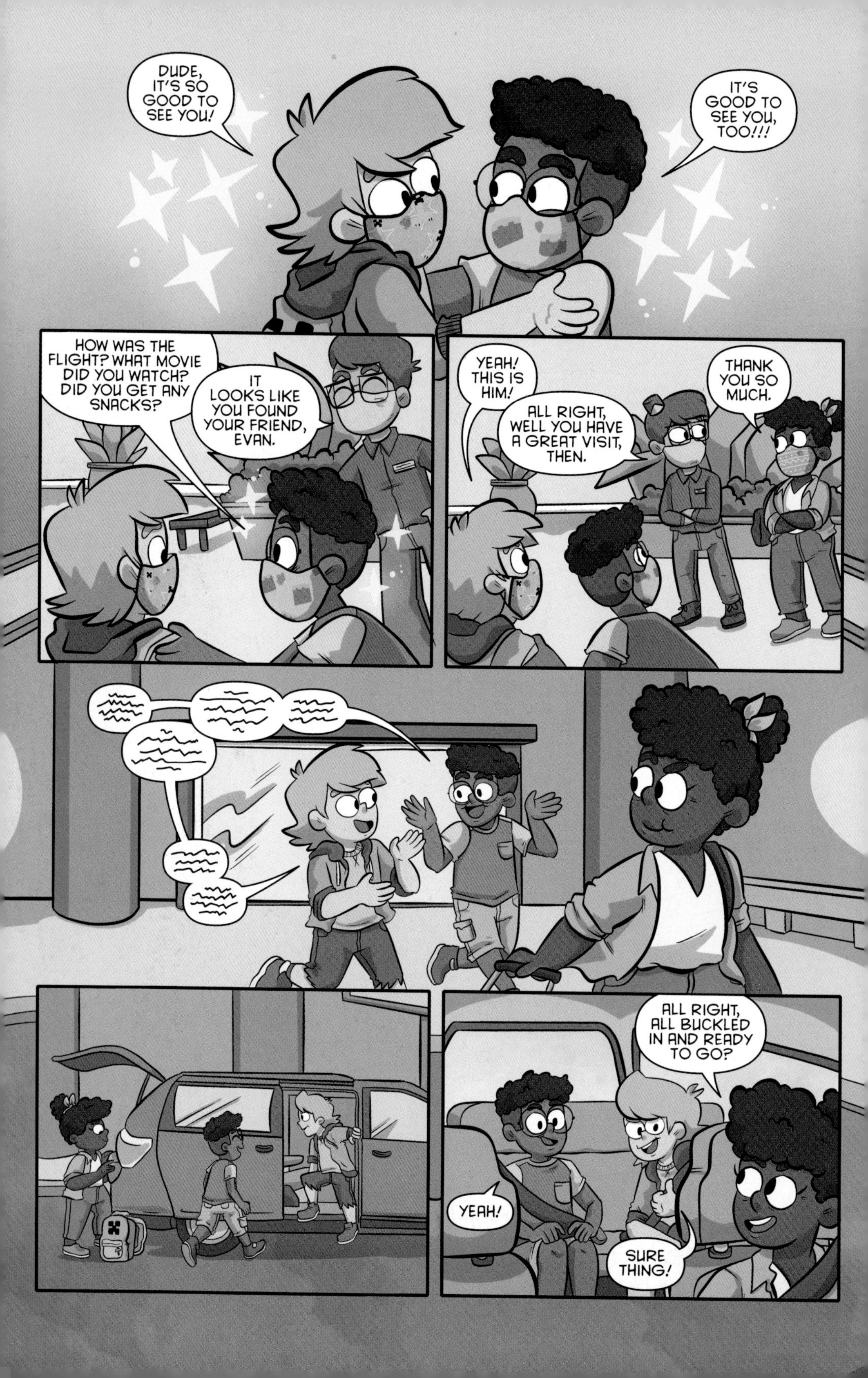
DUDE, IT'S SO GOOD TO SEE YOU!
IT'S GOOD TO SEE YOU, TOO!!!
HOW WAS THE FLIGHT? WHAT MOVIE DID YOU WATCH? DID YOU GET ANY SNACKS?
IT LOOKS LIKE YOU FOUND YOUR FRIEND, EVAN.
YEAH! THIS IS HIM!
ALL RIGHT, WELL YOU HAVE A GREAT VISIT, THEN.
THANK YOU SO MUCH.
ALL RIGHT, ALL BUCKLED IN AND READY TO GO?
YEAH!
SURE THING!

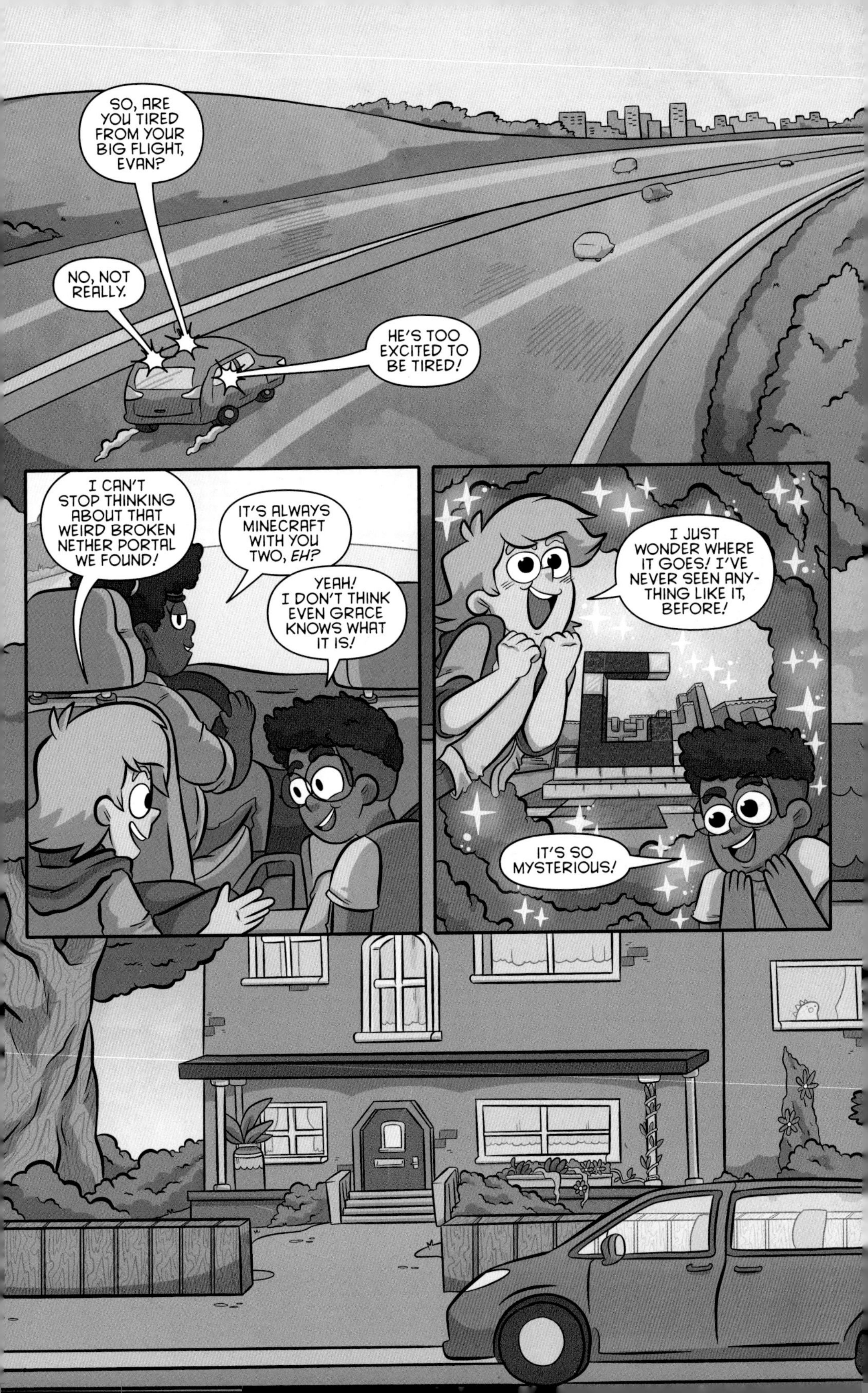
SO, ARE YOU TIRED FROM YOUR BIG FLIGHT, EVAN?
NO, NOT REALLY.
HE'S TOO EXCITED TO BE TIRED!
I CAN'T STOP THINKING ABOUT THAT WEIRD BROKEN NETHER PORTAL WE FOUND!
IT'S ALWAYS MINECRAFT WITH YOU TWO, *EH?*
YEAH! I DON'T THINK EVEN GRACE KNOWS WHAT IT IS!
I JUST WONDER WHERE IT GOES! I'VE NEVER SEEN ANYTHING LIKE IT, BEFORE!
IT'S SO MYSTERIOUS!

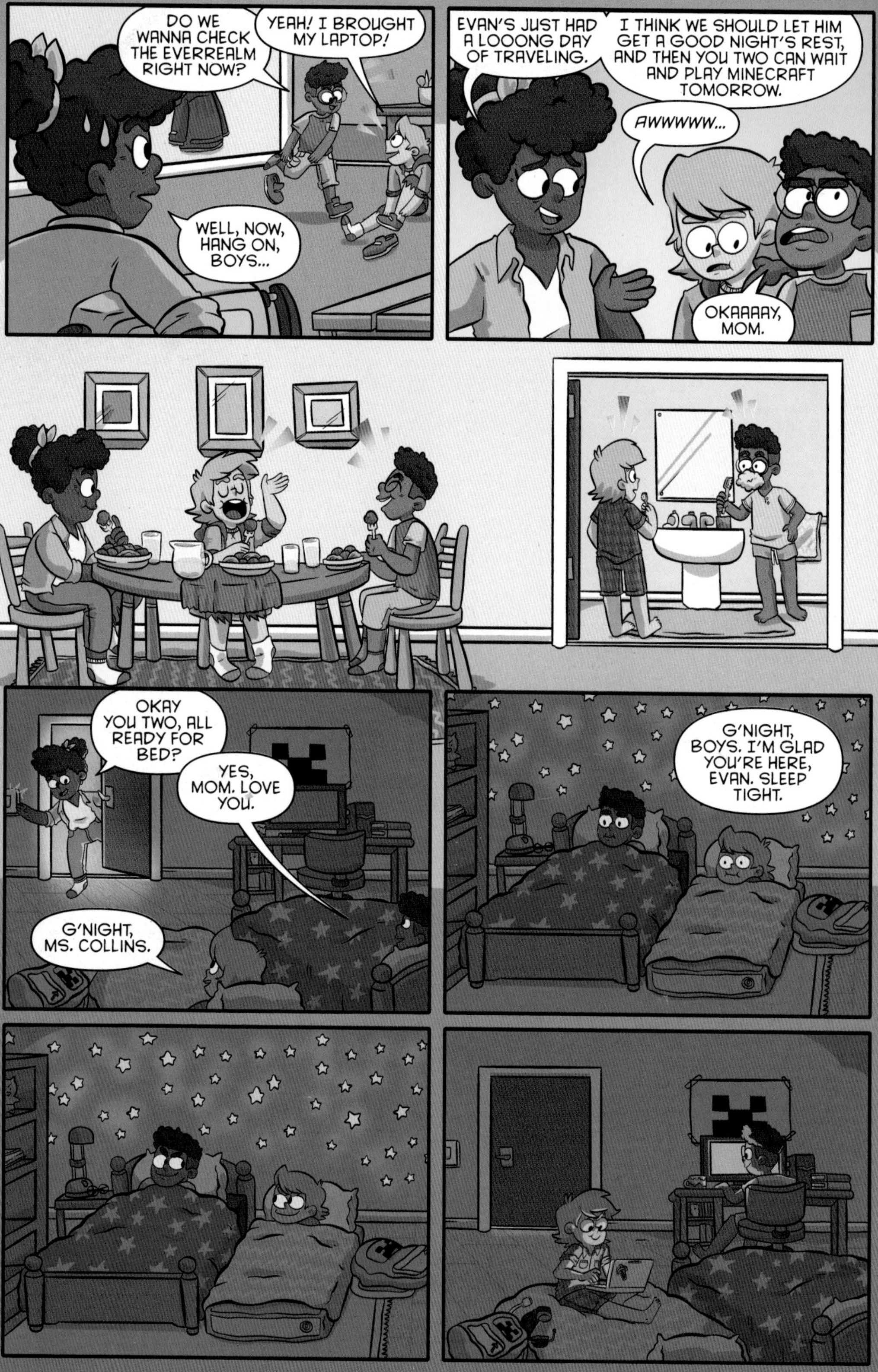
DO WE WANNA CHECK THE EVERREALM RIGHT NOW?
YEAH! I BROUGHT MY LAPTOP!
WELL, NOW, HANG ON, BOYS...
EVAN'S JUST HAD A LOOONG DAY OF TRAVELING.
I THINK WE SHOULD LET HIM GET A GOOD NIGHT'S REST, AND THEN YOU TWO CAN WAIT AND PLAY MINECRAFT TOMORROW.
AWWWWW...
OKAAAAY, MOM.
OKAY YOU TWO, ALL READY FOR BED?
YES, MOM. LOVE YOU.
G'NIGHT, MS. COLLINS.
G'NIGHT, BOYS. I'M GLAD YOU'RE HERE, EVAN. SLEEP TIGHT.

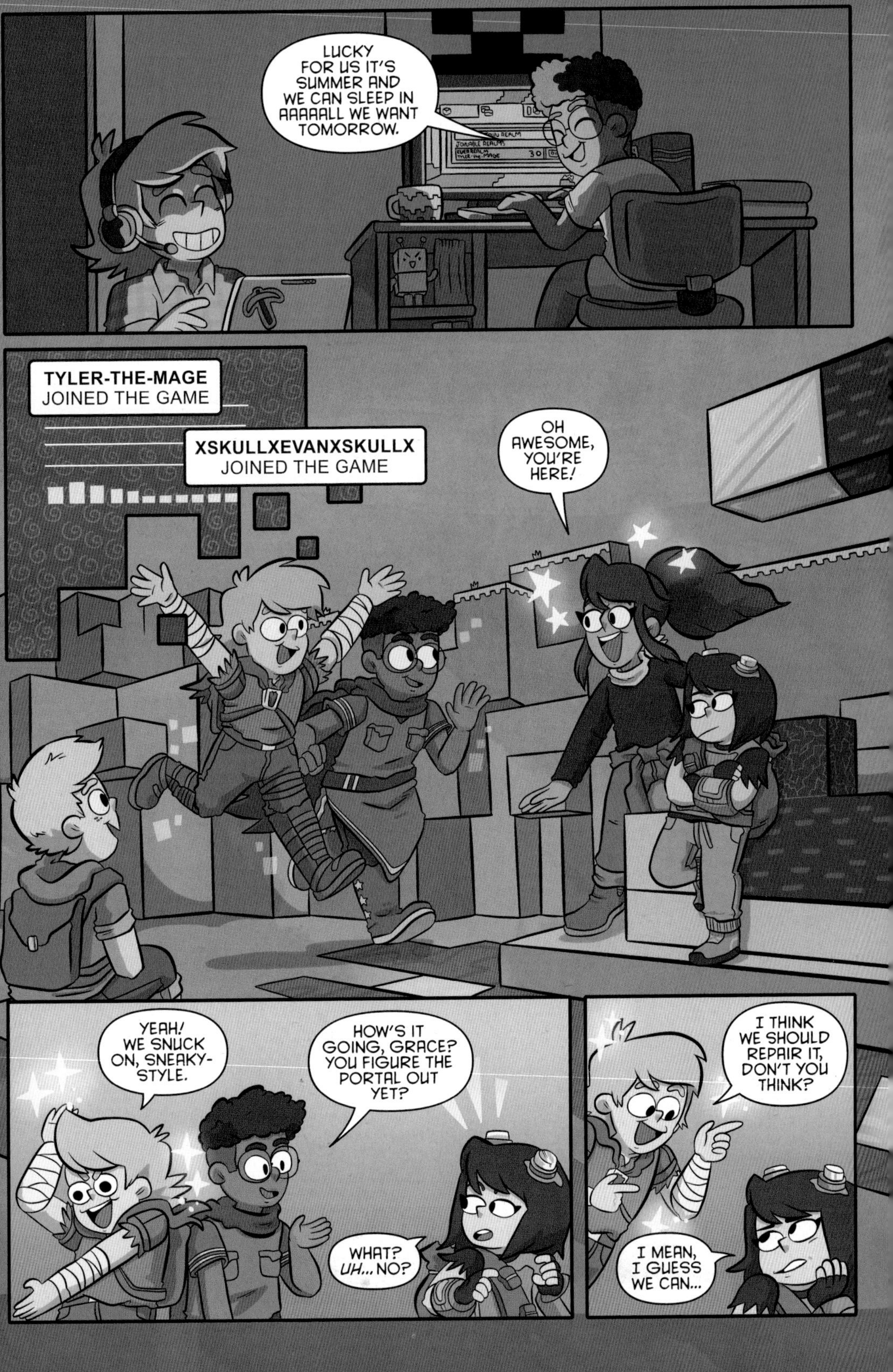

LUCKY FOR US IT'S SUMMER AND WE CAN SLEEP IN AAAAALL WE WANT TOMORROW.
TYLER-THE-MAGE JOINED THE GAME
XSKULLXEVANXSKULLX JOINED THE GAME
OH AWESOME, YOU'RE HERE!
YEAH! WE SNUCK ON, SNEAKY-STYLE.
HOW'S IT GOING, GRACE? YOU FIGURE THE PORTAL OUT YET?
WHAT? *UH...* NO?
I THINK WE SHOULD REPAIR IT, DON'T YOU THINK?
I MEAN, I GUESS WE CAN...

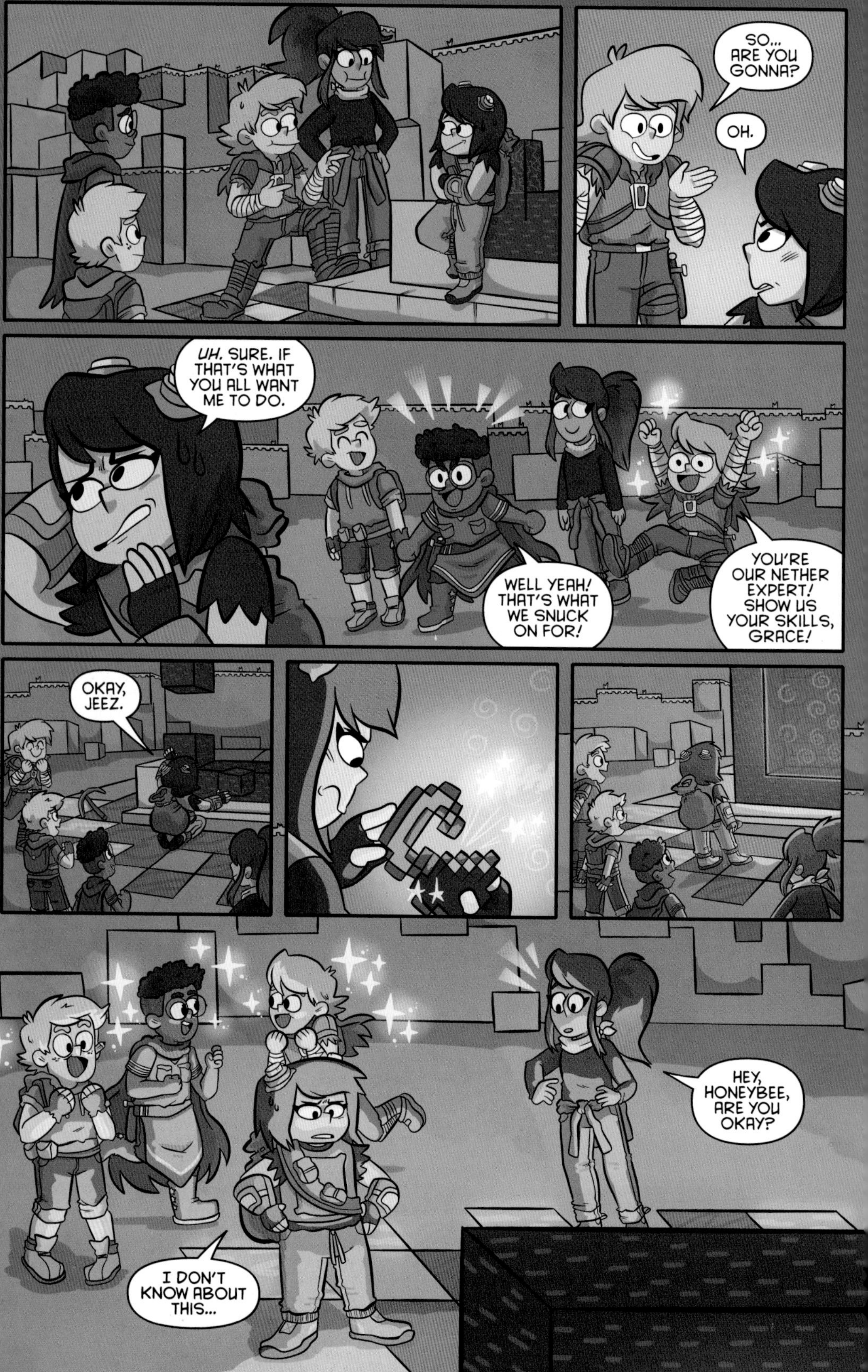
SO... ARE YOU GONNA?
OH.
UH. SURE. IF THAT'S WHAT YOU ALL WANT ME TO DO.
WELL YEAH! THAT'S WHAT WE SNUCK ON FOR!
YOU'RE OUR NETHER EXPERT! SHOW US YOUR SKILLS, GRACE!
OKAY, JEEZ.
HEY, HONEYBEE, ARE YOU OKAY?
I DON'T KNOW ABOUT THIS...

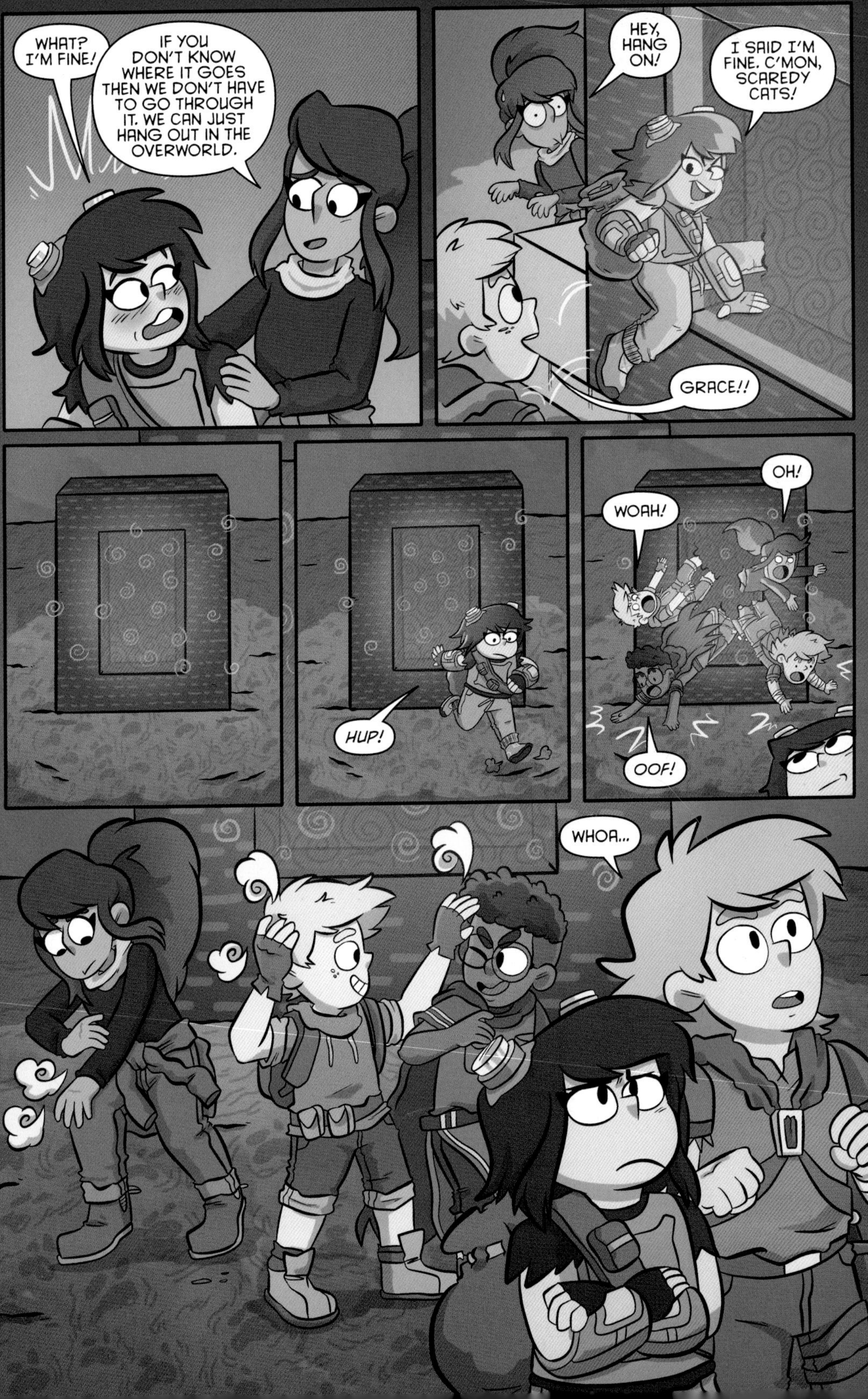
WHAT? I'M FINE!
IF YOU DON'T KNOW WHERE IT GOES THEN WE DON'T HAVE TO GO THROUGH IT. WE CAN JUST HANG OUT IN THE OVERWORLD.
HEY, HANG ON!
I SAID I'M FINE. C'MON, SCAREDY CATS!
GRACE!!
HUP!
WOAH!
OH!
OOF!
WHOA...

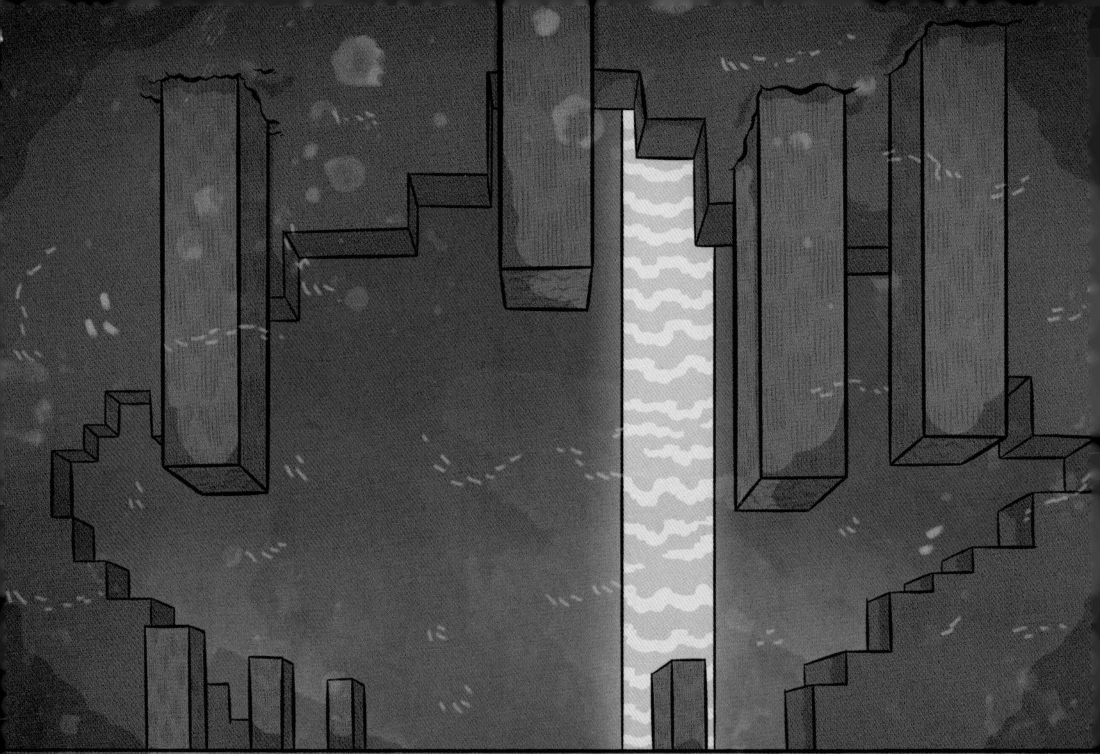

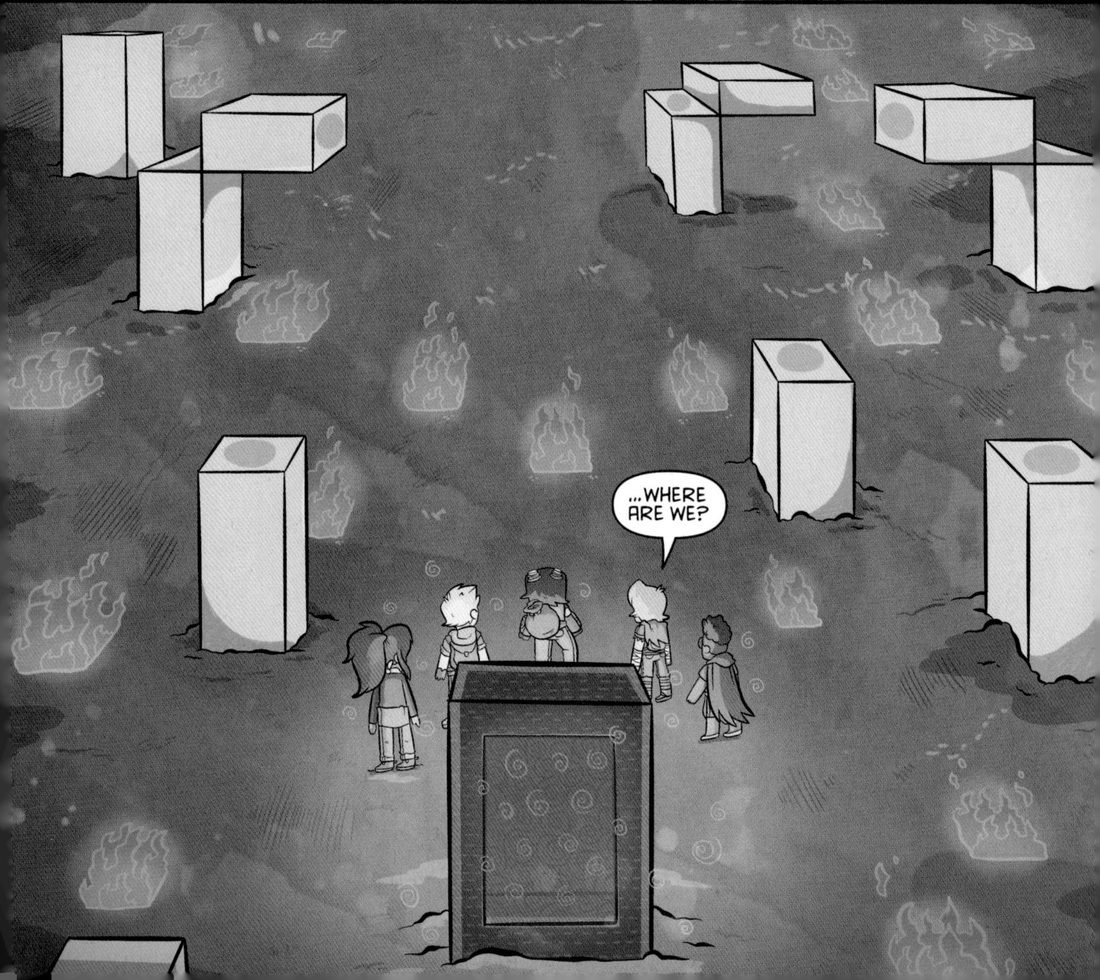
...WHERE ARE WE?

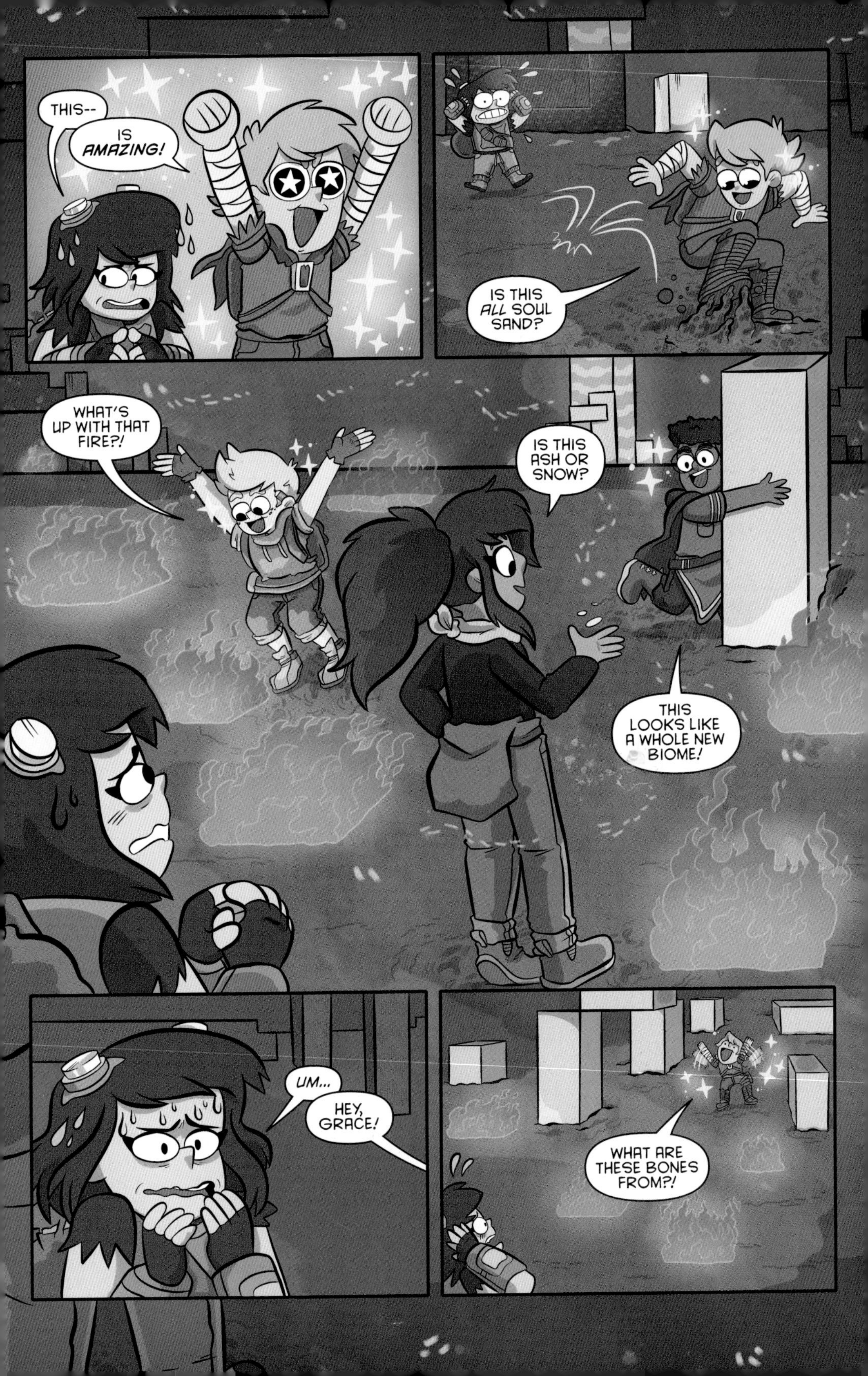
THIS--
IS AMAZING!
IS THIS ALL SOUL SAND?
WHAT'S UP WITH THAT FIRE?!
IS THIS ASH OR SNOW?
THIS LOOKS LIKE A WHOLE NEW BIOME!
UM...
HEY, GRACE!
WHAT ARE THESE BONES FROM?!

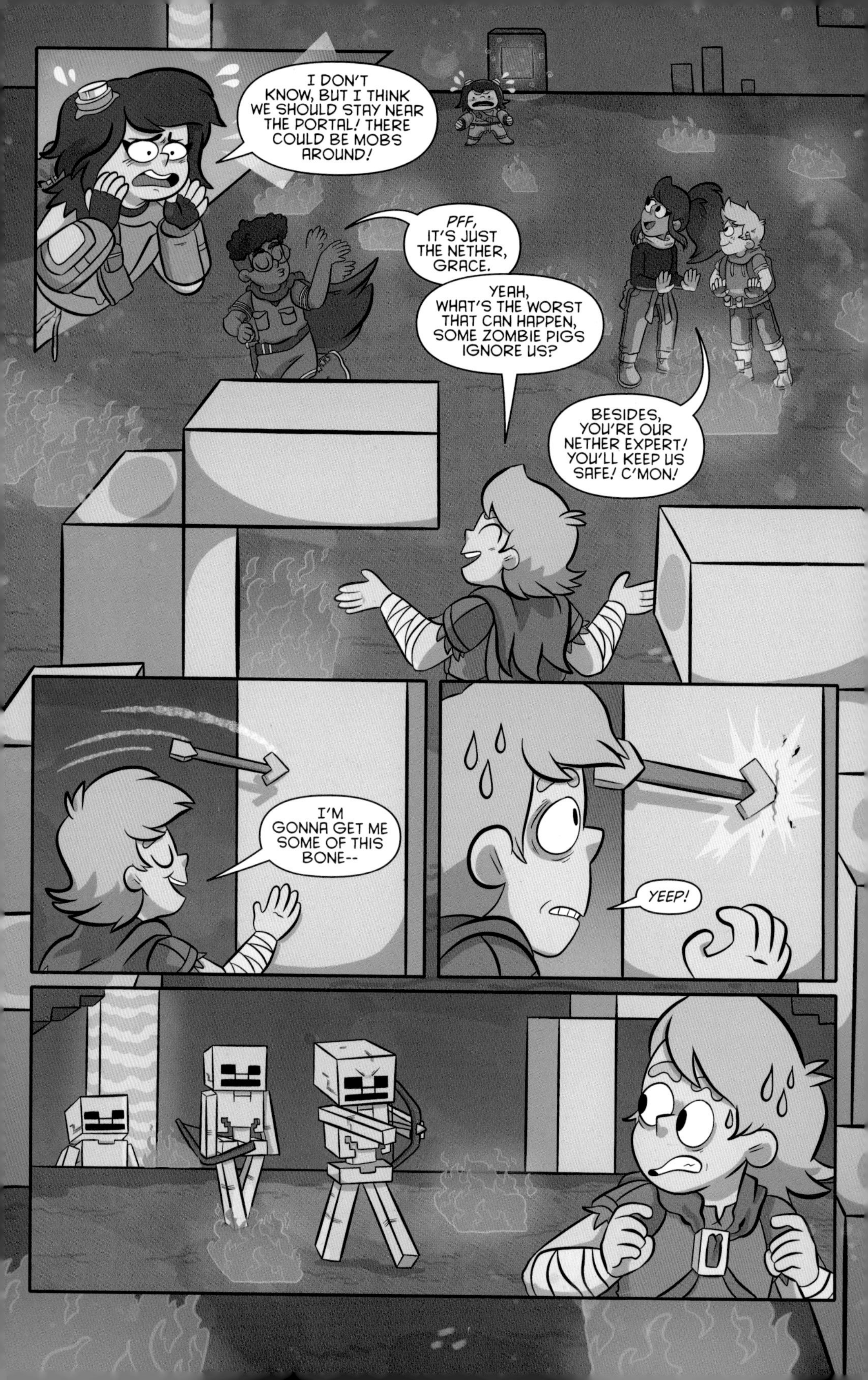
I DON'T KNOW, BUT I THINK WE SHOULD STAY NEAR THE PORTAL! THERE COULD BE MOBS AROUND!
PFF, IT'S JUST THE NETHER, GRACE.
YEAH, WHAT'S THE WORST THAT CAN HAPPEN, SOME ZOMBIE PIGS IGNORE US?
BESIDES, YOU'RE OUR NETHER EXPERT! YOU'LL KEEP US SAFE! C'MON!
I'M GONNA GET ME SOME OF THIS BONE--
YEEP!

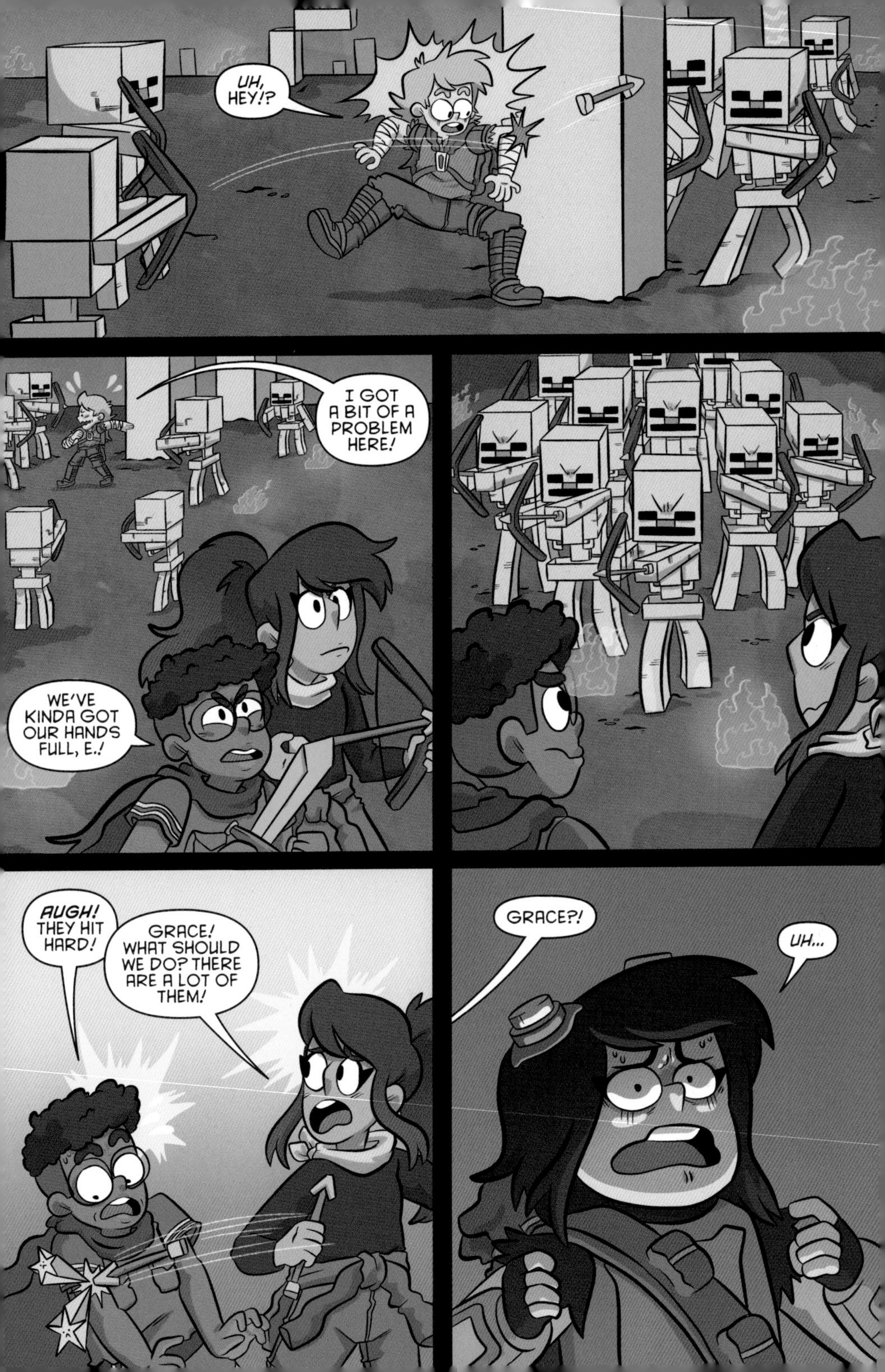
UH, HEY!?
I GOT A BIT OF A PROBLEM HERE!
WE'VE KINDA GOT OUR HANDS FULL, E.!
AUGH! THEY HIT HARD!
GRACE! WHAT SHOULD WE DO? THERE ARE A LOT OF THEM!
GRACE?!
UH...

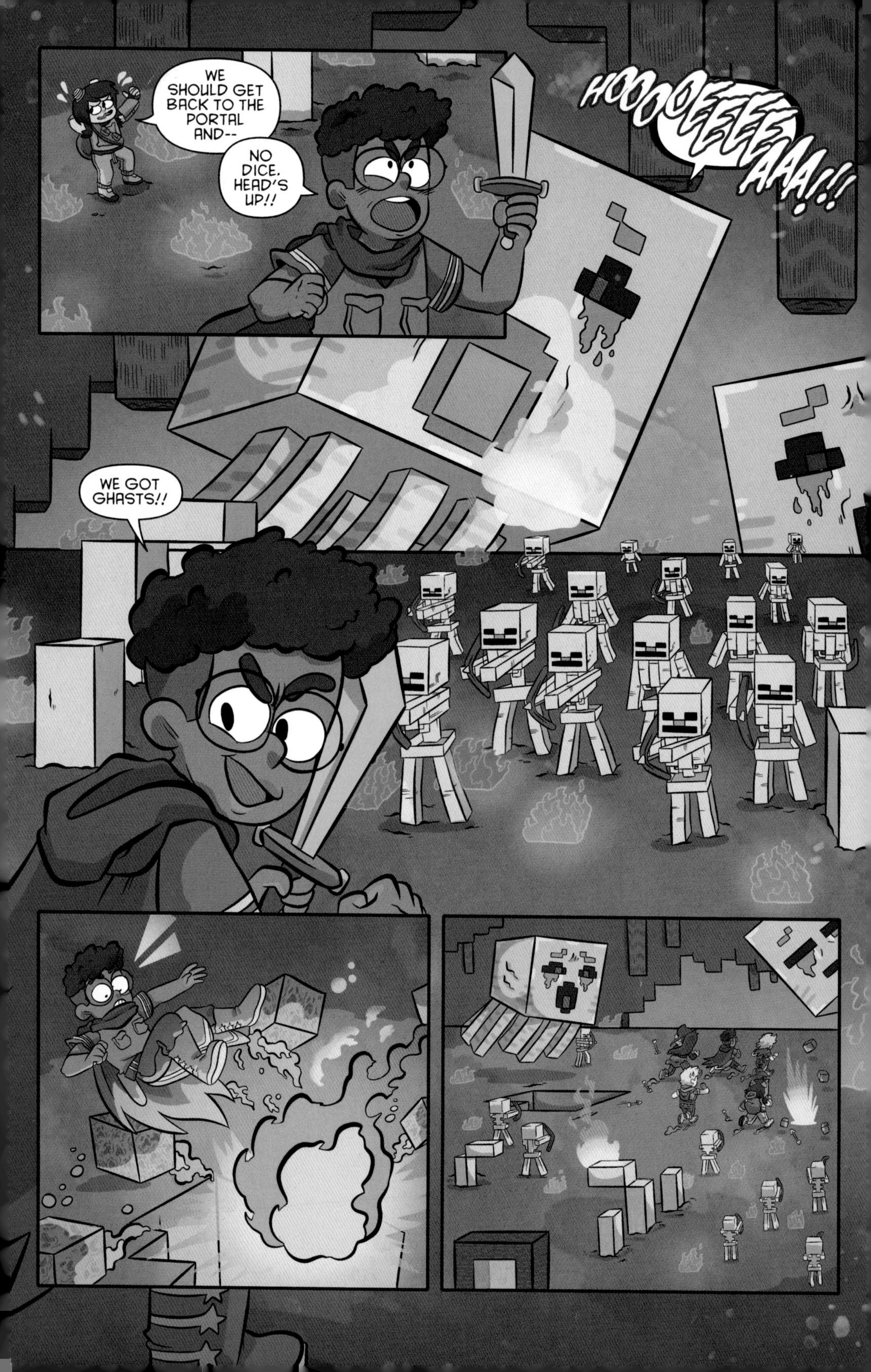
WE SHOULD GET BACK TO THE PORTAL AND--
NO DICE. HEAD'S UP!!
HOOOOEEEEAAA!!!
WE GOT GHASTS!!

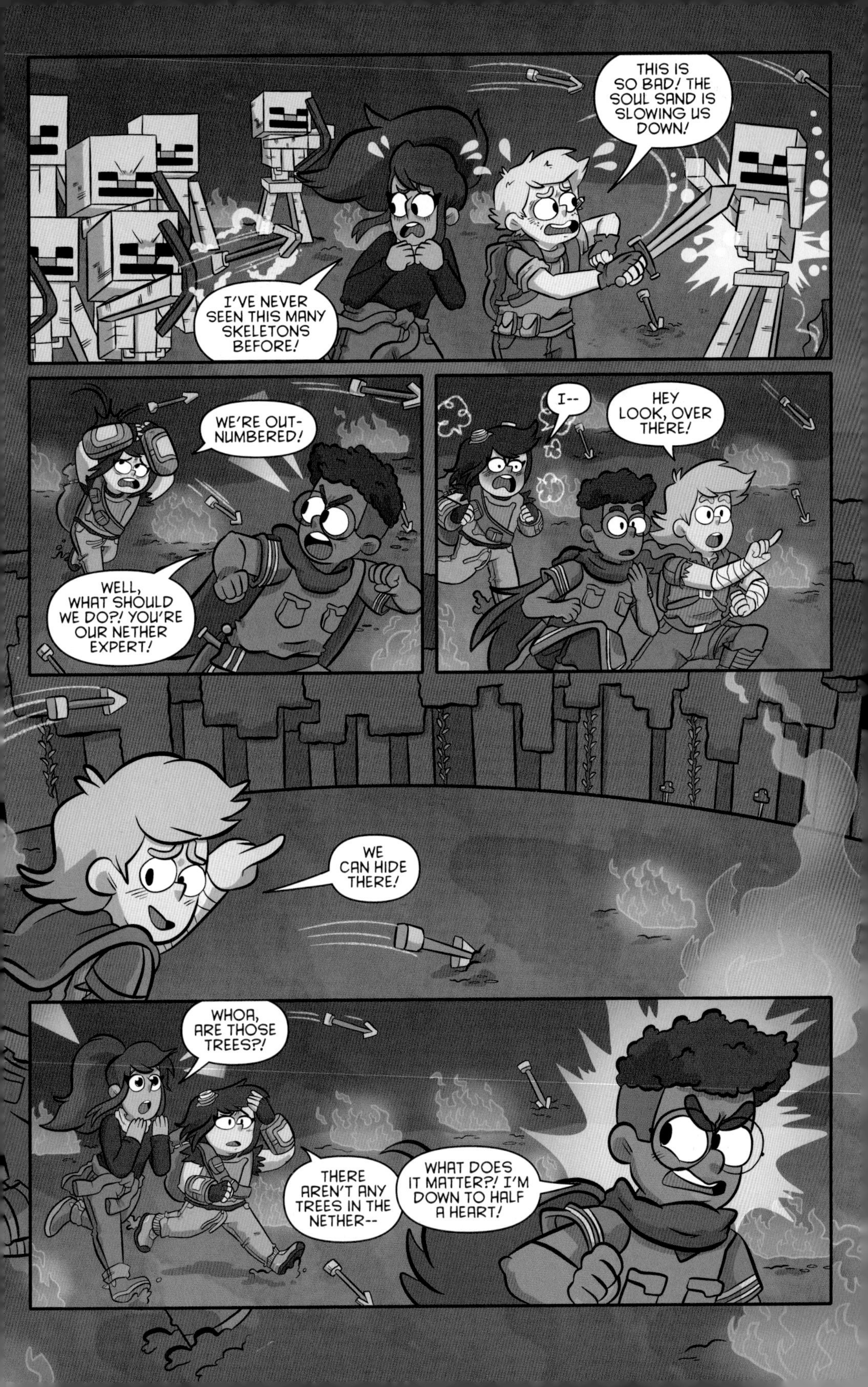
I'VE NEVER SEEN THIS MANY SKELETONS BEFORE!
THIS IS SO BAD! THE SOUL SAND IS SLOWING US DOWN!
WE'RE OUT-NUMBERED!
WELL, WHAT SHOULD WE DO?! YOU'RE OUR NETHER EXPERT!
I--
HEY LOOK, OVER THERE!
WE CAN HIDE THERE!
WHOA, ARE THOSE TREES?!
THERE AREN'T ANY TREES IN THE NETHER--
WHAT DOES IT MATTER?! I'M DOWN TO HALF A HEART!

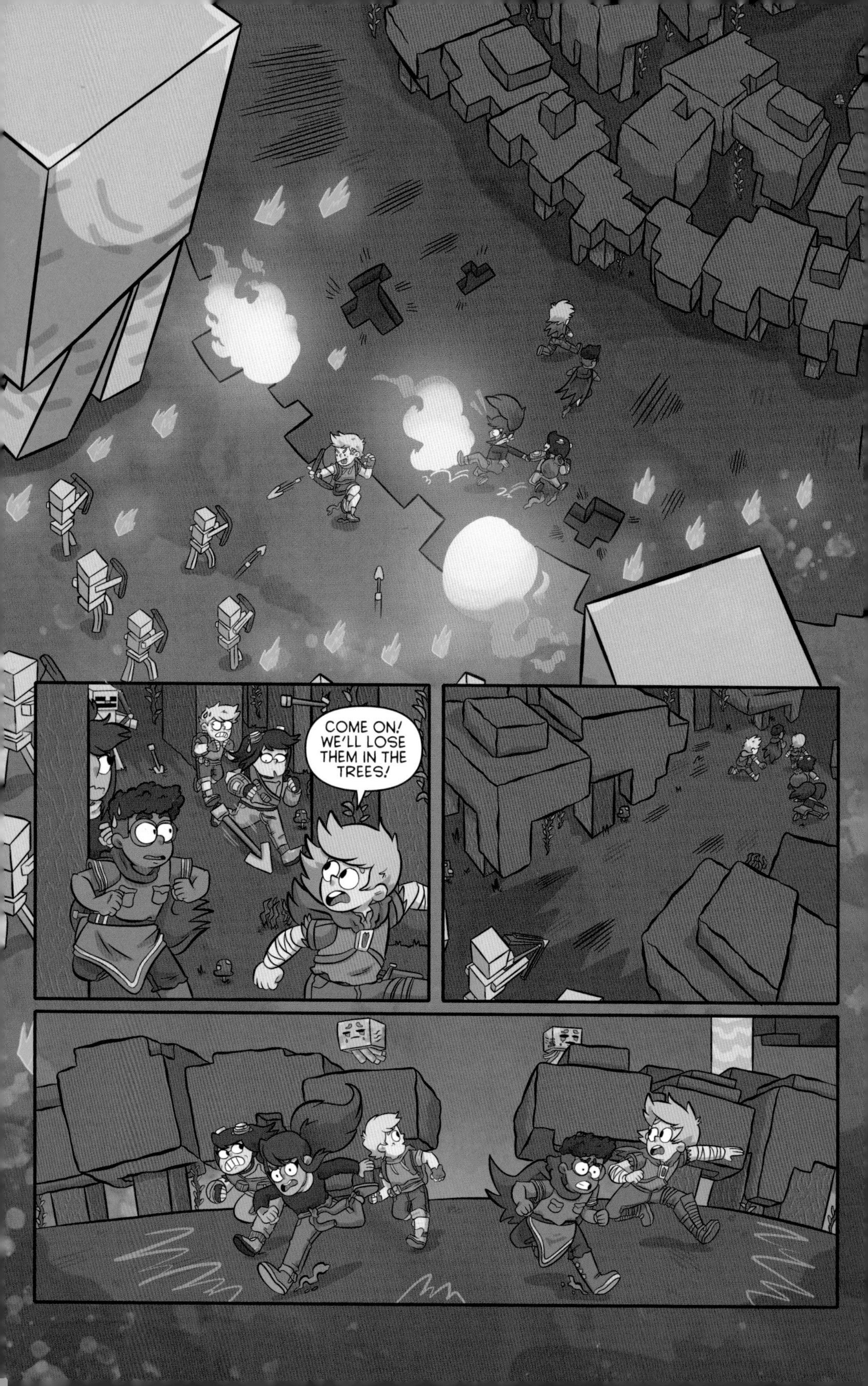
COME ON! WE'LL LOSE THEM IN THE TREES!

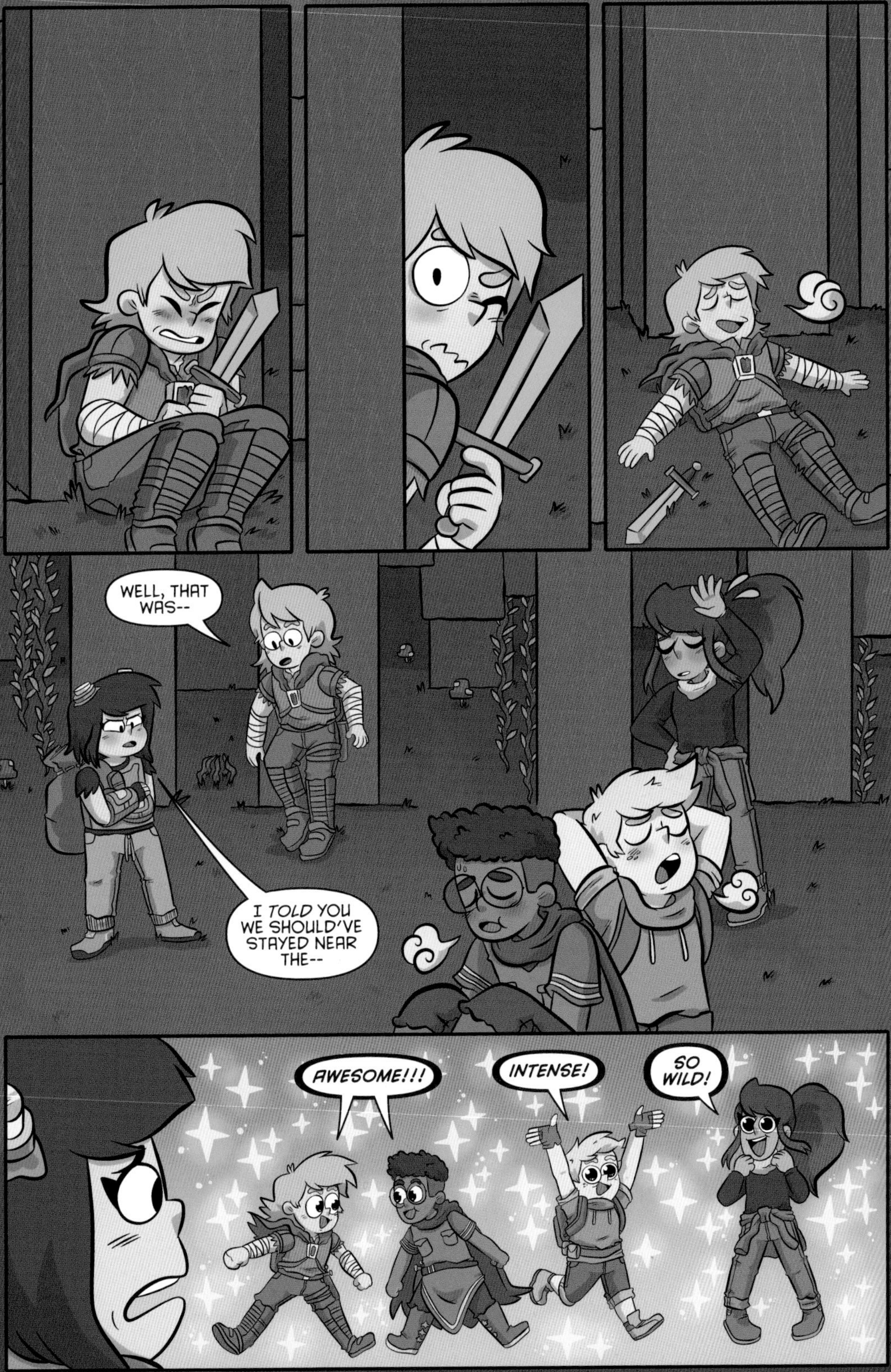
WELL, THAT WAS--
I *TOLD* YOU WE SHOULD'VE STAYED NEAR THE--
AWESOME!!!
INTENSE!
SO WILD!

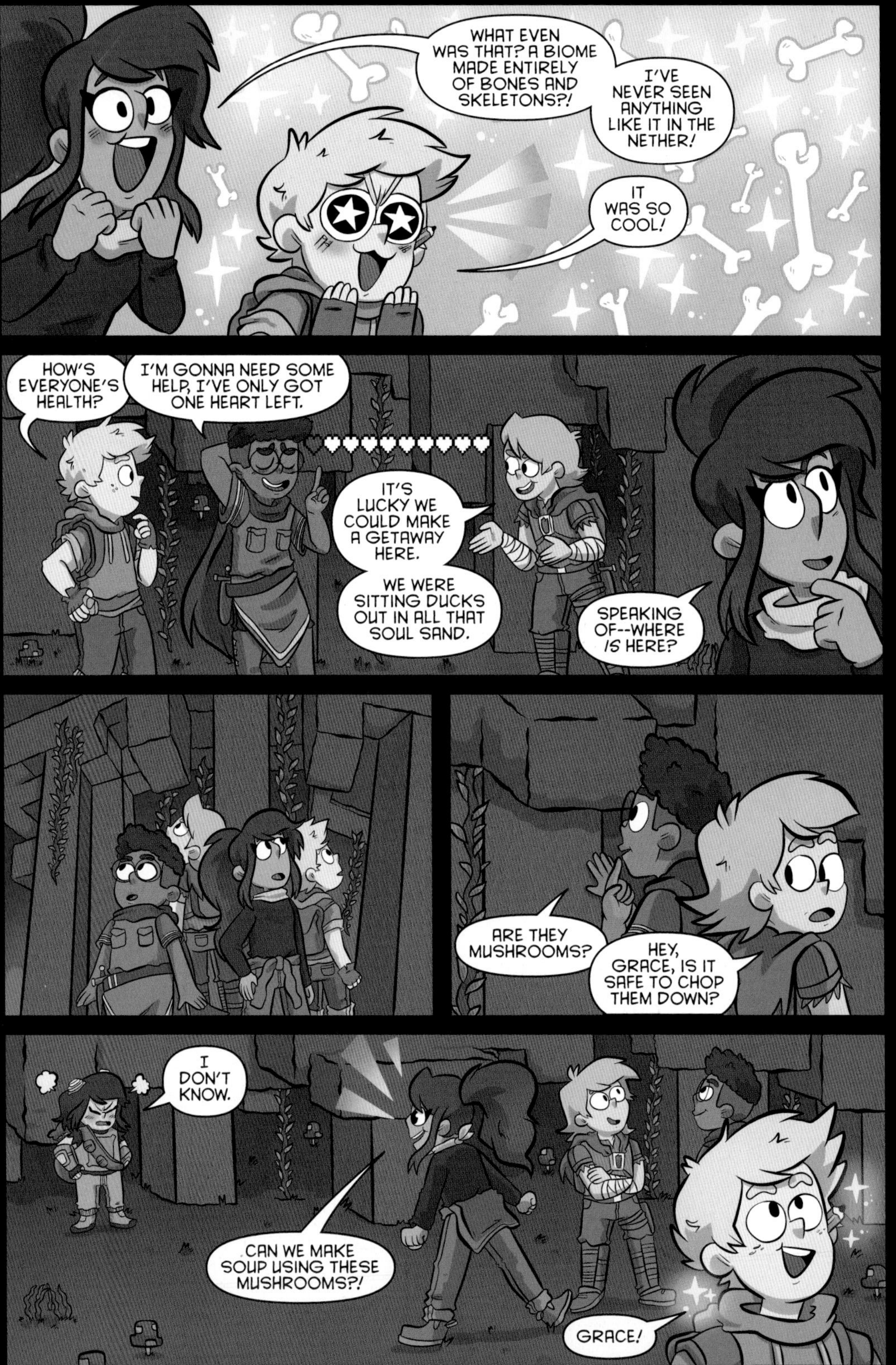
WHAT EVEN WAS THAT? A BIOME MADE ENTIRELY OF BONES AND SKELETONS?!
I'VE NEVER SEEN ANYTHING LIKE IT IN THE NETHER!
IT WAS SO COOL!
HOW'S EVERYONE'S HEALTH?
I'M GONNA NEED SOME HELP, I'VE ONLY GOT ONE HEART LEFT.
IT'S LUCKY WE COULD MAKE A GETAWAY HERE.
WE WERE SITTING DUCKS OUT IN ALL THAT SOUL SAND.
SPEAKING OF--WHERE IS HERE?
ARE THEY MUSHROOMS?
HEY, GRACE, IS IT SAFE TO CHOP THEM DOWN?
I DON'T KNOW.
CAN WE MAKE SOUP USING THESE MUSHROOMS?!
GRACE!

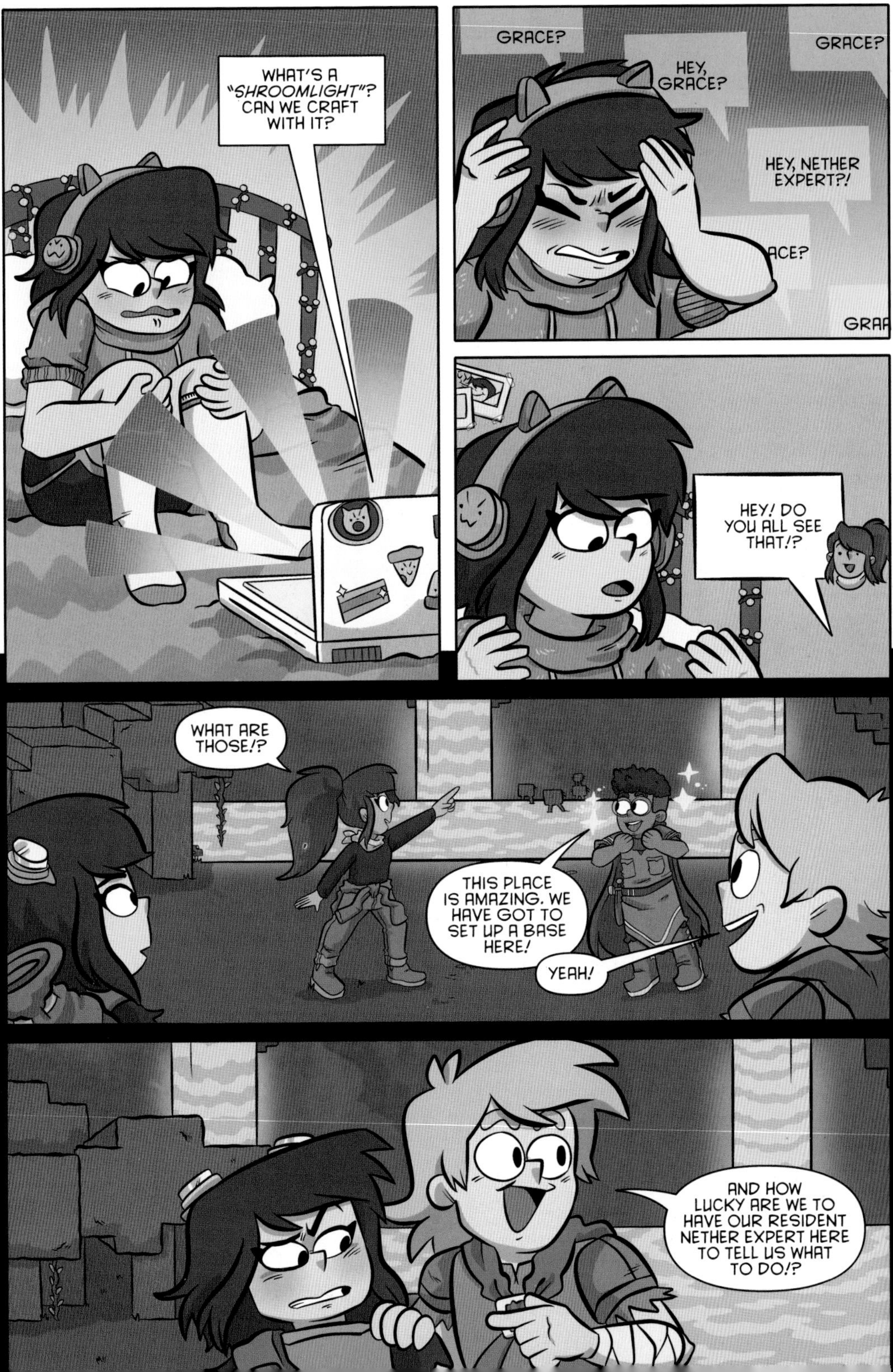

WHAT'S A "SHROOMLIGHT"? CAN WE CRAFT WITH IT?
GRACE?
HEY, GRACE?
GRACE?
HEY, NETHER EXPERT?!
ACE?
GRAA
HEY! DO YOU ALL SEE THAT!?
WHAT ARE THOSE!?
THIS PLACE IS AMAZING. WE HAVE GOT TO SET UP A BASE HERE!
YEAH!
AND HOW LUCKY ARE WE TO HAVE OUR RESIDENT NETHER EXPERT HERE TO TELL US WHAT TO DO!?

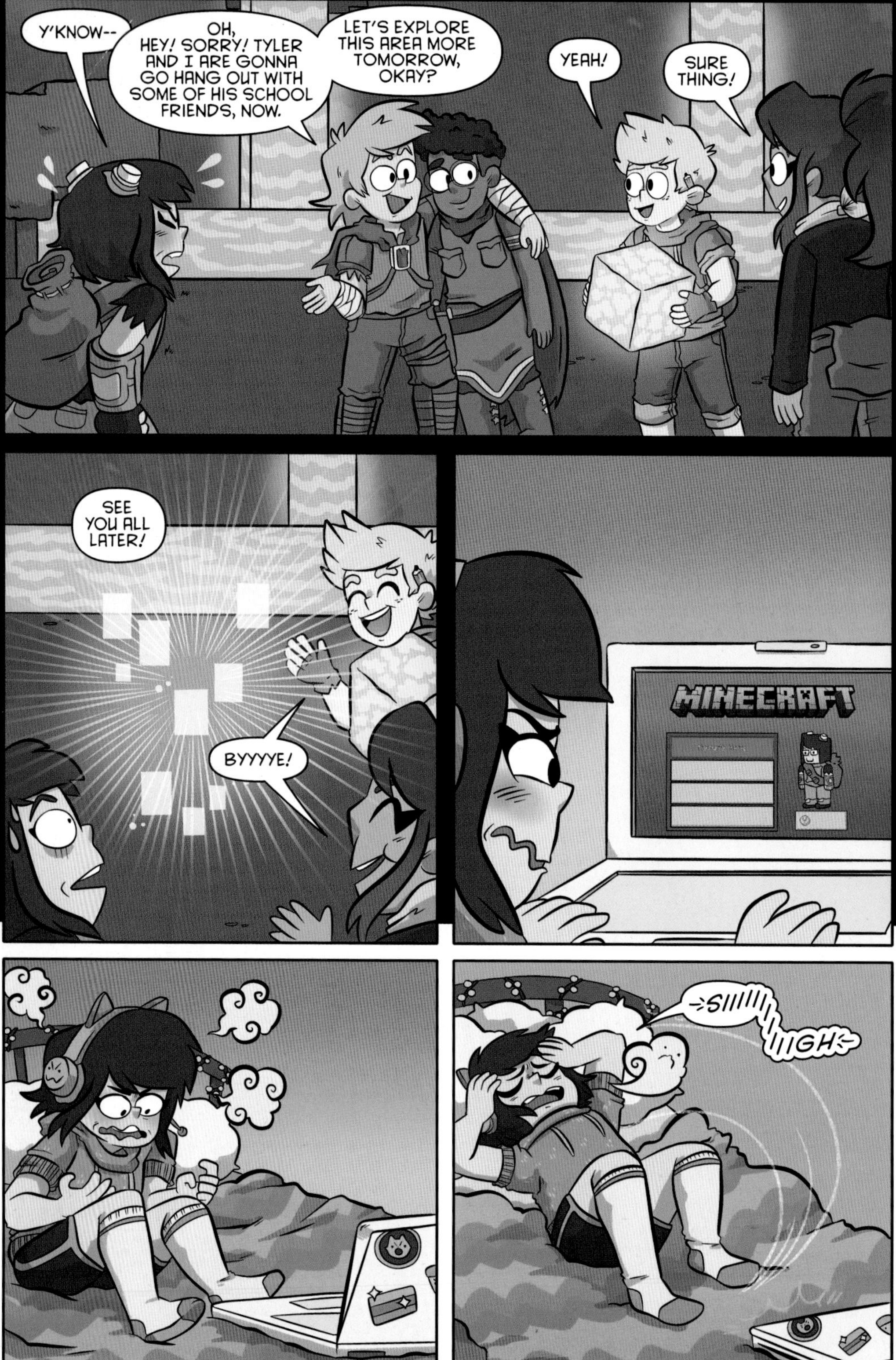
Y'KNOW--
OH, HEY! SORRY! TYLER AND I ARE GONNA GO HANG OUT WITH SOME OF HIS SCHOOL FRIENDS, NOW.
LET'S EXPLORE THIS AREA MORE TOMORROW, OKAY?
YEAH!
SURE THING!
SEE YOU ALL LATER!
BYYYYE!
MINECRAFT
SIIIIIIIIGH

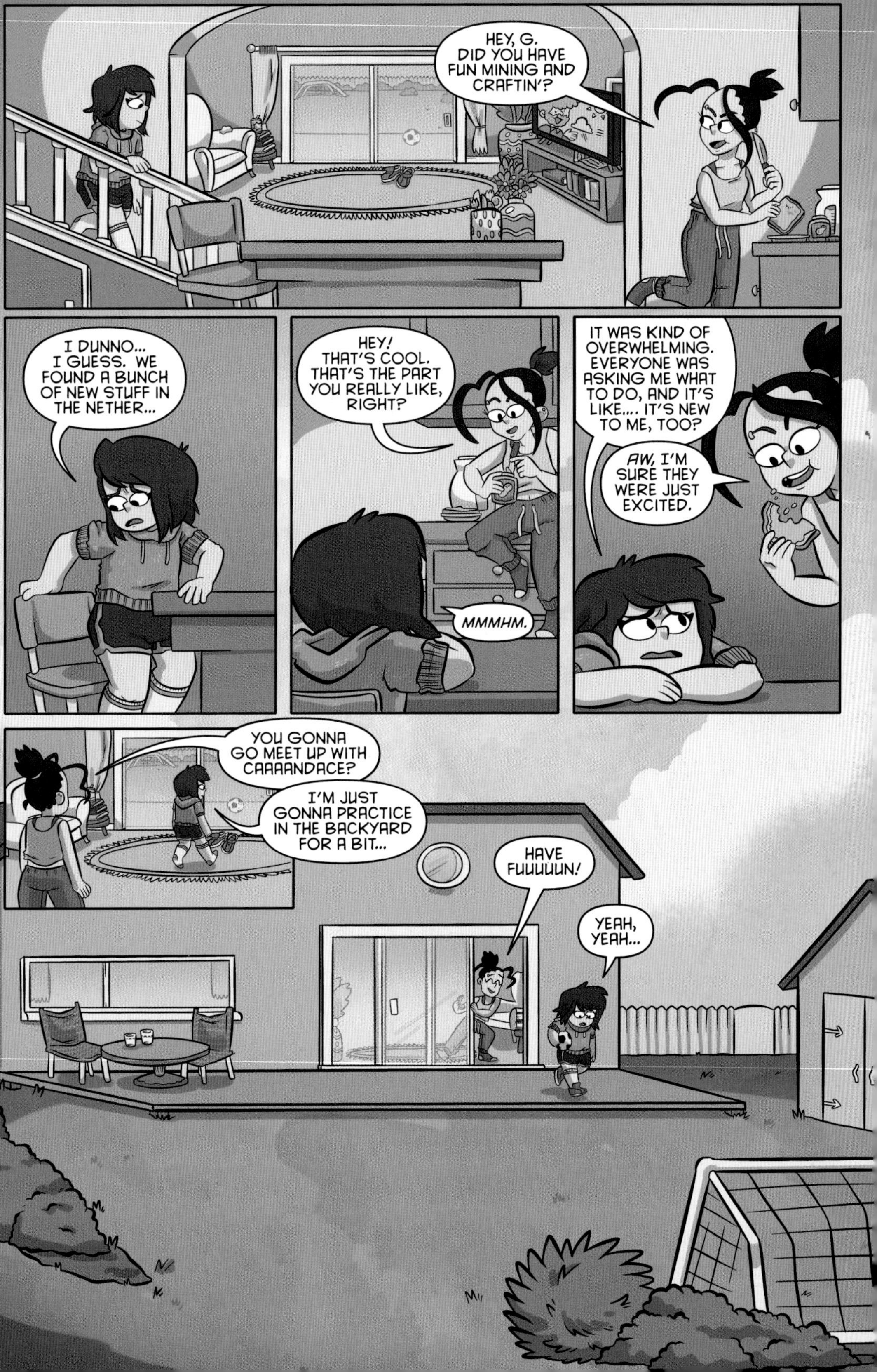
HEY, G. DID YOU HAVE FUN MINING AND CRAFTIN'?
I DUNNO... I GUESS. WE FOUND A BUNCH OF NEW STUFF IN THE NETHER...
HEY! THAT'S COOL. THAT'S THE PART YOU REALLY LIKE, RIGHT?
MMMHM.
IT WAS KIND OF OVERWHELMING. EVERYONE WAS ASKING ME WHAT TO DO, AND IT'S LIKE.... IT'S NEW TO ME, TOO?
AW, I'M SURE THEY WERE JUST EXCITED.
YOU GONNA GO MEET UP WITH CAAAANDACE?
I'M JUST GONNA PRACTICE IN THE BACKYARD FOR A BIT...
HAVE FUUUUUN!
YEAH, YEAH...

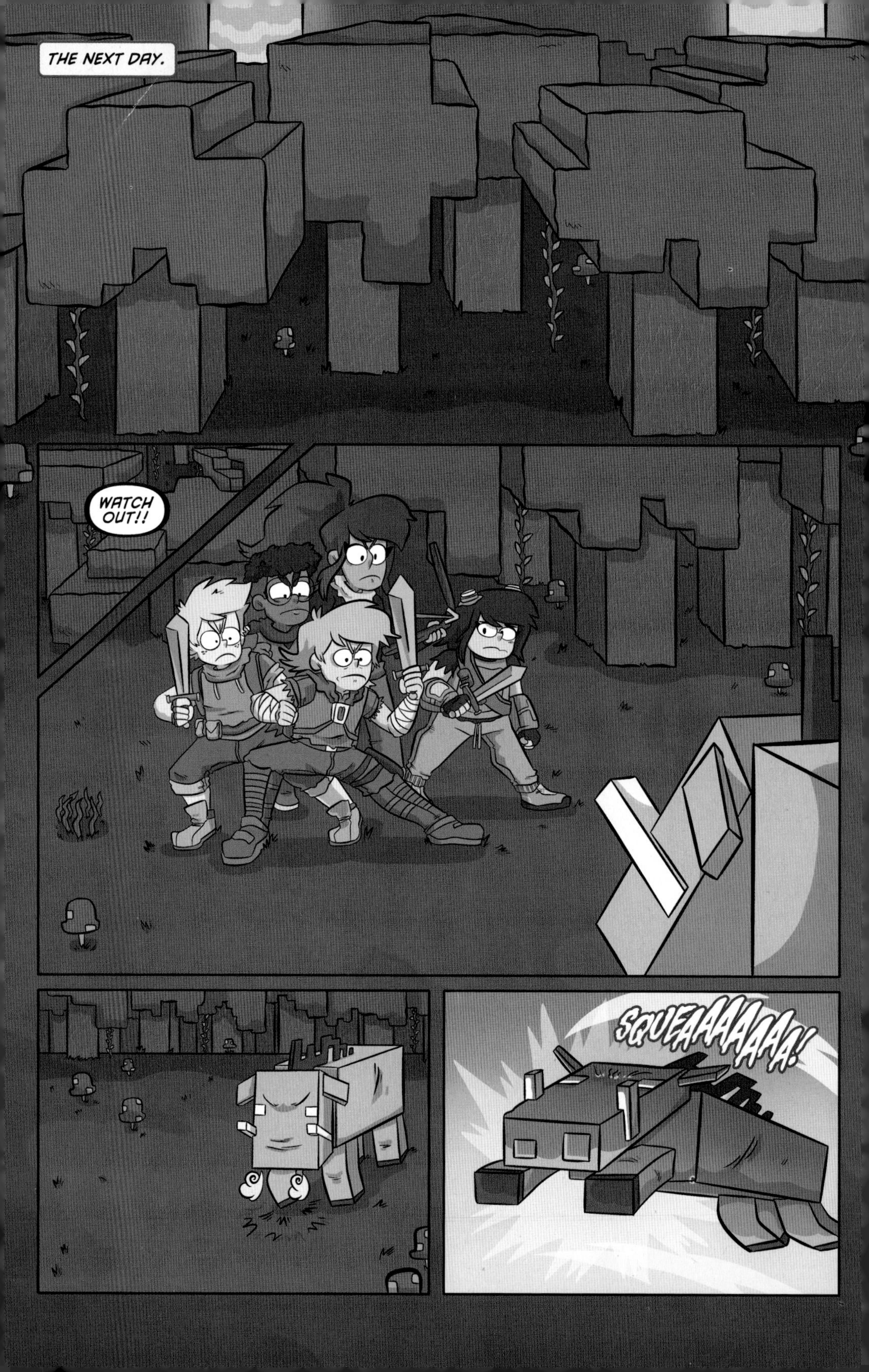
THE NEXT DAY.
WATCH OUT!!
SQUEAAAAAAAA!

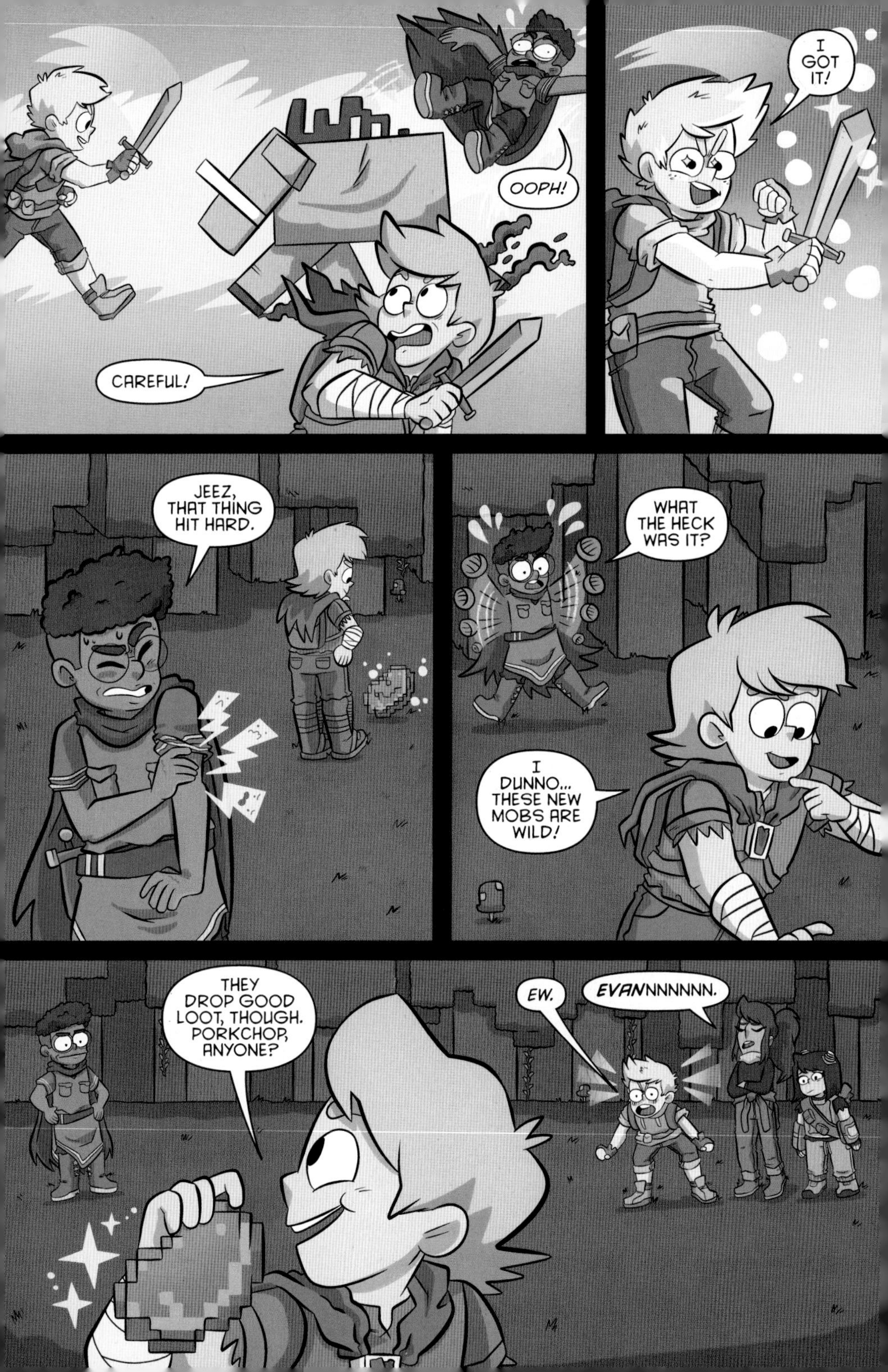
OOPH!
CAREFUL!
I GOT IT!
JEEZ, THAT THING HIT HARD.
WHAT THE HECK WAS IT?
I DUNNO... THESE NEW MOBS ARE WILD!
THEY DROP GOOD LOOT, THOUGH. PORKCHOP, ANYONE?
EW.
EVANNNNNNN.

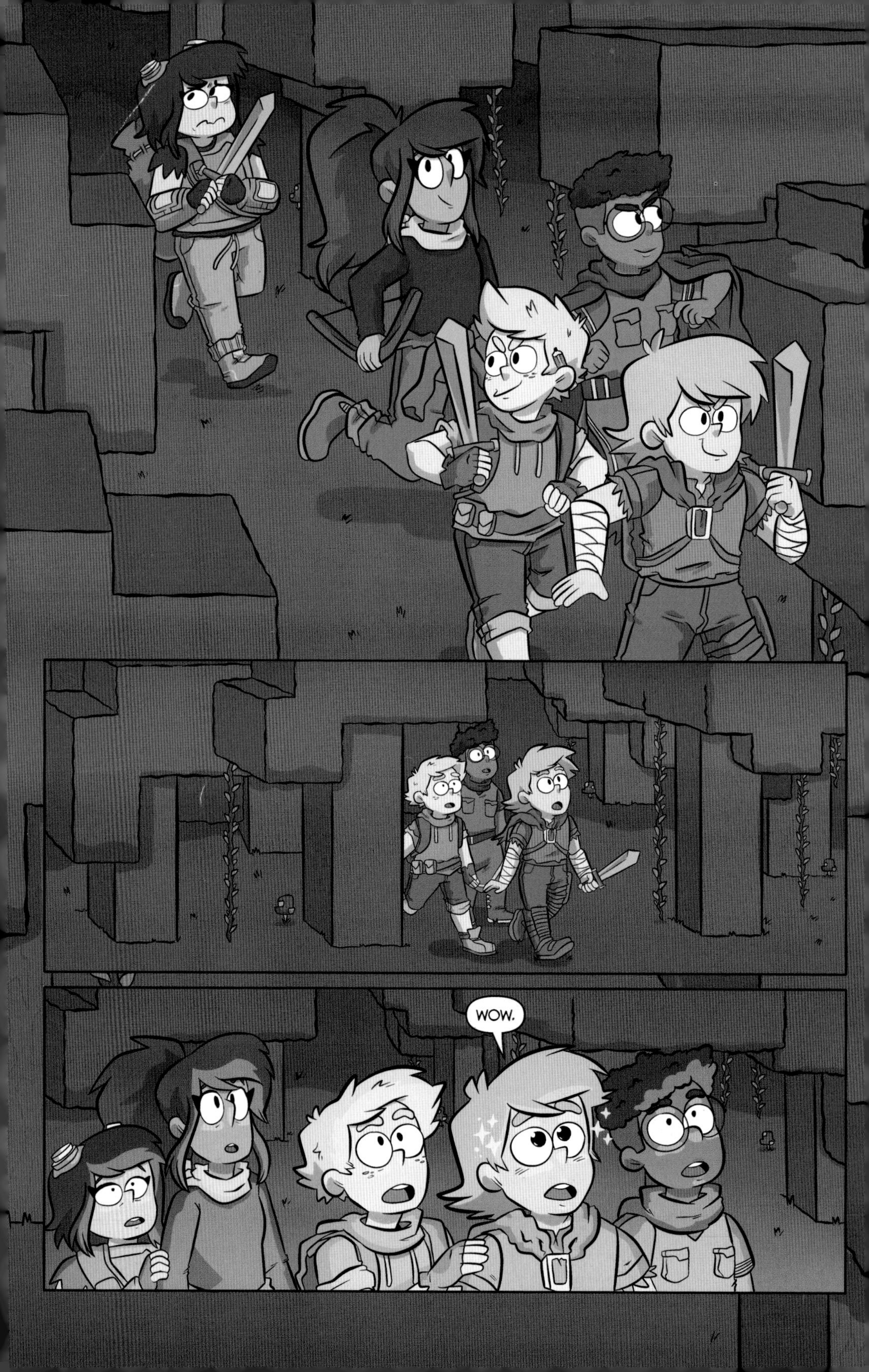
WOW.

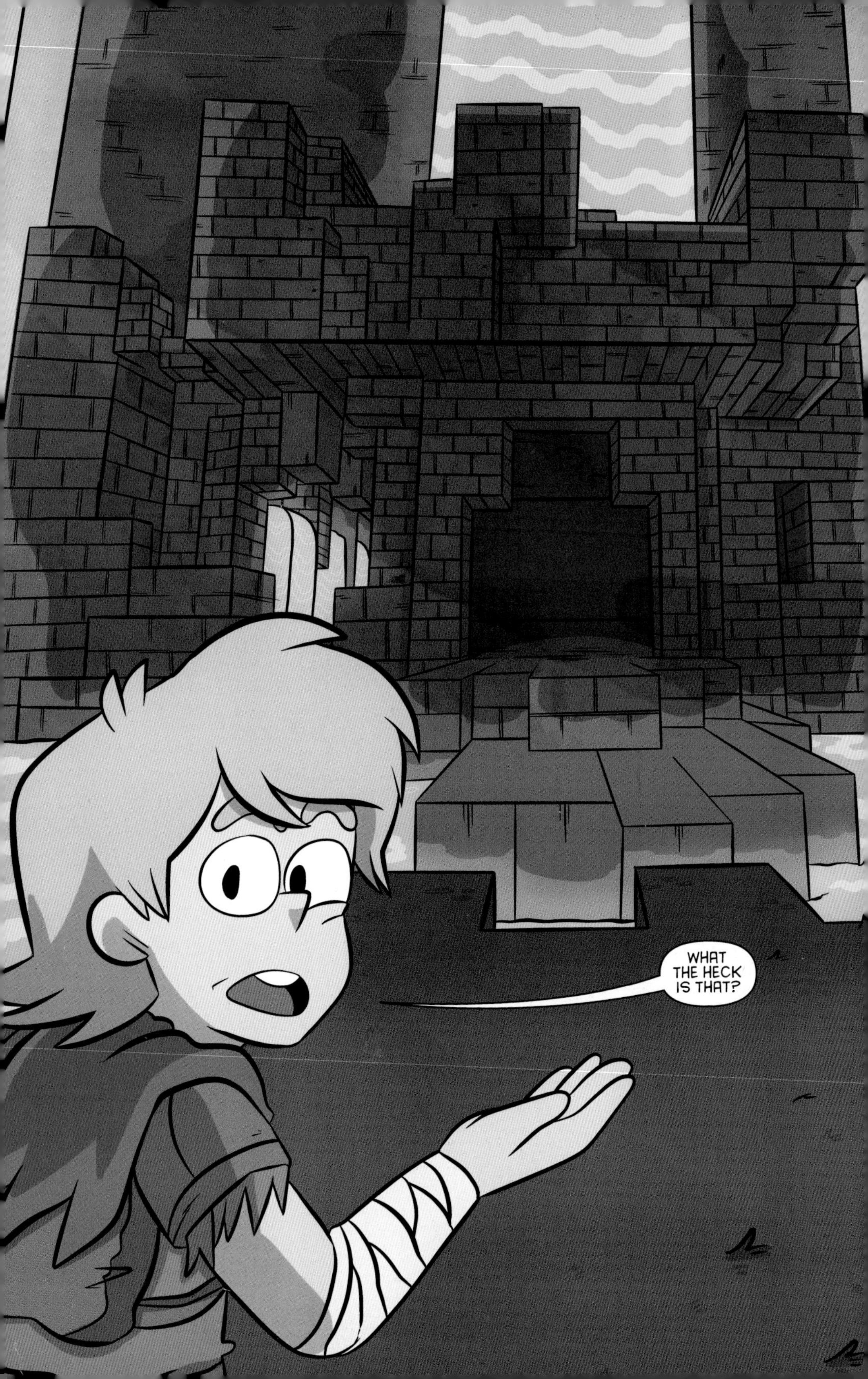
WHAT THE HECK IS THAT?

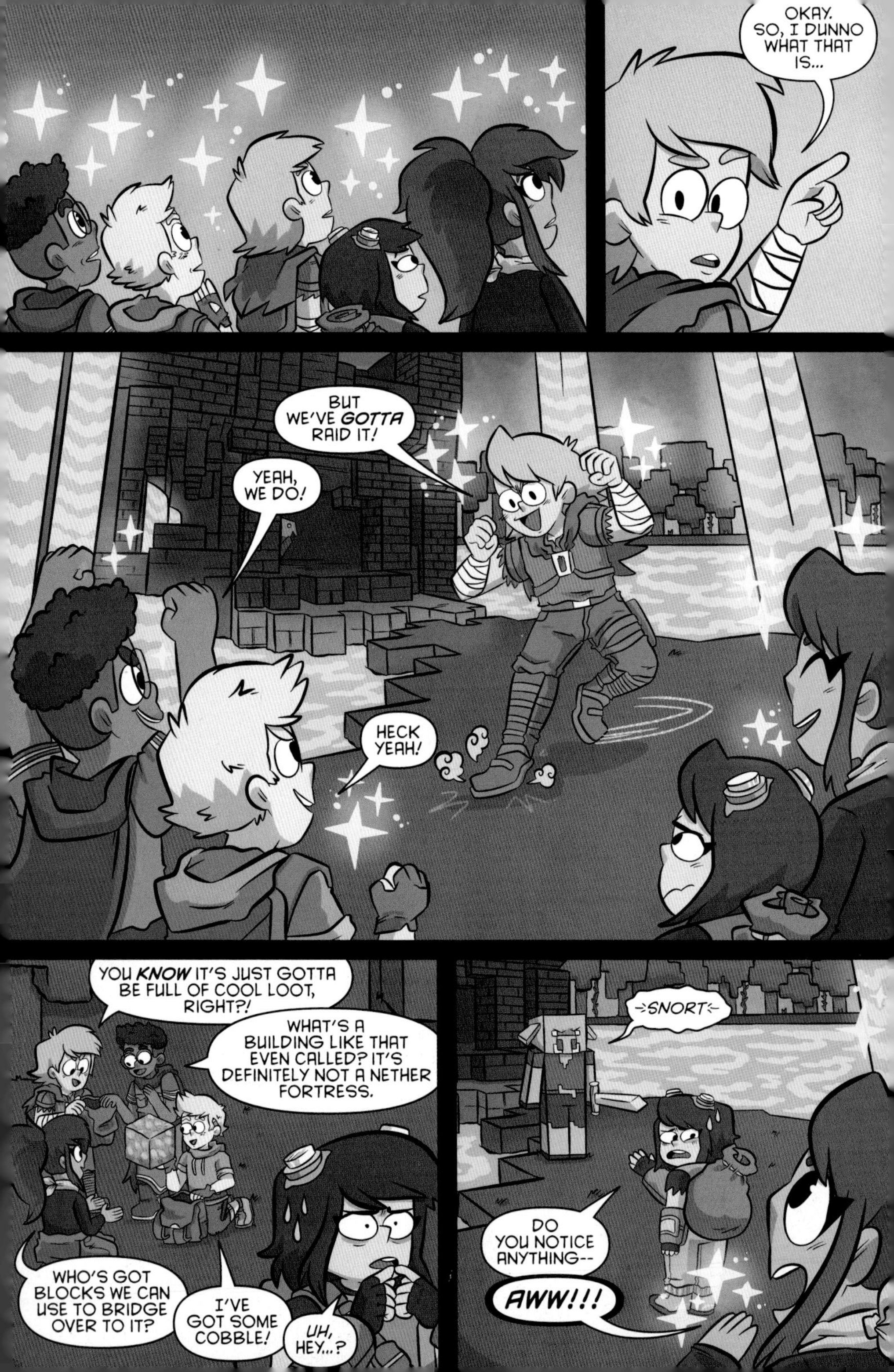
OKAY. SO, I DUNNO WHAT THAT IS...
BUT WE'VE *GOTTA* RAID IT!
YEAH, WE DO!
HECK YEAH!
YOU *KNOW* IT'S JUST GOTTA BE FULL OF COOL LOOT, RIGHT?!
WHAT'S A BUILDING LIKE THAT EVEN CALLED? IT'S DEFINITELY NOT A NETHER FORTRESS.
WHO'S GOT BLOCKS WE CAN USE TO BRIDGE OVER TO IT?
I'VE GOT SOME COBBLE!
UH, HEY...?
SNORT
DO YOU NOTICE ANYTHING--
AWW!!!

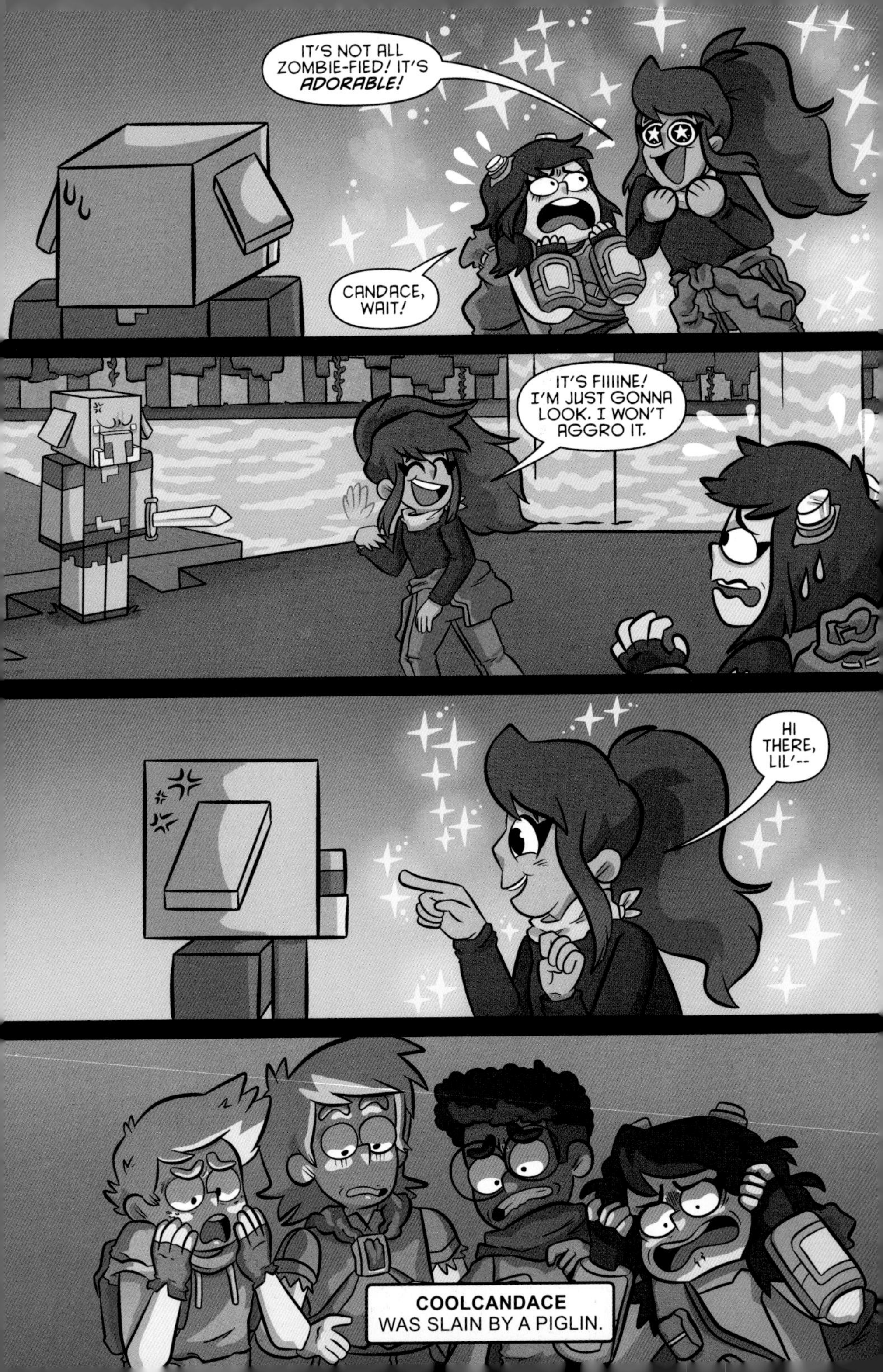
IT'S NOT ALL ZOMBIE-FIED! IT'S ADORABLE!
CANDACE, WAIT!
IT'S FIIIINE! I'M JUST GONNA LOOK. I WON'T AGGRO IT.
HI THERE, LIL'--
COOLCANDACE WAS SLAIN BY A PIGLIN.

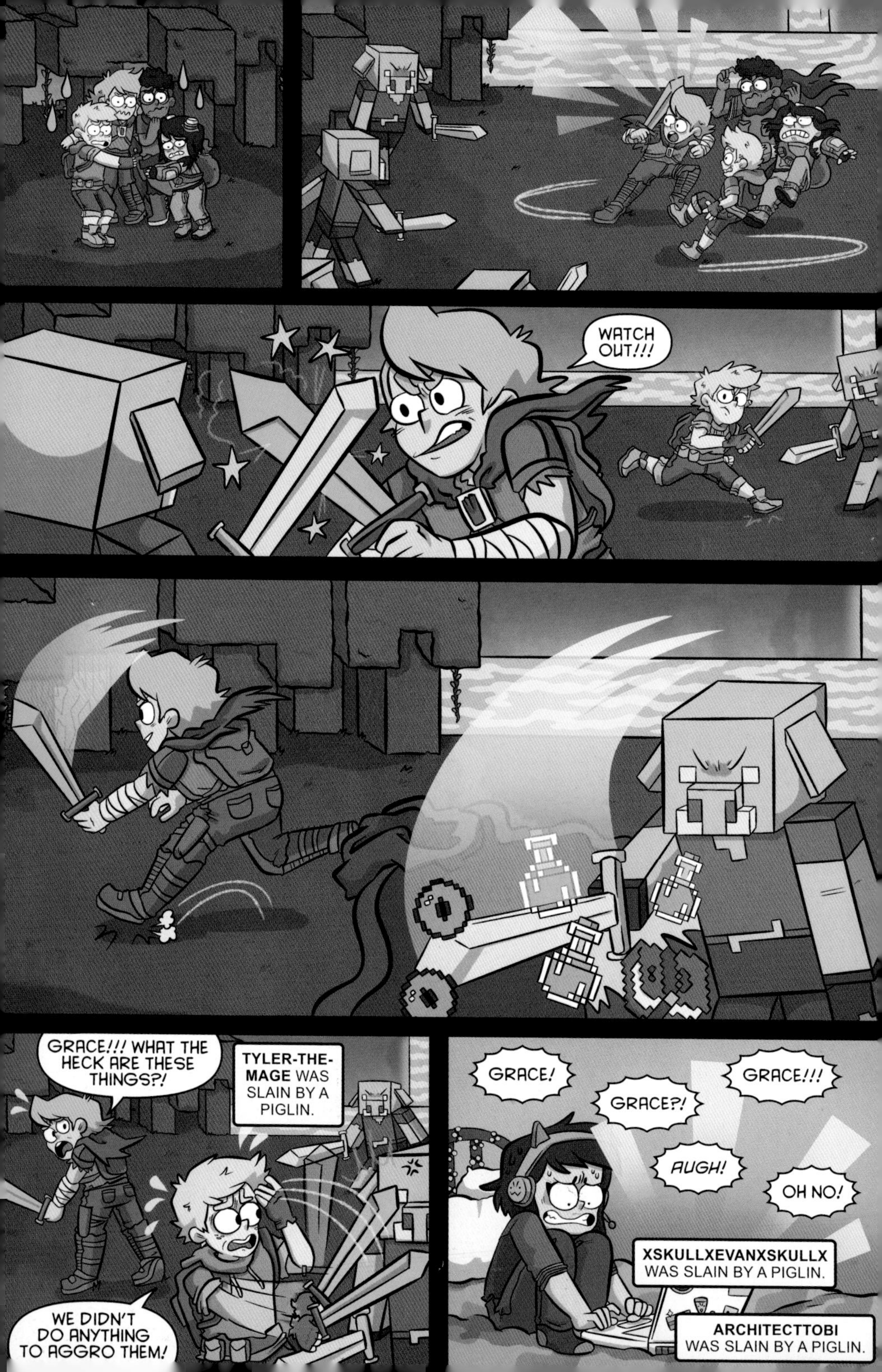
WATCH OUT!!!
GRACE!!! WHAT THE HECK ARE THESE THINGS?!
TYLER-THE-MAGE WAS SLAIN BY A PIGLIN.
WE DIDN'T DO ANYTHING TO AGGRO THEM!
GRACE!
GRACE?!
GRACE!!!
AUGH!
OH NO!
XSKULLXEVANXSKULLX WAS SLAIN BY A PIGLIN.
ARCHITECTTOBI WAS SLAIN BY A PIGLIN.

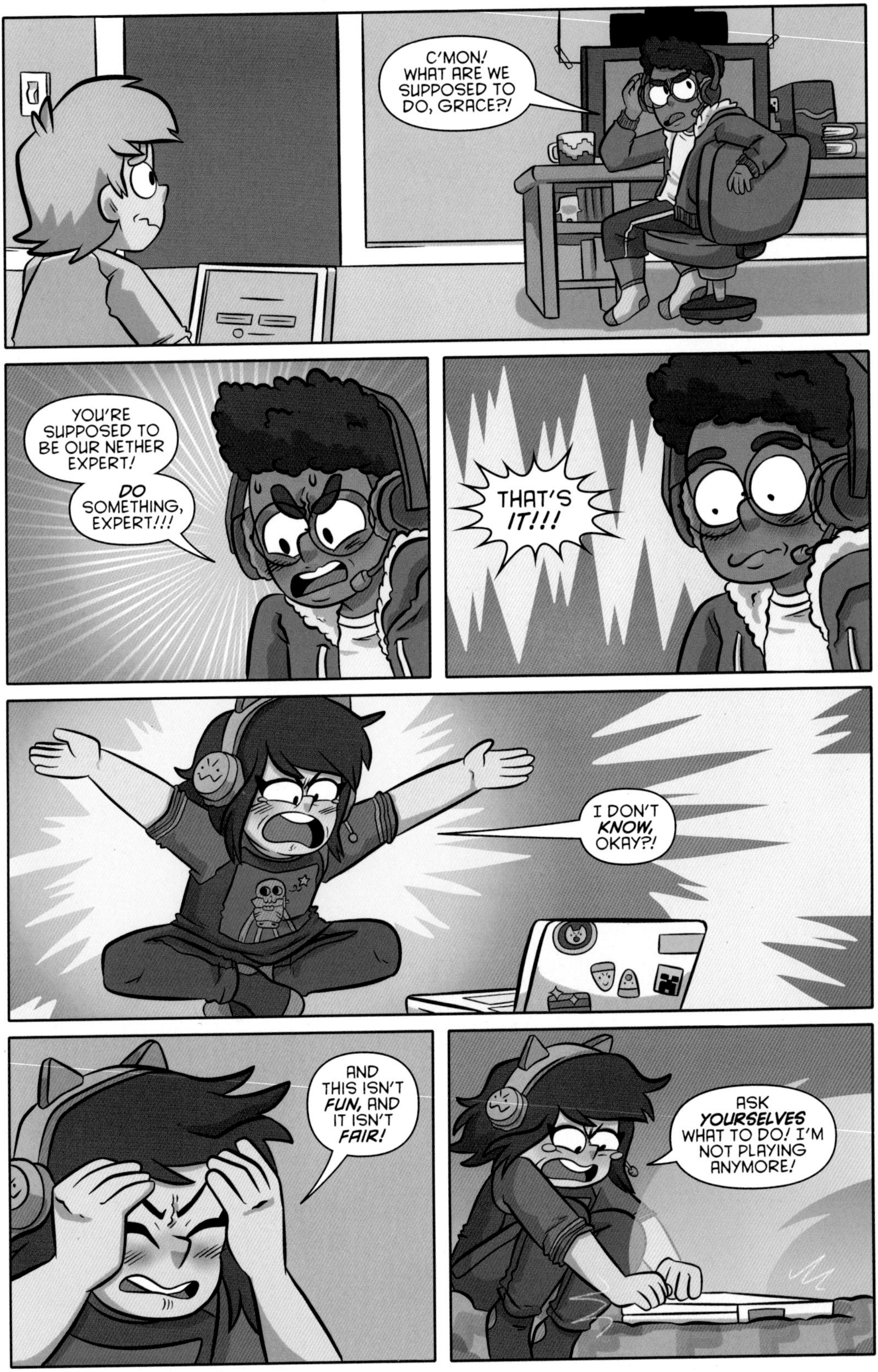

C'MON! WHAT ARE WE SUPPOSED TO DO, GRACE?!
YOU'RE SUPPOSED TO BE OUR NETHER EXPERT!
DO SOMETHING, EXPERT!!!
THAT'S *IT*!!!
I DON'T ***KNOW,*** OKAY?!
AND THIS ISN'T ***FUN,*** AND IT ISN'T ***FAIR!***
ASK ***YOURSELVES*** WHAT TO DO! I'M NOT PLAYING ANYMORE!

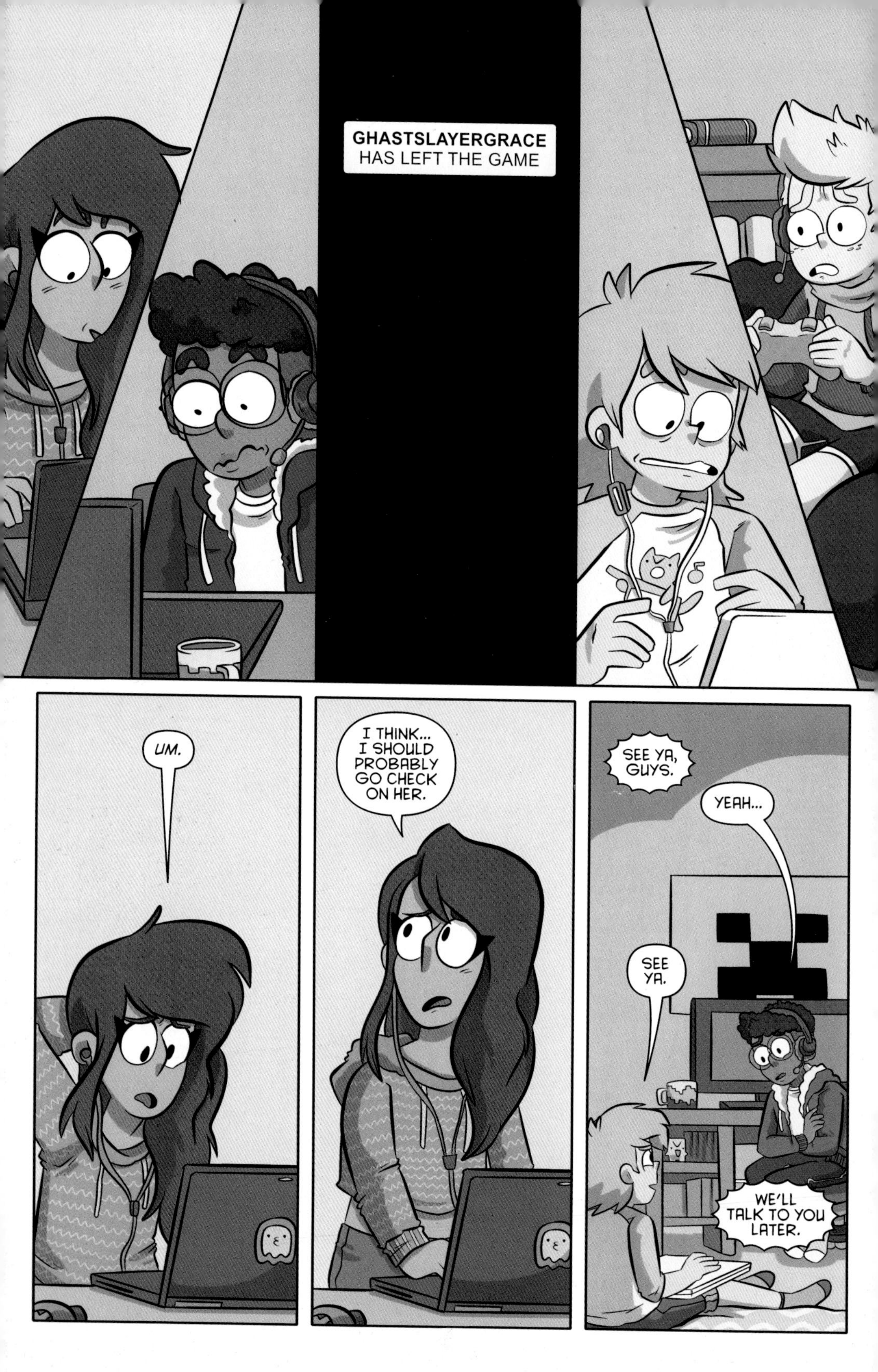
GHASTSLAYERGRACE
HAS LEFT THE GAME
UM.
I THINK... I SHOULD PROBABLY GO CHECK ON HER.
SEE YA, GUYS.
YEAH...
SEE YA.
WE'LL TALK TO YOU LATER.

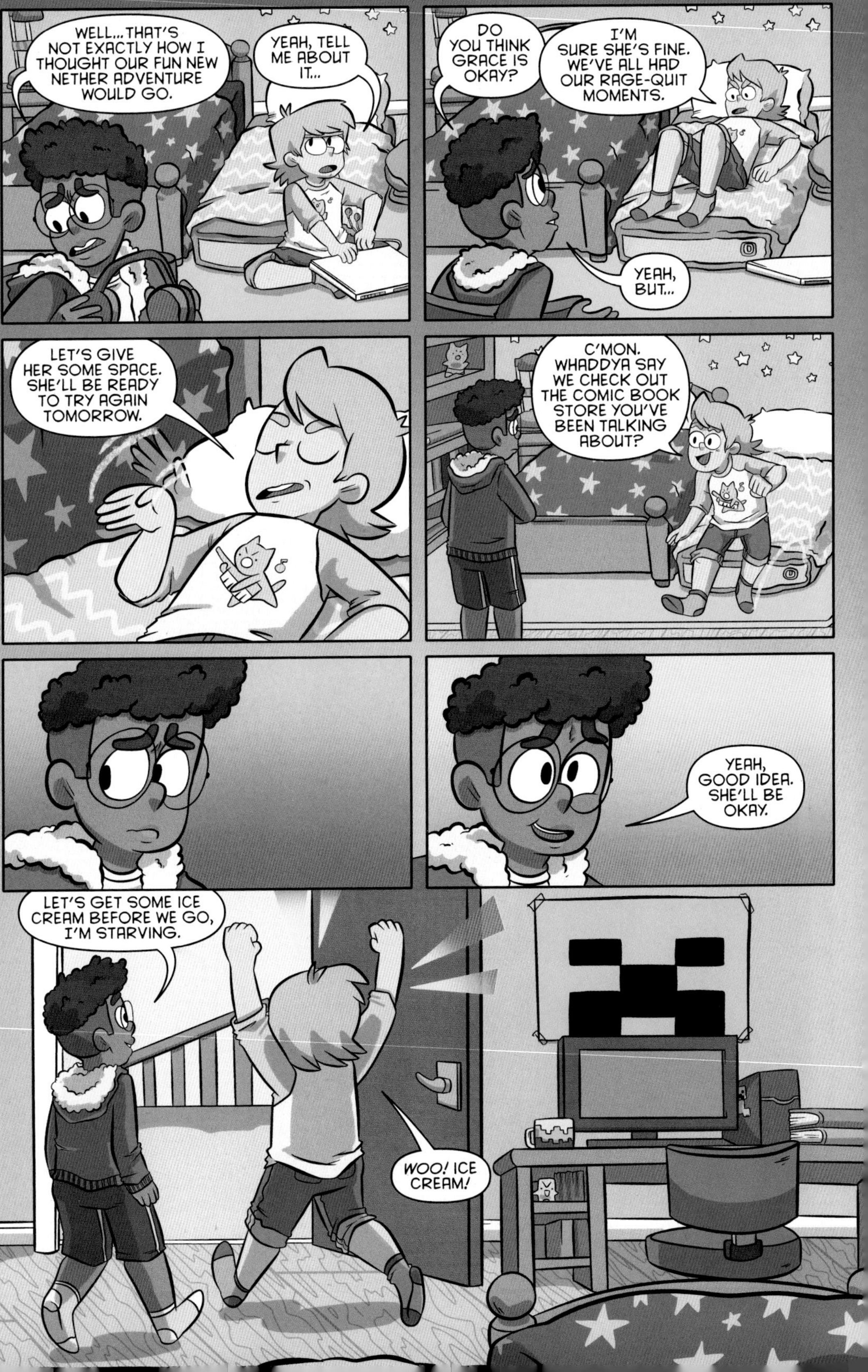
WELL... THAT'S NOT EXACTLY HOW I THOUGHT OUR FUN NEW NETHER ADVENTURE WOULD GO.
YEAH, TELL ME ABOUT IT...
DO YOU THINK GRACE IS OKAY?
I'M SURE SHE'S FINE. WE'VE ALL HAD OUR RAGE-QUIT MOMENTS.
YEAH, BUT...
LET'S GIVE HER SOME SPACE. SHE'LL BE READY TO TRY AGAIN TOMORROW.
C'MON. WHADDYA SAY WE CHECK OUT THE COMIC BOOK STORE YOU'VE BEEN TALKING ABOUT?
YEAH, GOOD IDEA. SHE'LL BE OKAY.
LET'S GET SOME ICE CREAM BEFORE WE GO, I'M STARVING.
WOO! ICE CREAM!

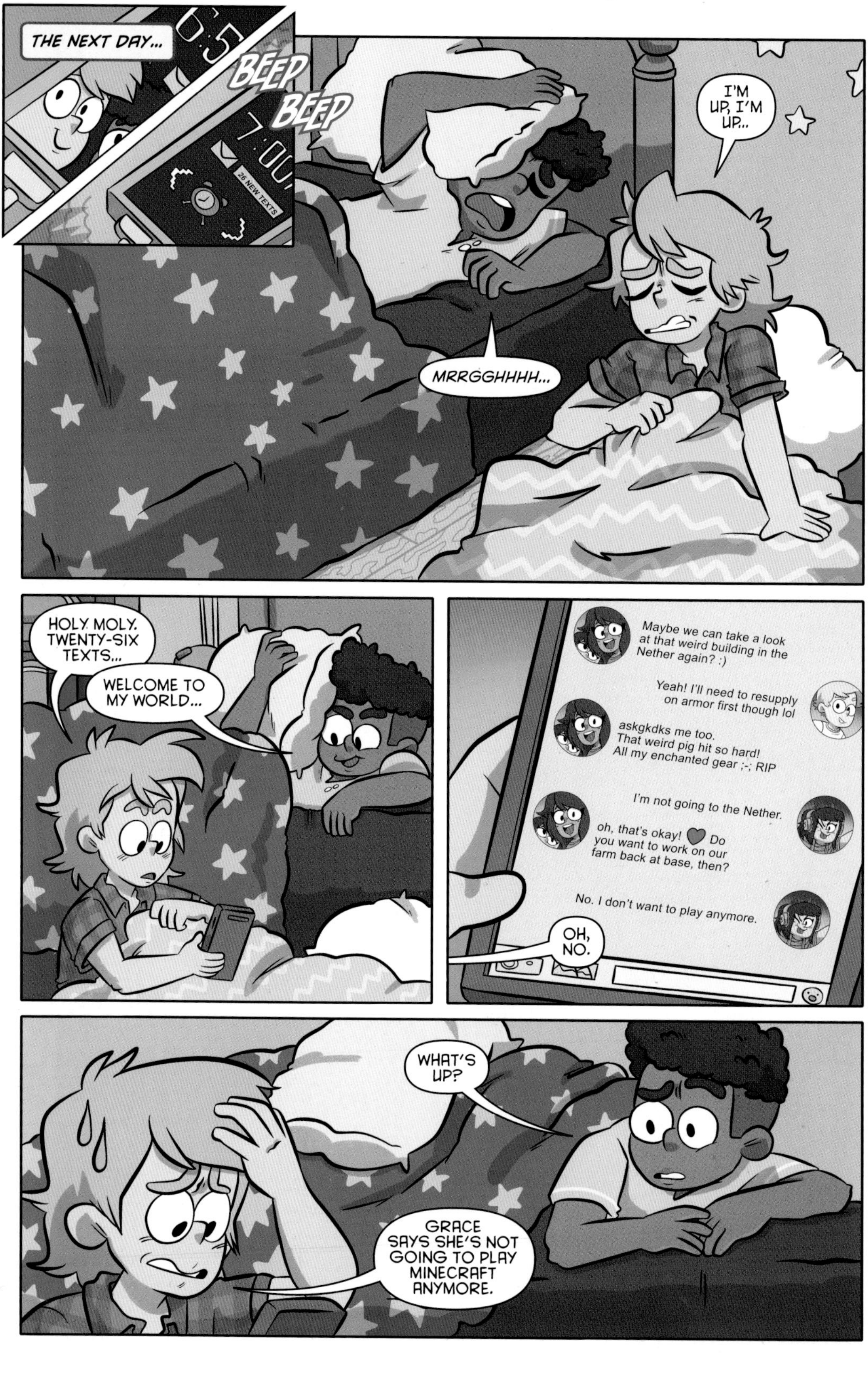
THE NEXT DAY...
6:5
BEEP BEEP
7:00
26 NEW TEXTS
I'M UP, I'M UP...
MRRGGHHHH...
HOLY MOLY. TWENTY-SIX TEXTS...
WELCOME TO MY WORLD...
Maybe we can take a look at that weird building in the Nether again? :)
Yeah! I'll need to resupply on armor first though lol
askgkdks me too. That weird pig hit so hard! All my enchanted gear ;-; RIP
I'm not going to the Nether.
oh, that's okay! ♥ Do you want to work on our farm back at base, then?
No. I don't want to play anymore.
OH, NO.
WHAT'S UP?
GRACE SAYS SHE'S NOT GOING TO PLAY MINECRAFT ANYMORE.

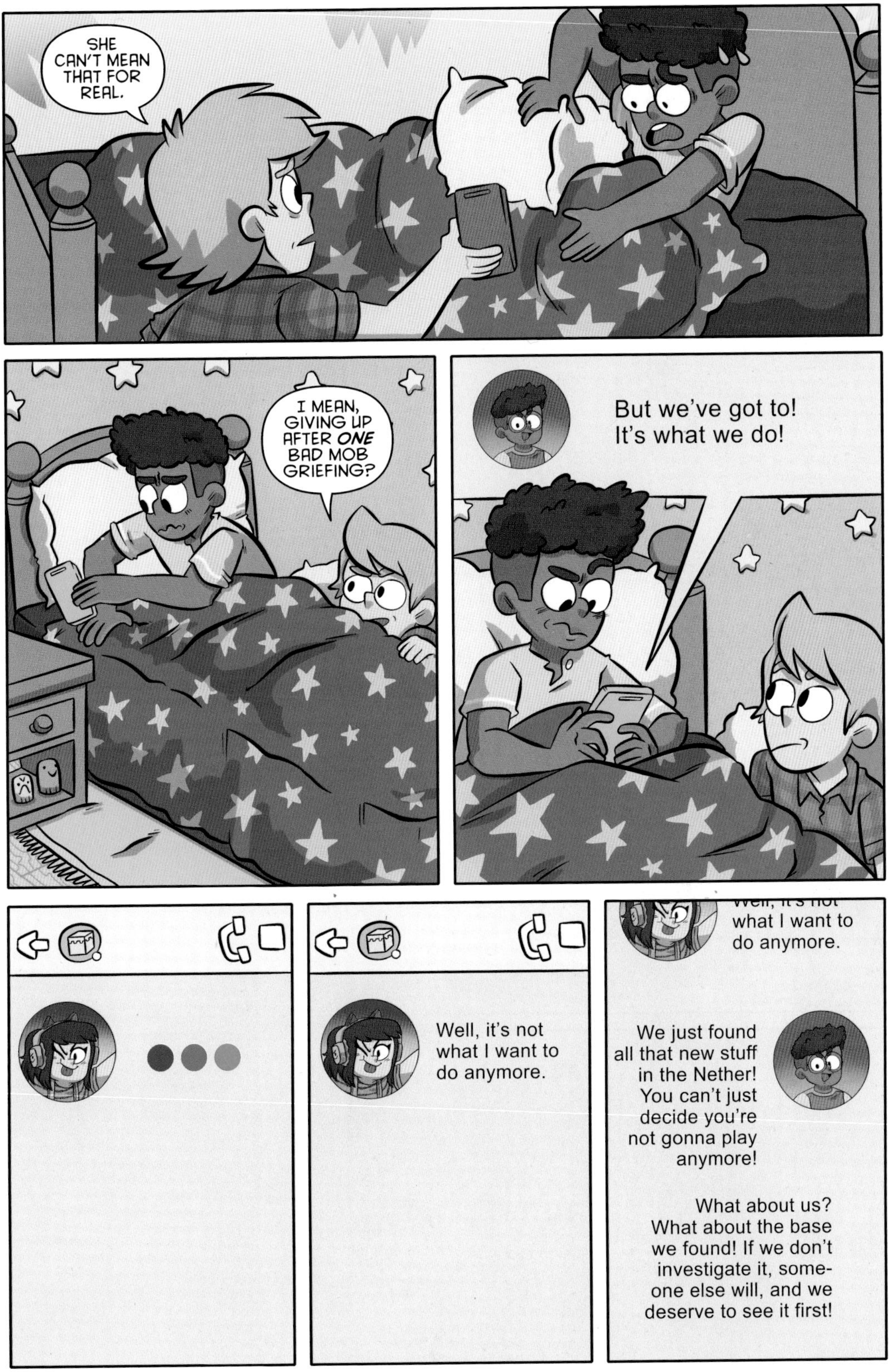

SHE CAN'T MEAN THAT FOR REAL.
I MEAN, GIVING UP AFTER *ONE* BAD MOB GRIEFING?
But we've got to! It's what we do!
Well, it's not what I want to do anymore.
what I want to do anymore.
We just found all that new stuff in the Nether! You can't just decide you're not gonna play anymore!
What about us? What about the base we found! If we don't investigate it, some-one else will, and we deserve to see it first!

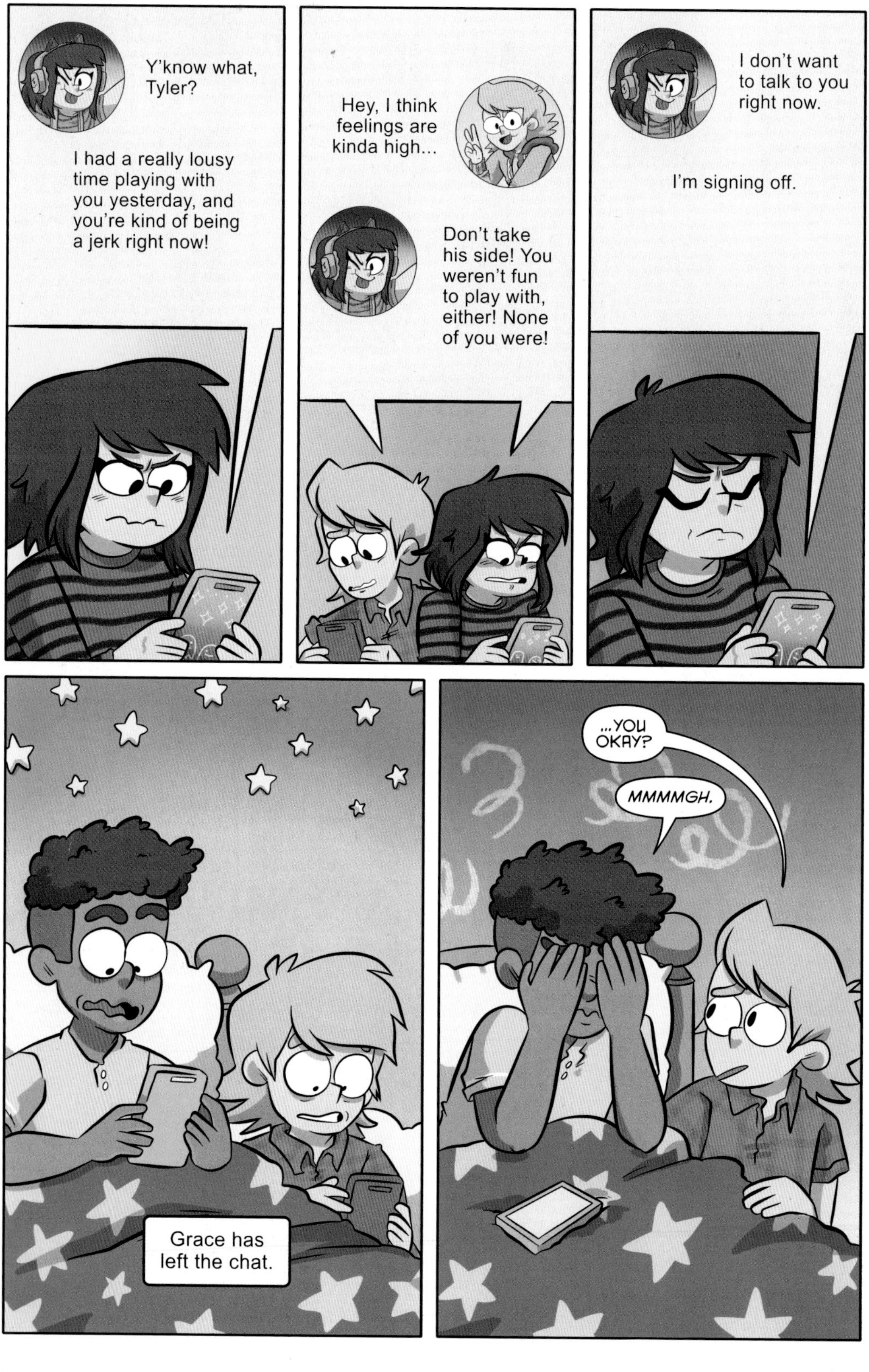
Y'know what, Tyler?
I had a really lousy time playing with you yesterday, and you're kind of being a jerk right now!
Hey, I think feelings are kinda high...
Don't take his side! You weren't fun to play with, either! None of you were!
I don't want to talk to you right now.
I'm signing off.
Grace has left the chat.
...YOU OKAY?
MMMMGH.

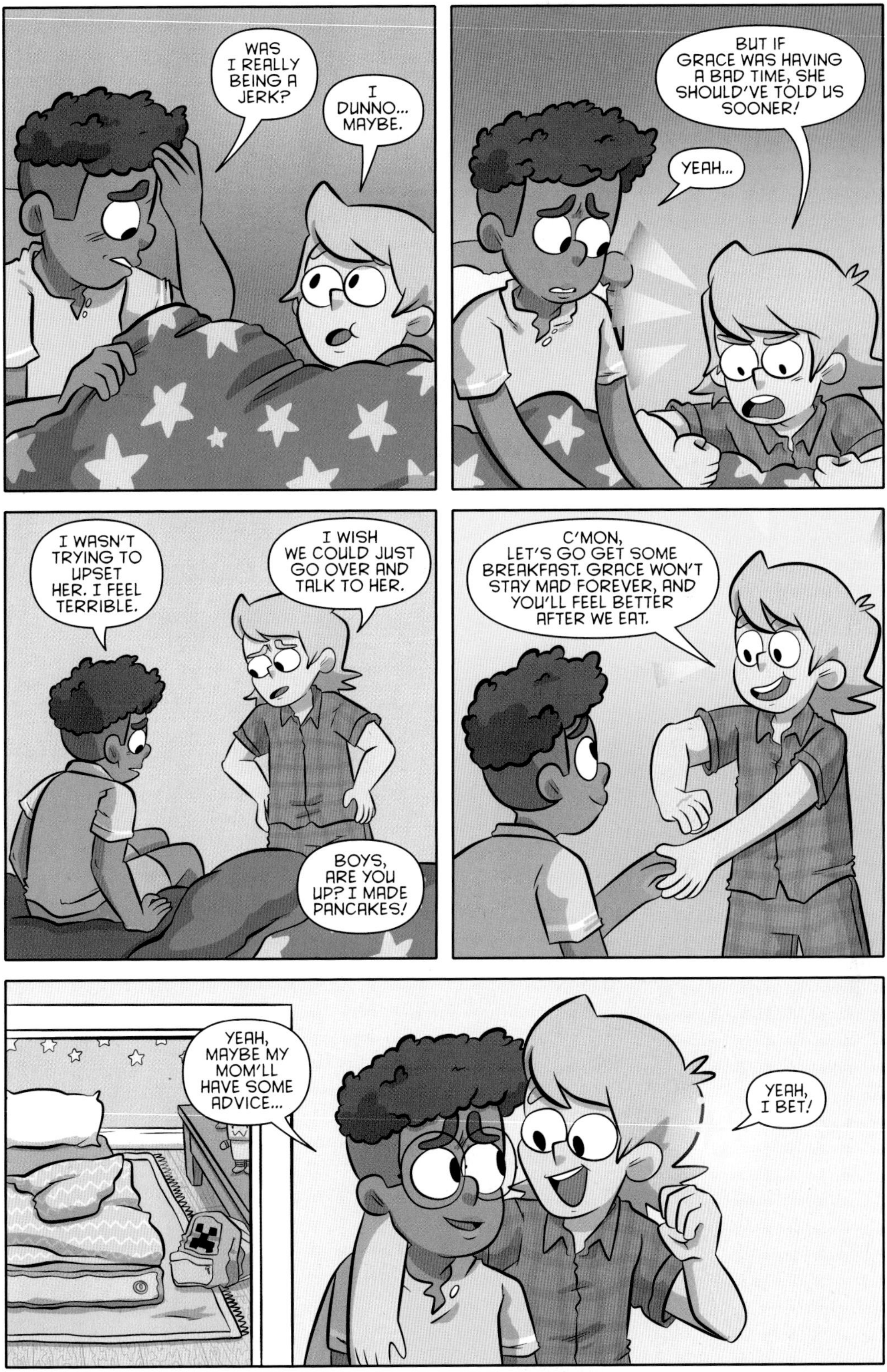
WAS I REALLY BEING A JERK?
I DUNNO... MAYBE.
BUT IF GRACE WAS HAVING A BAD TIME, SHE SHOULD'VE TOLD US SOONER!
YEAH...
I WASN'T TRYING TO UPSET HER. I FEEL TERRIBLE.
I WISH WE COULD JUST GO OVER AND TALK TO HER.
BOYS, ARE YOU UP? I MADE PANCAKES!
C'MON, LET'S GO GET SOME BREAKFAST. GRACE WON'T STAY MAD FOREVER, AND YOU'LL FEEL BETTER AFTER WE EAT.
YEAH, MAYBE MY MOM'LL HAVE SOME ADVICE...
YEAH, I BET!

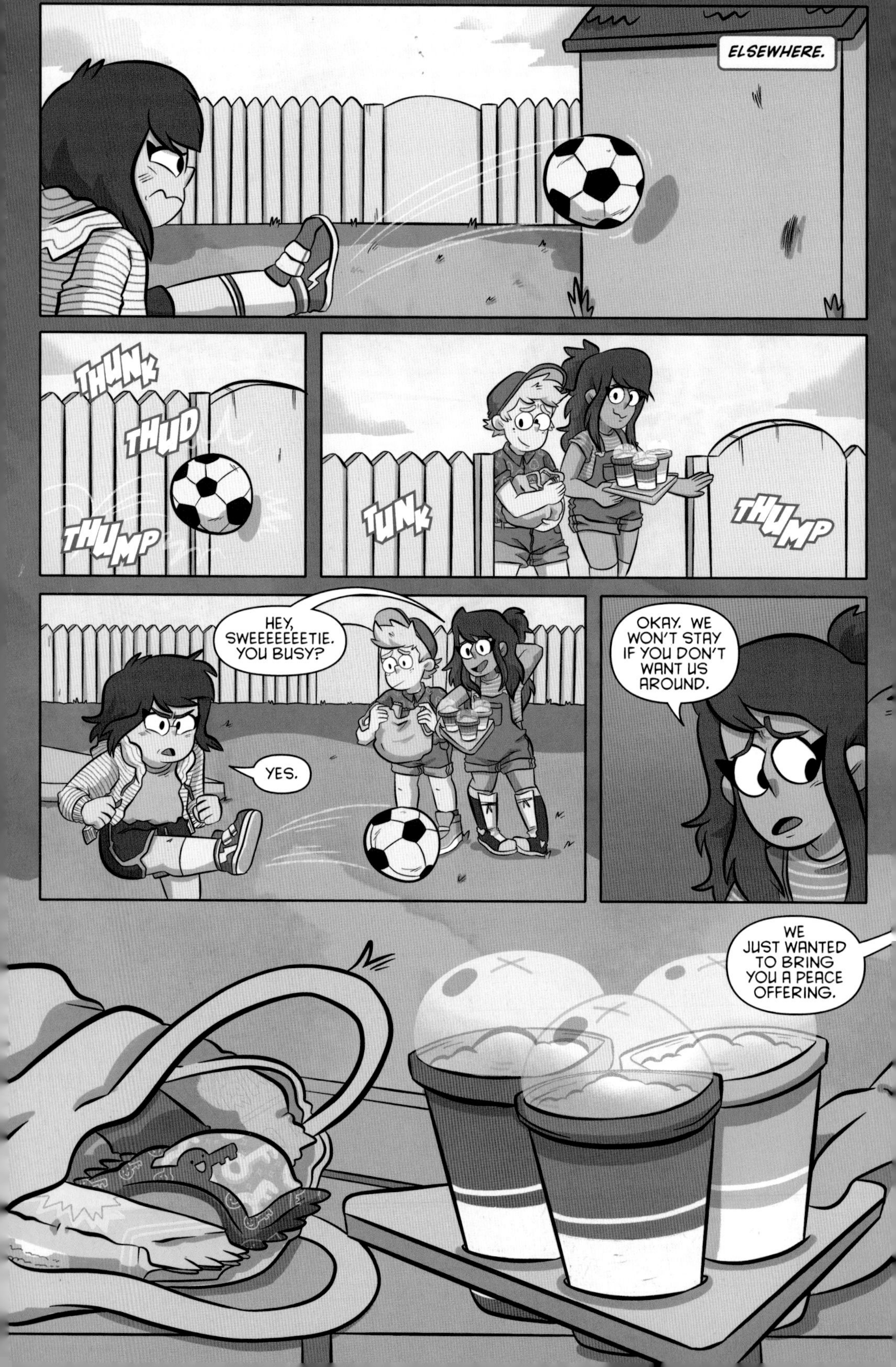
ELSEWHERE.
THUNK
THUD
THUMP
TUNK
THUMP
HEY, SWEEEEEEETIE. YOU BUSY?
YES.
OKAY. WE WON'T STAY IF YOU DON'T WANT US AROUND.
WE JUST WANTED TO BRING YOU A PEACE OFFERING.

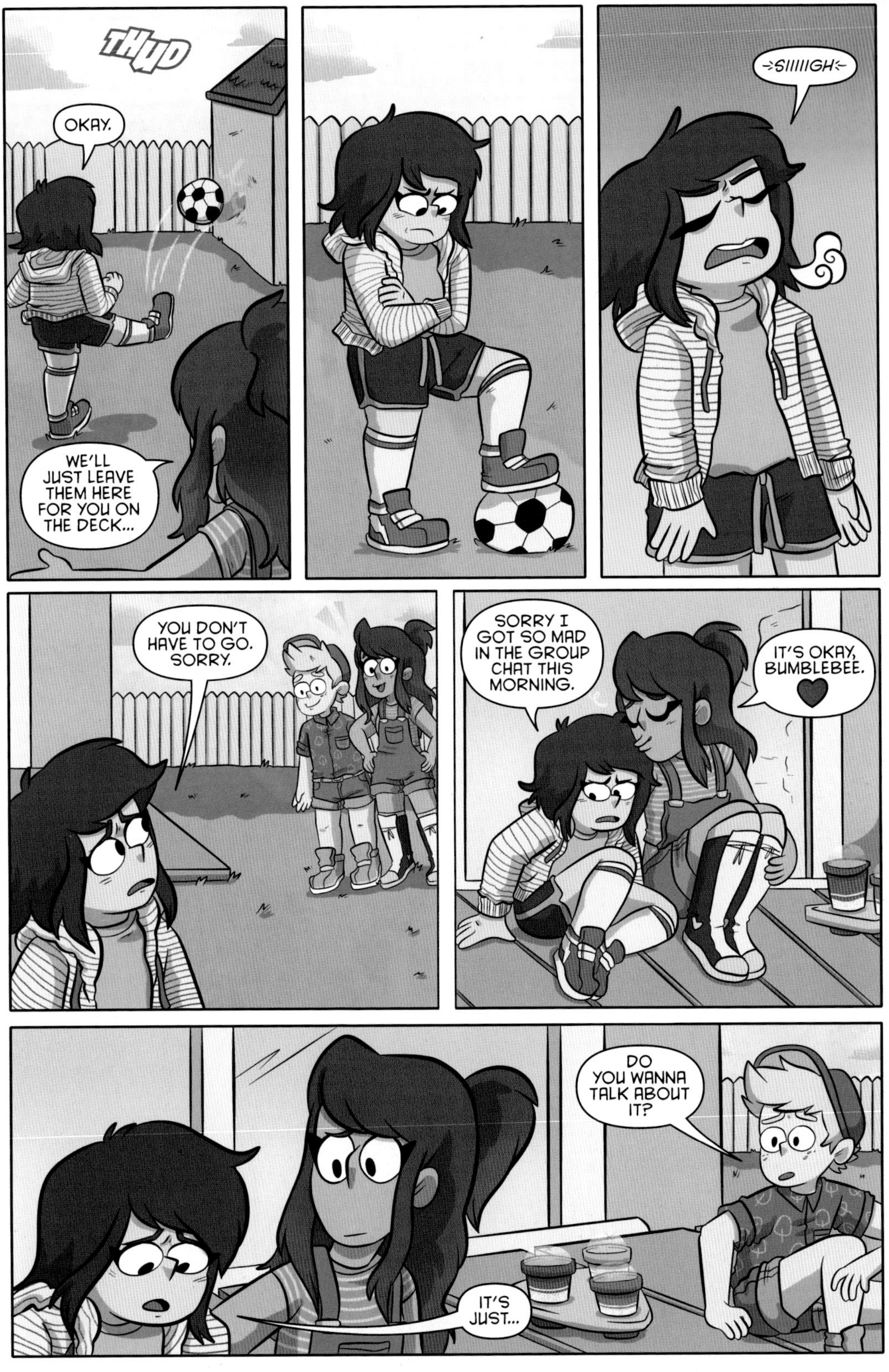
THUD
OKAY.
WE'LL JUST LEAVE THEM HERE FOR YOU ON THE DECK...
SIIIIIGH
YOU DON'T HAVE TO GO. SORRY.
SORRY I GOT SO MAD IN THE GROUP CHAT THIS MORNING.
IT'S OKAY, BUMBLEBEE.
DO YOU WANNA TALK ABOUT IT?
IT'S JUST...

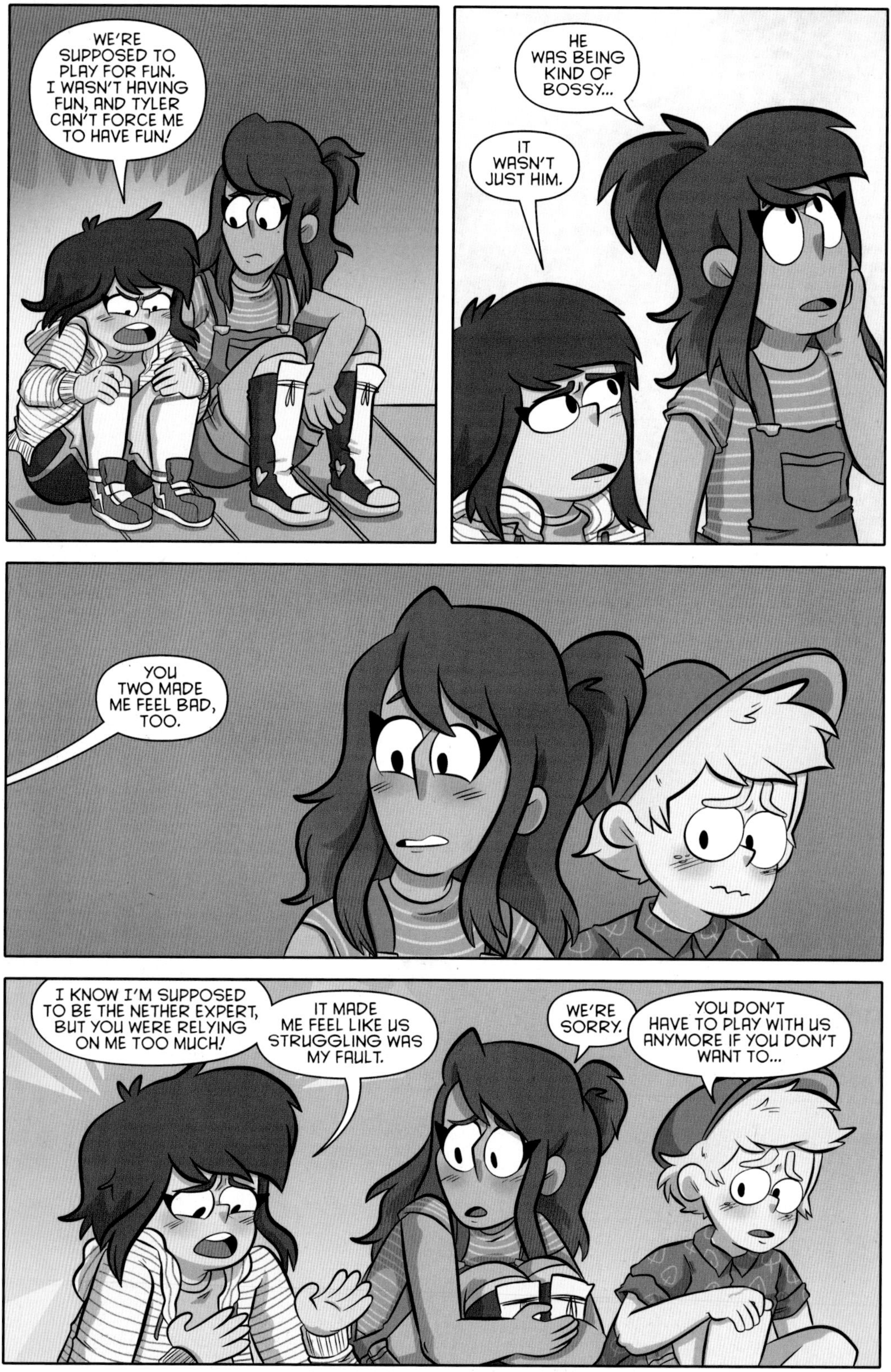
WE'RE SUPPOSED TO PLAY FOR FUN. I WASN'T HAVING FUN, AND TYLER CAN'T FORCE ME TO HAVE FUN!
HE WAS BEING KIND OF BOSSY...
IT WASN'T JUST HIM.
YOU TWO MADE ME FEEL BAD, TOO.
I KNOW I'M SUPPOSED TO BE THE NETHER EXPERT, BUT YOU WERE RELYING ON ME TOO MUCH!
IT MADE ME FEEL LIKE US STRUGGLING WAS MY FAULT.
WE'RE SORRY.
YOU DON'T HAVE TO PLAY WITH US ANYMORE IF YOU DON'T WANT TO...

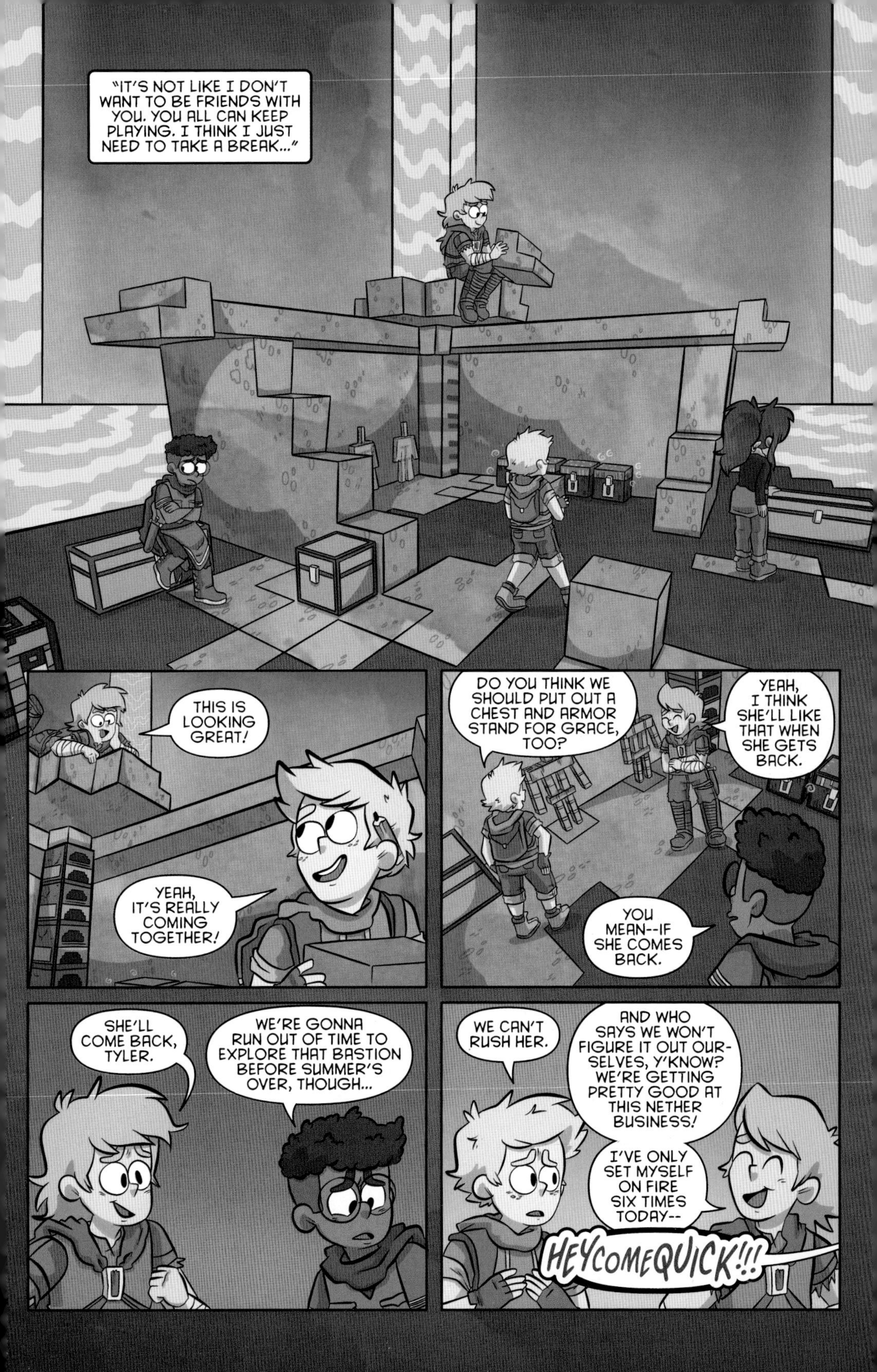
"IT'S NOT LIKE I DON'T WANT TO BE FRIENDS WITH YOU. YOU ALL CAN KEEP PLAYING. I THINK I JUST NEED TO TAKE A BREAK..."
THIS IS LOOKING GREAT!
YEAH, IT'S REALLY COMING TOGETHER!
DO YOU THINK WE SHOULD PUT OUT A CHEST AND ARMOR STAND FOR GRACE, TOO?
YEAH, I THINK SHE'LL LIKE THAT WHEN SHE GETS BACK.
YOU MEAN--IF SHE COMES BACK.
SHE'LL COME BACK, TYLER.
WE'RE GONNA RUN OUT OF TIME TO EXPLORE THAT BASTION BEFORE SUMMER'S OVER, THOUGH...
WE CAN'T RUSH HER.
AND WHO SAYS WE WON'T FIGURE IT OUT OUR-SELVES, Y'KNOW? WE'RE GETTING PRETTY GOOD AT THIS NETHER BUSINESS!
I'VE ONLY SET MYSELF ON FIRE SIX TIMES TODAY--
HEYCOMEQUICK!!!

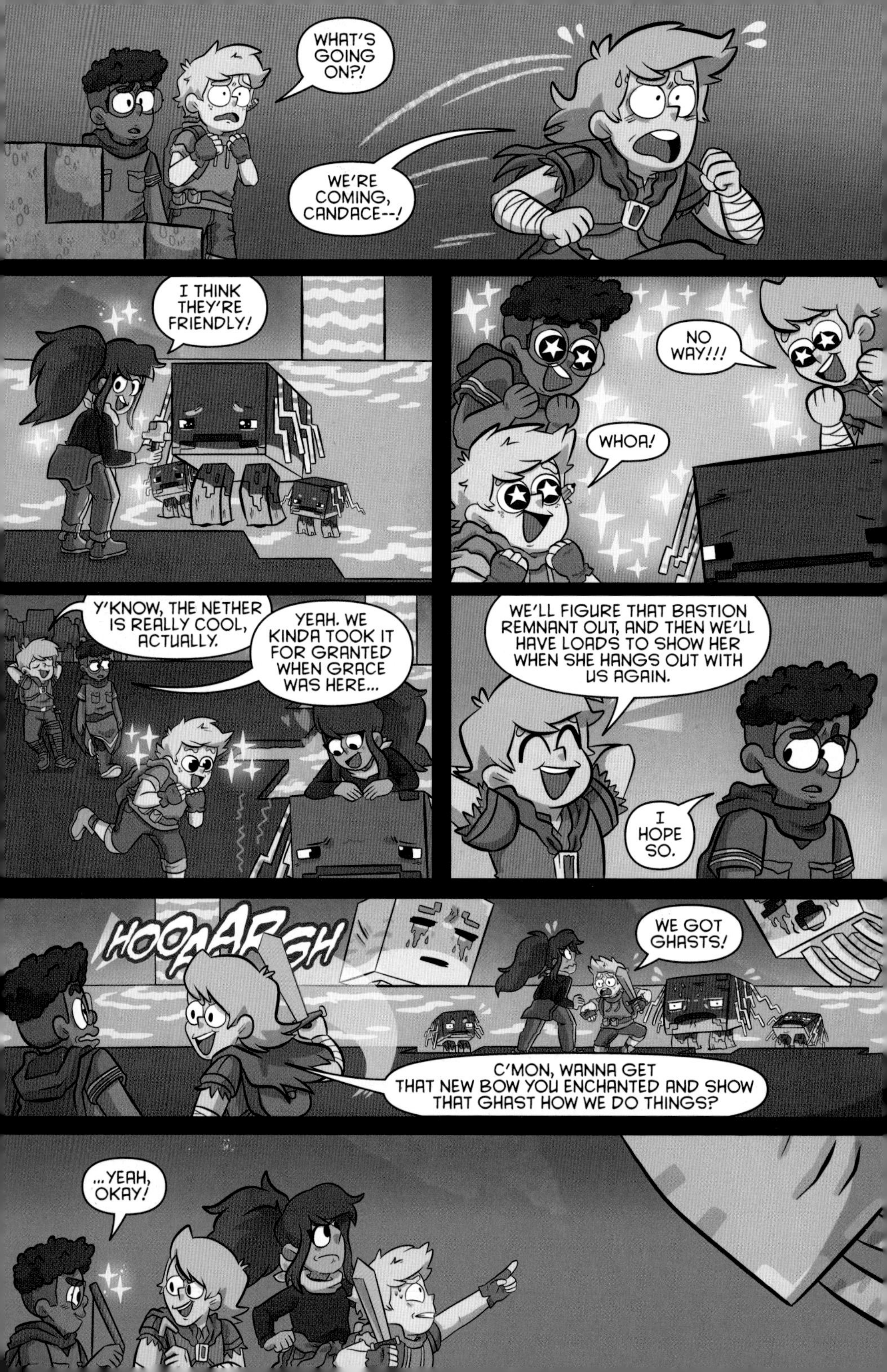
WHAT'S GOING ON?!
WE'RE COMING, CANDACE--!
I THINK THEY'RE FRIENDLY!
NO WAY!!!
WHOA!
Y'KNOW, THE NETHER IS REALLY COOL, ACTUALLY.
YEAH. WE KINDA TOOK IT FOR GRANTED WHEN GRACE WAS HERE...
WE'LL FIGURE THAT BASTION REMNANT OUT, AND THEN WE'LL HAVE LOADS TO SHOW HER WHEN SHE HANGS OUT WITH US AGAIN.
I HOPE SO.
WE GOT GHASTS!
C'MON, WANNA GET THAT NEW BOW YOU ENCHANTED AND SHOW THAT GHAST HOW WE DO THINGS?
...YEAH, OKAY!

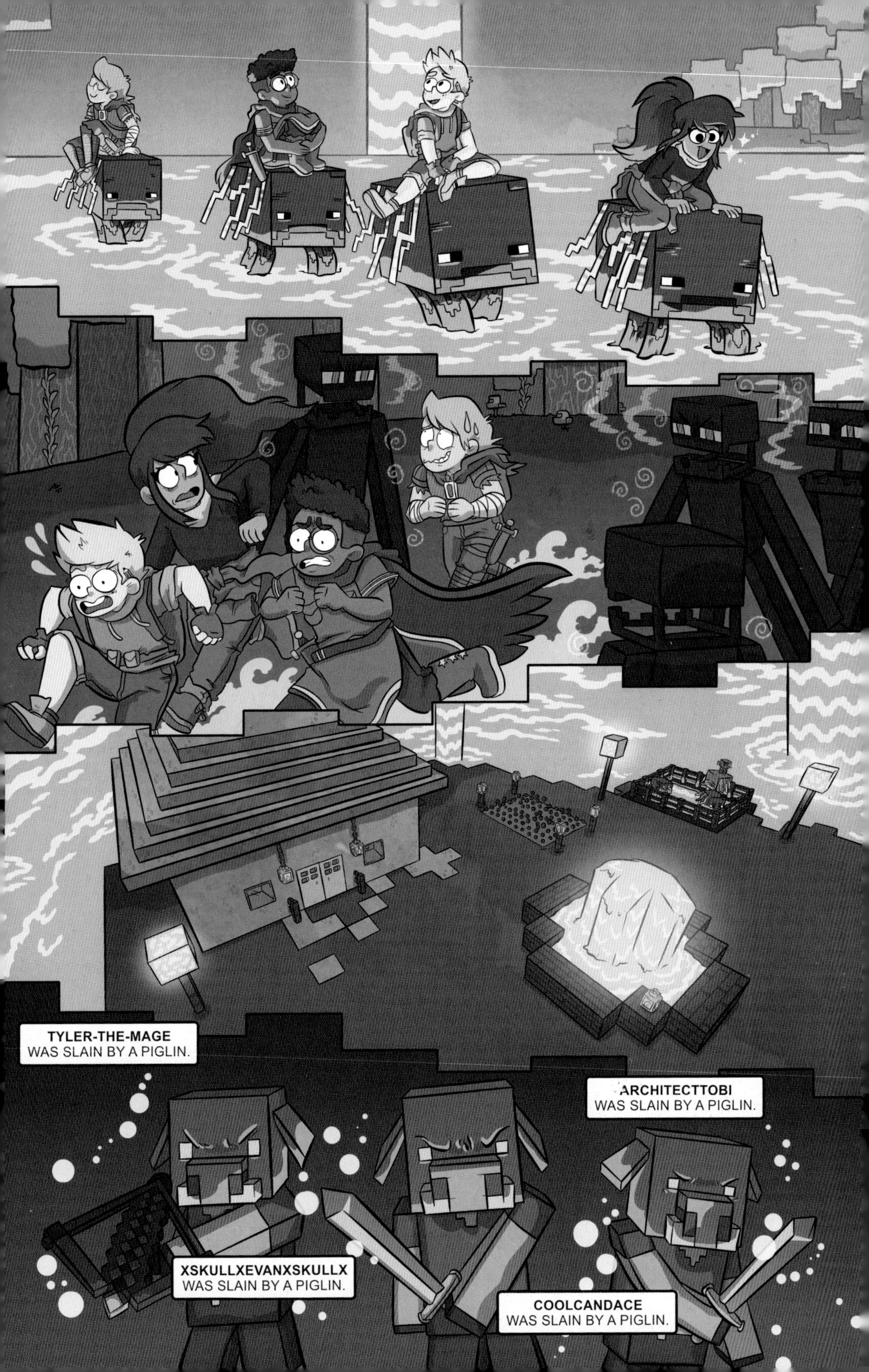
TYLER-THE-MAGE
WAS SLAIN BY A PIGLIN.
ARCHITECTTOBI
WAS SLAIN BY A PIGLIN.
XSKULLXEVANXSKULLX
WAS SLAIN BY A PIGLIN.
COOLCANDACE
WAS SLAIN BY A PIGLIN.

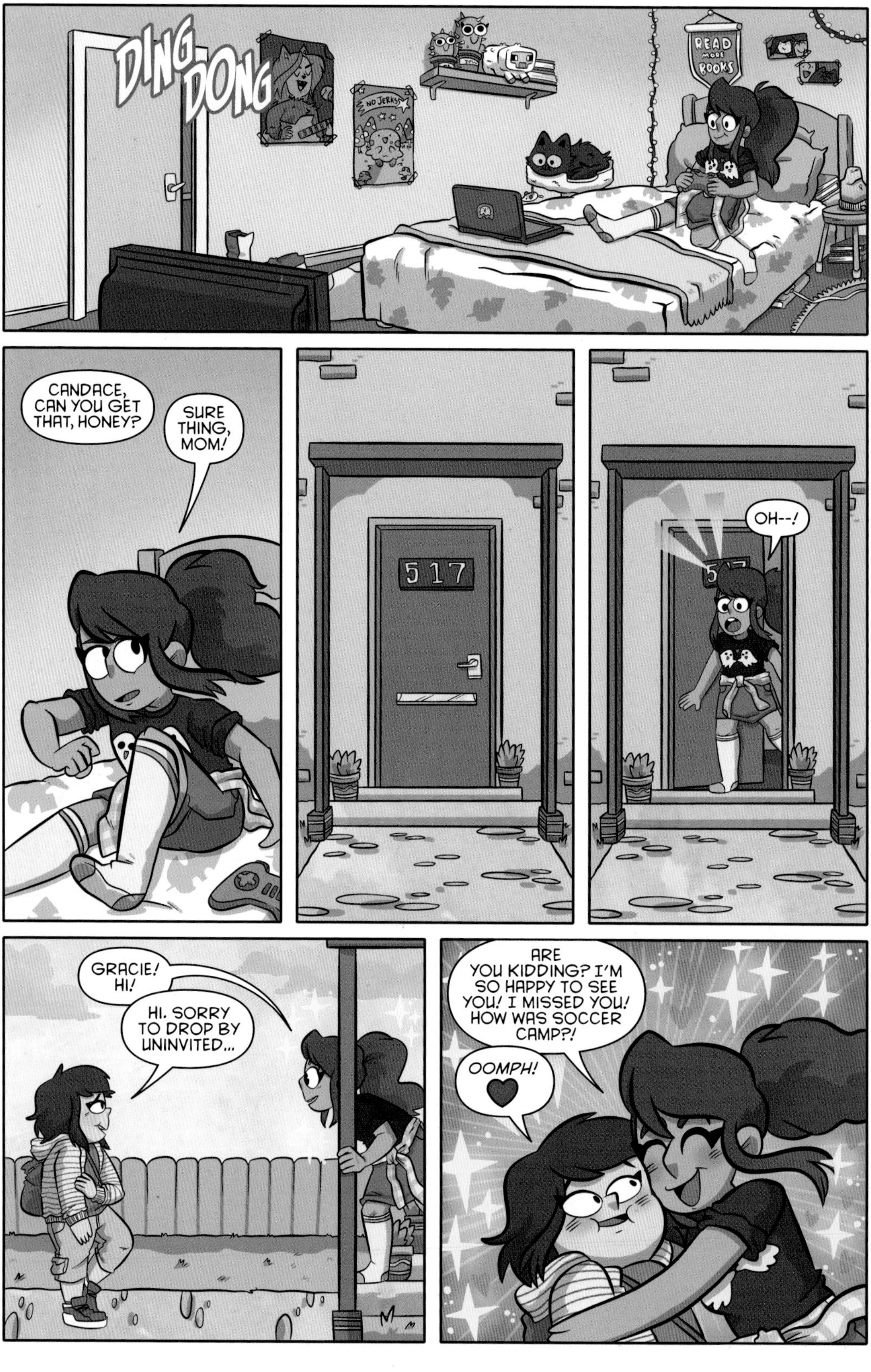
DING DONG
READ MORE BOOKS
NO JERKS
CANDACE, CAN YOU GET THAT, HONEY?
SURE THING, MOM!
517
OH--!
GRACIE! HI!
HI. SORRY TO DROP BY UNINVITED...
ARE YOU KIDDING? I'M SO HAPPY TO SEE YOU! I MISSED YOU! HOW WAS SOCCER CAMP?!
OOMPH!

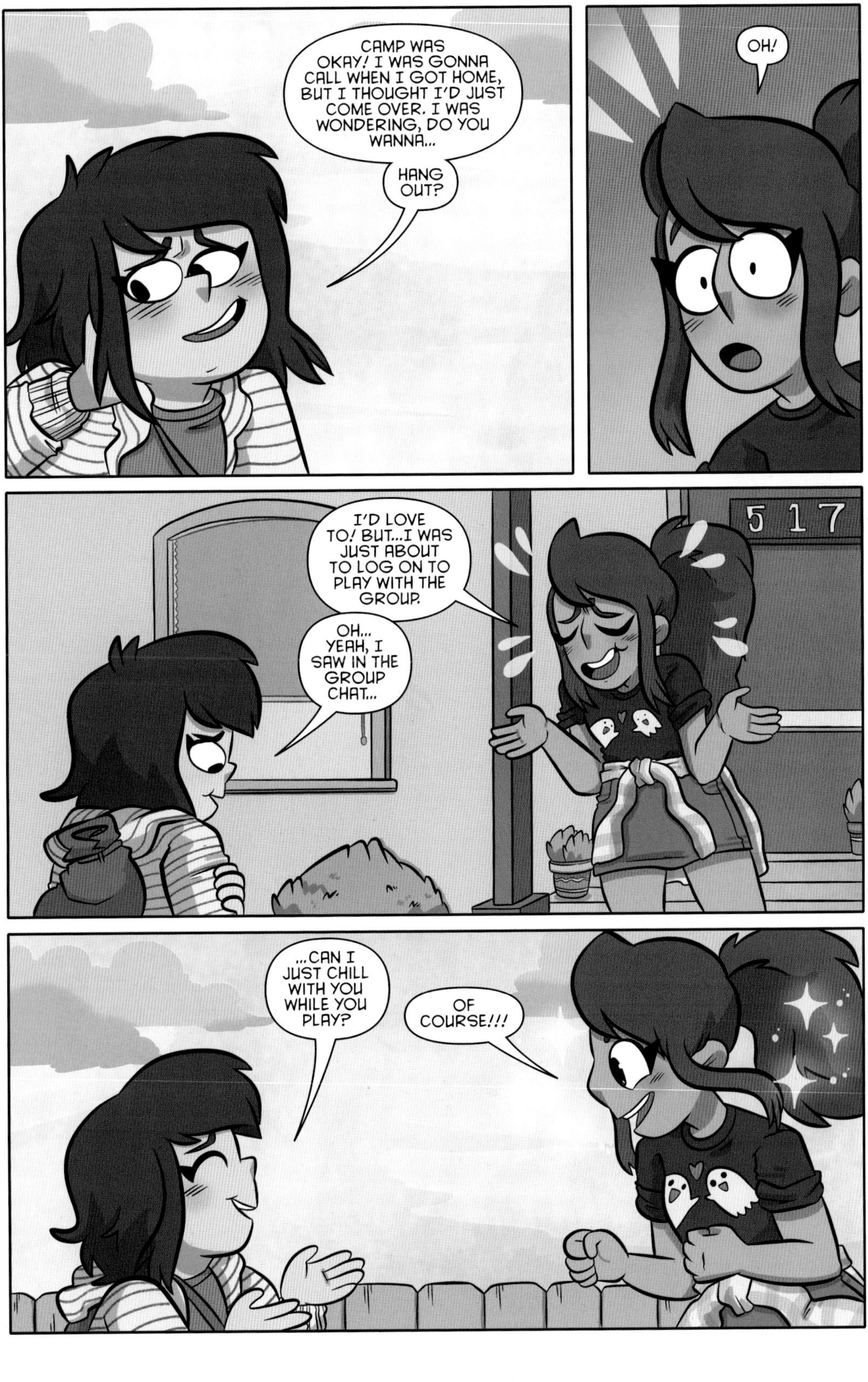
CAMP WAS OKAY! I WAS GONNA CALL WHEN I GOT HOME, BUT I THOUGHT I'D JUST COME OVER. I WAS WONDERING, DO YOU WANNA...
HANG OUT?
OH!
I'D LOVE TO! BUT...I WAS JUST ABOUT TO LOG ON TO PLAY WITH THE GROUP.
OH... YEAH, I SAW IN THE GROUP CHAT...
517
...CAN I JUST CHILL WITH YOU WHILE YOU PLAY?
OF COURSE!!!

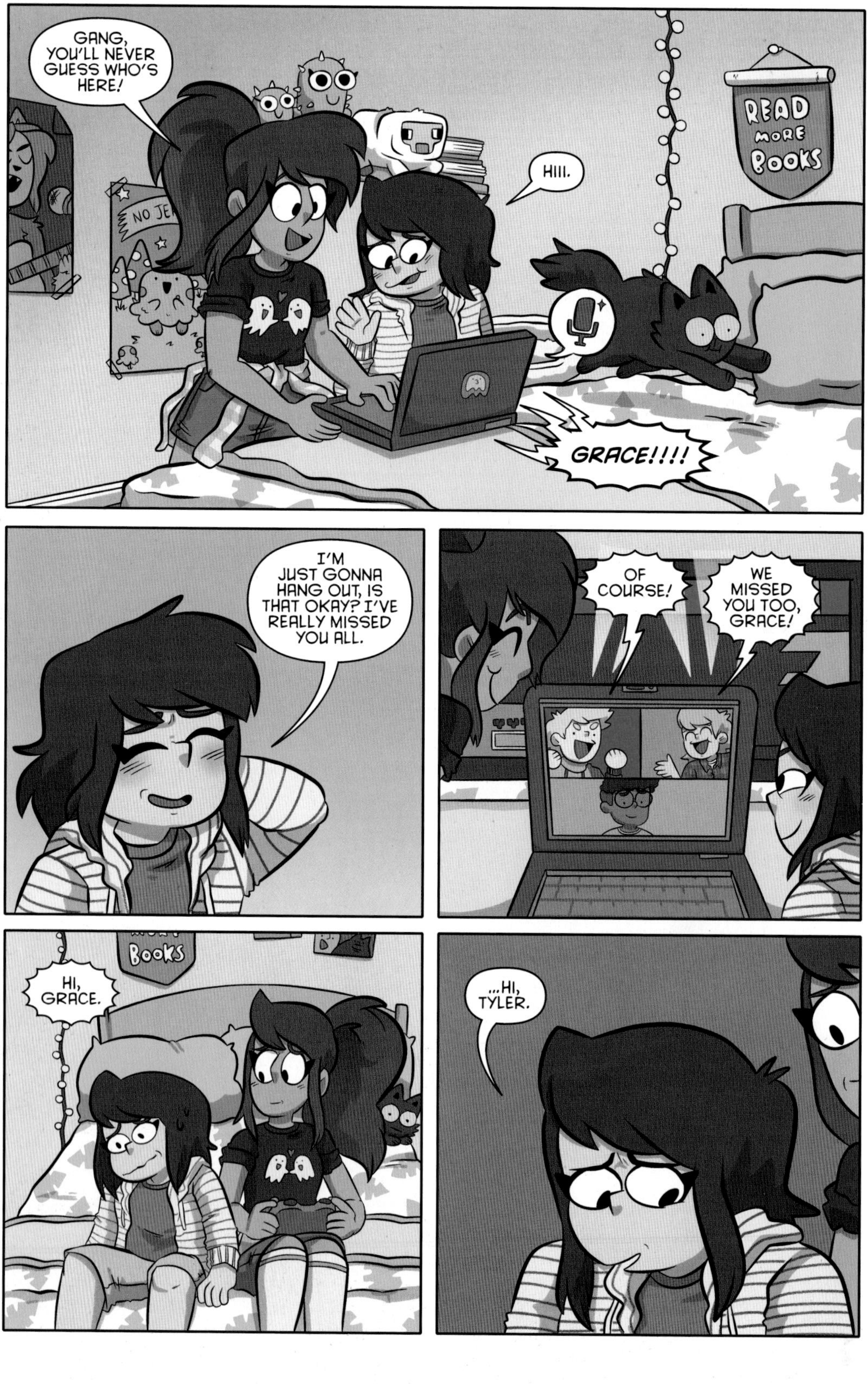
GANG, YOU'LL NEVER GUESS WHO'S HERE!
HIII.
READ MORE BOOKS
GRACE!!!!
I'M JUST GONNA HANG OUT, IS THAT OKAY? I'VE REALLY MISSED YOU ALL.
OF COURSE!
WE MISSED YOU TOO, GRACE!
BOOKS
HI, GRACE.
...HI, TYLER.

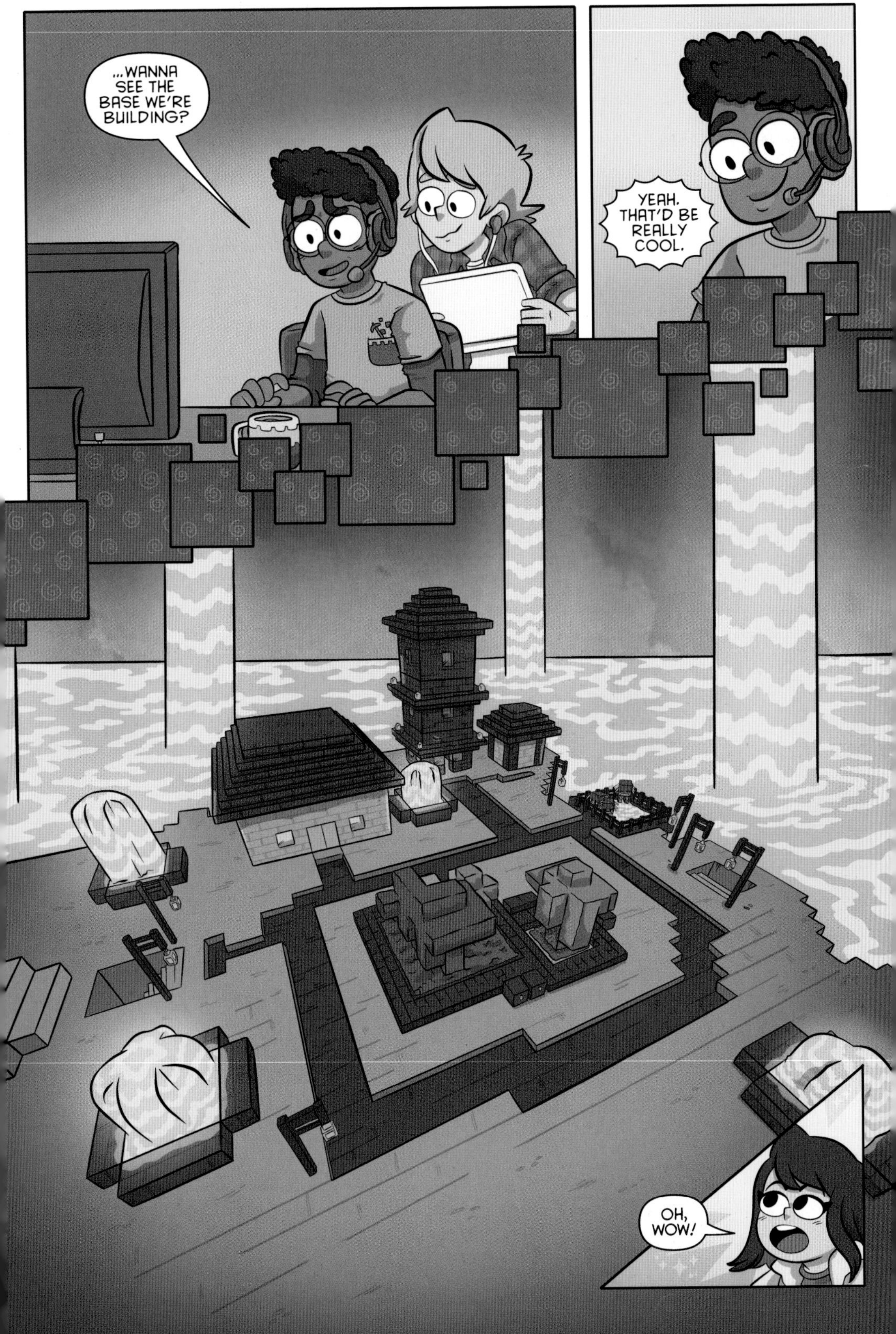
...WANNA SEE THE BASE WE'RE BUILDING?
YEAH. THAT'D BE REALLY COOL.
OH, WOW!

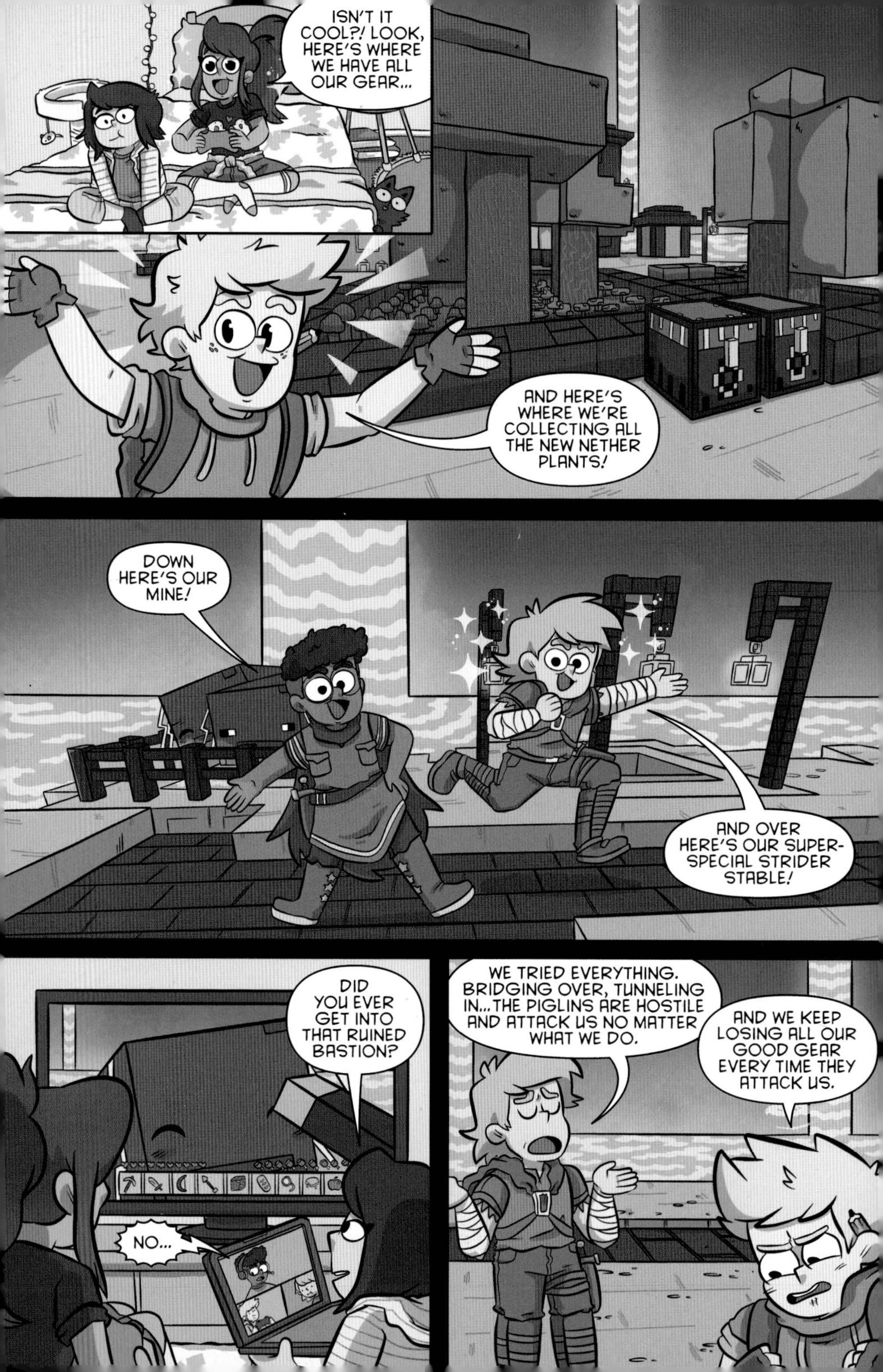

ISN'T IT COOL?! LOOK, HERE'S WHERE WE HAVE ALL OUR GEAR...
AND HERE'S WHERE WE'RE COLLECTING ALL THE NEW NETHER PLANTS!
DOWN HERE'S OUR MINE!
AND OVER HERE'S OUR SUPER-SPECIAL STRIDER STABLE!
DID YOU EVER GET INTO THAT RUINED BASTION?
NO...
WE TRIED EVERYTHING. BRIDGING OVER, TUNNELING IN... THE PIGLINS ARE HOSTILE AND ATTACK US NO MATTER WHAT WE DO.
AND WE KEEP LOSING ALL OUR GOOD GEAR EVERY TIME THEY ATTACK US.

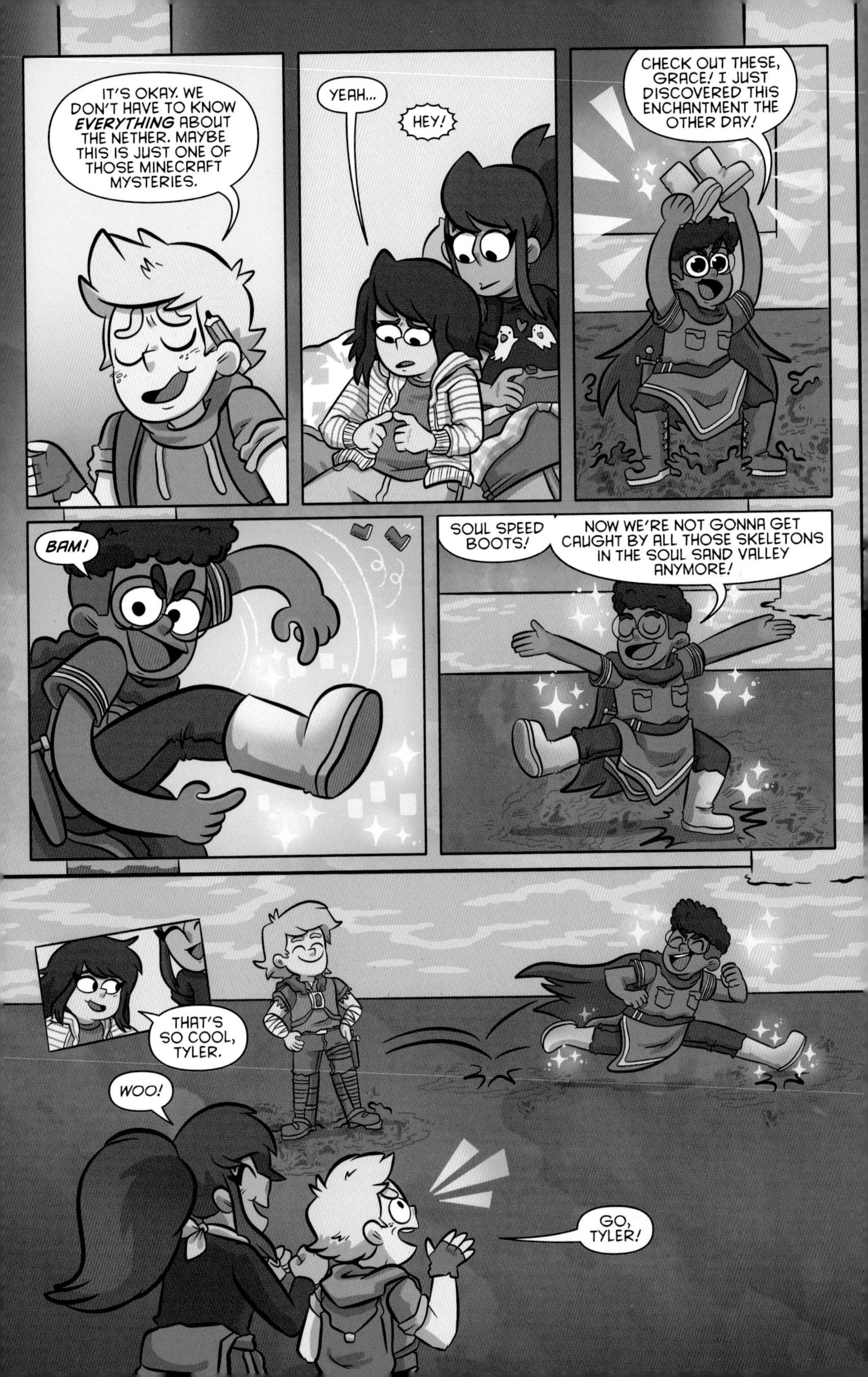
IT'S OKAY. WE DON'T HAVE TO KNOW EVERYTHING ABOUT THE NETHER. MAYBE THIS IS JUST ONE OF THOSE MINECRAFT MYSTERIES.
YEAH...
HEY!
CHECK OUT THESE, GRACE! I JUST DISCOVERED THIS ENCHANTMENT THE OTHER DAY!
BAM!
SOUL SPEED BOOTS!
NOW WE'RE NOT GONNA GET CAUGHT BY ALL THOSE SKELETONS IN THE SOUL SAND VALLEY ANYMORE!
THAT'S SO COOL, TYLER.
WOO!
GO, TYLER!

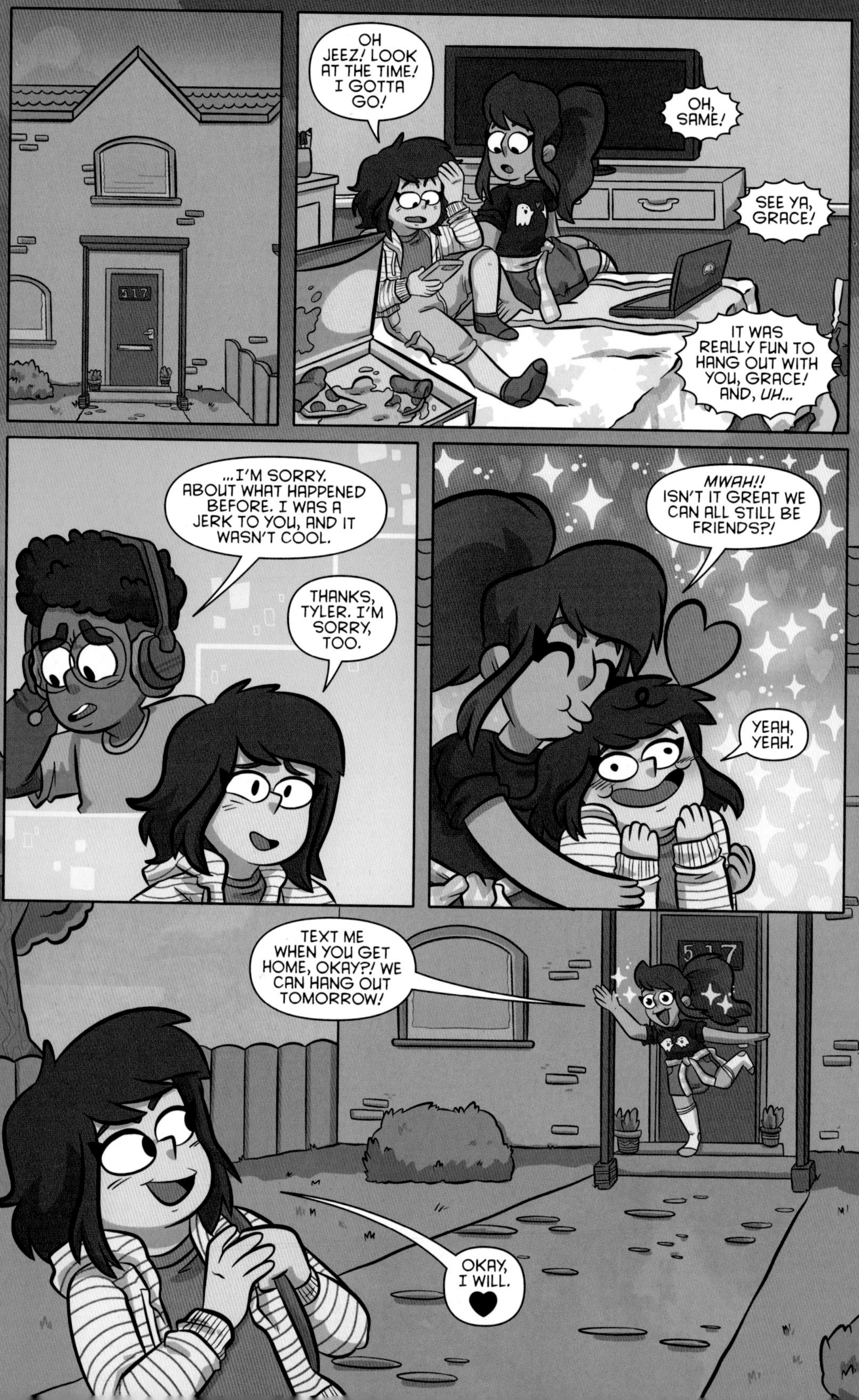
OH JEEZ! LOOK AT THE TIME! I GOTTA GO!
OH, SAME!
SEE YA, GRACE!
IT WAS REALLY FUN TO HANG OUT WITH YOU, GRACE! AND, *UH*...
...I'M SORRY. ABOUT WHAT HAPPENED BEFORE. I WAS A JERK TO YOU, AND IT WASN'T COOL.
THANKS, TYLER. I'M SORRY, TOO.
MWAH!! ISN'T IT GREAT WE CAN ALL STILL BE FRIENDS?!
YEAH, YEAH.
TEXT ME WHEN YOU GET HOME, OKAY?! WE CAN HANG OUT TOMORROW!
OKAY, I WILL.

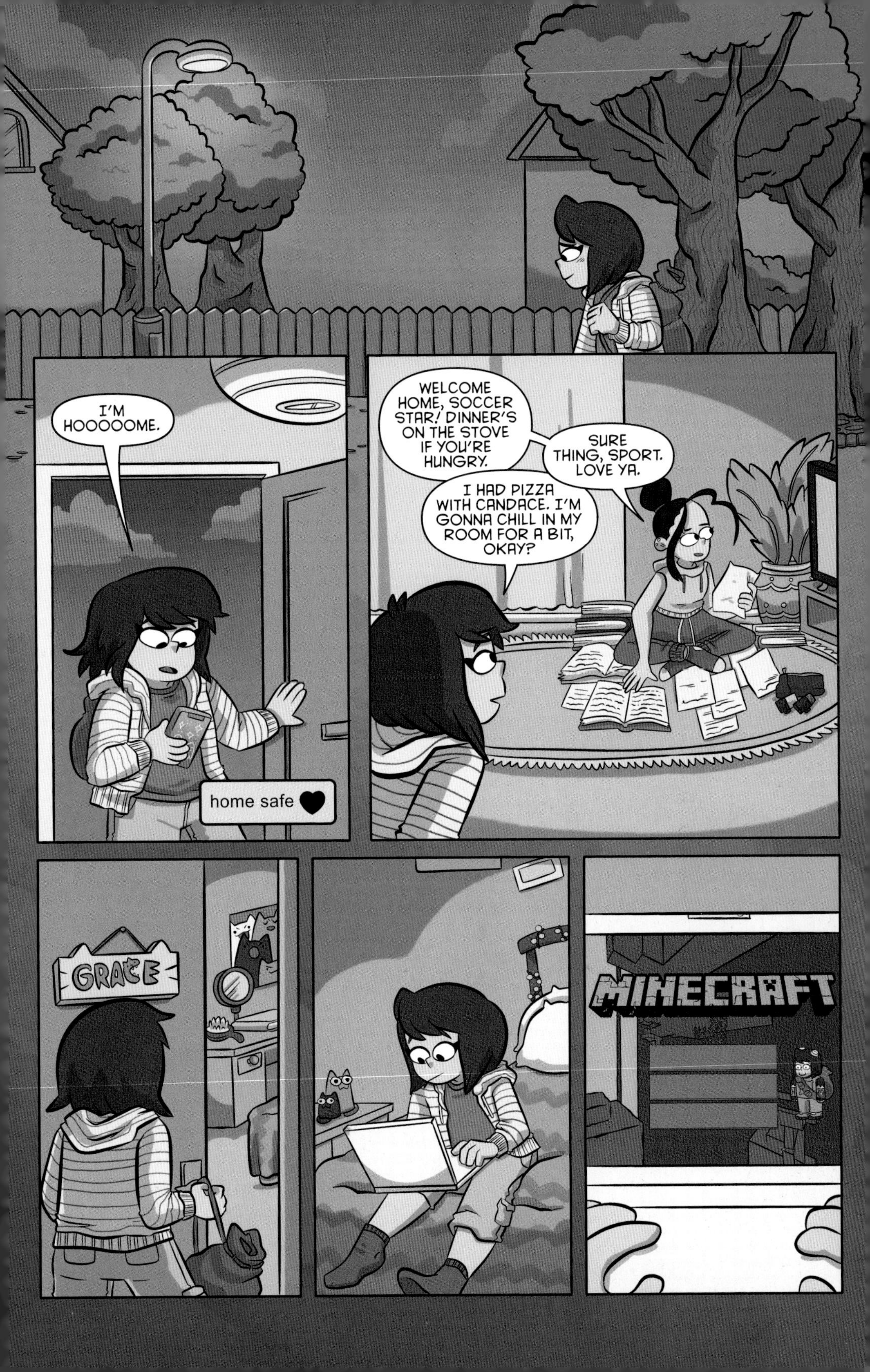
I'M HOOOOOME.
home safe
WELCOME HOME, SOCCER STAR! DINNER'S ON THE STOVE IF YOU'RE HUNGRY.
I HAD PIZZA WITH CANDACE. I'M GONNA CHILL IN MY ROOM FOR A BIT, OKAY?
SURE THING, SPORT. LOVE YA.
GRACE
MINECRAFT

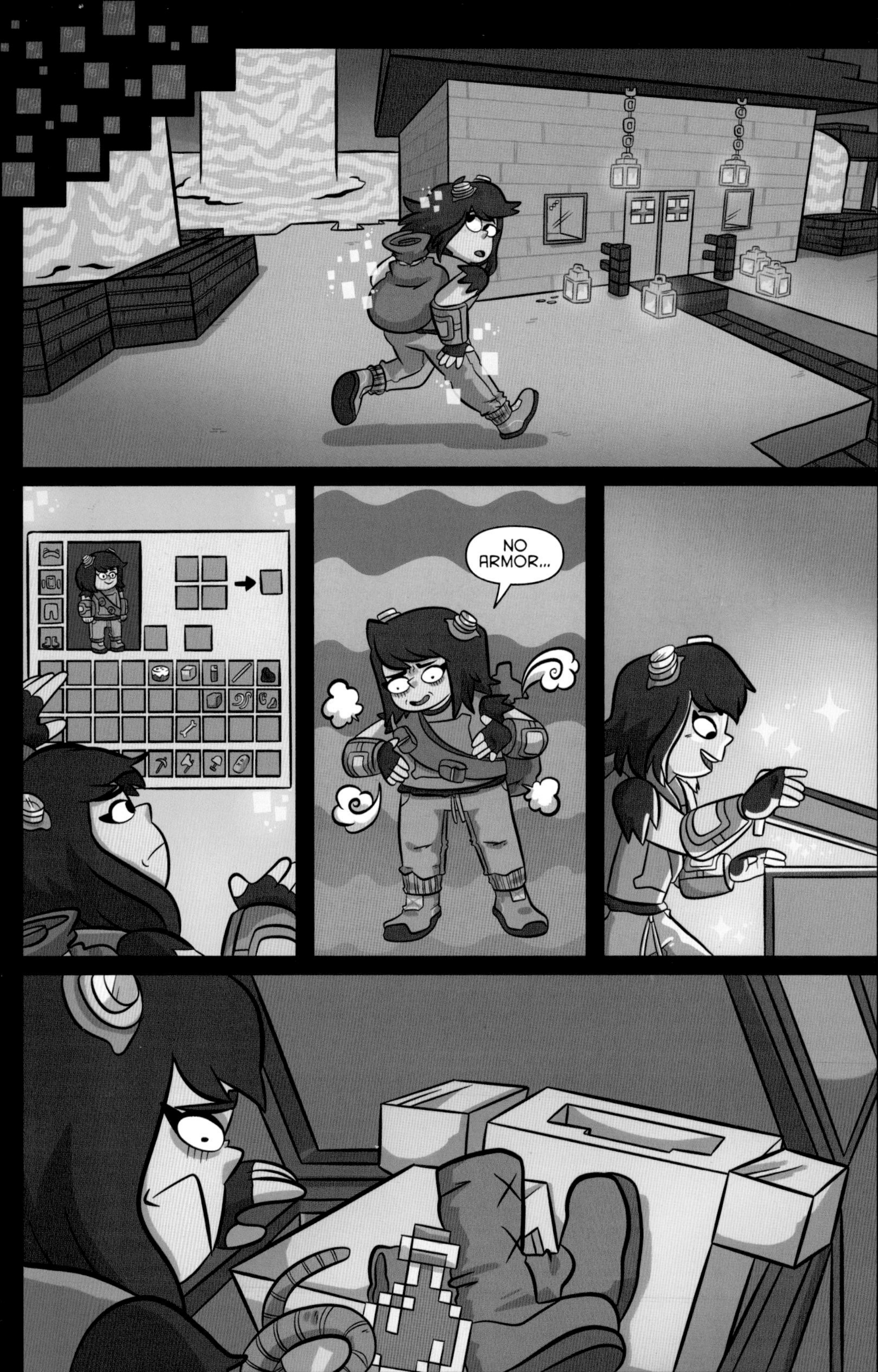
NO ARMOR...

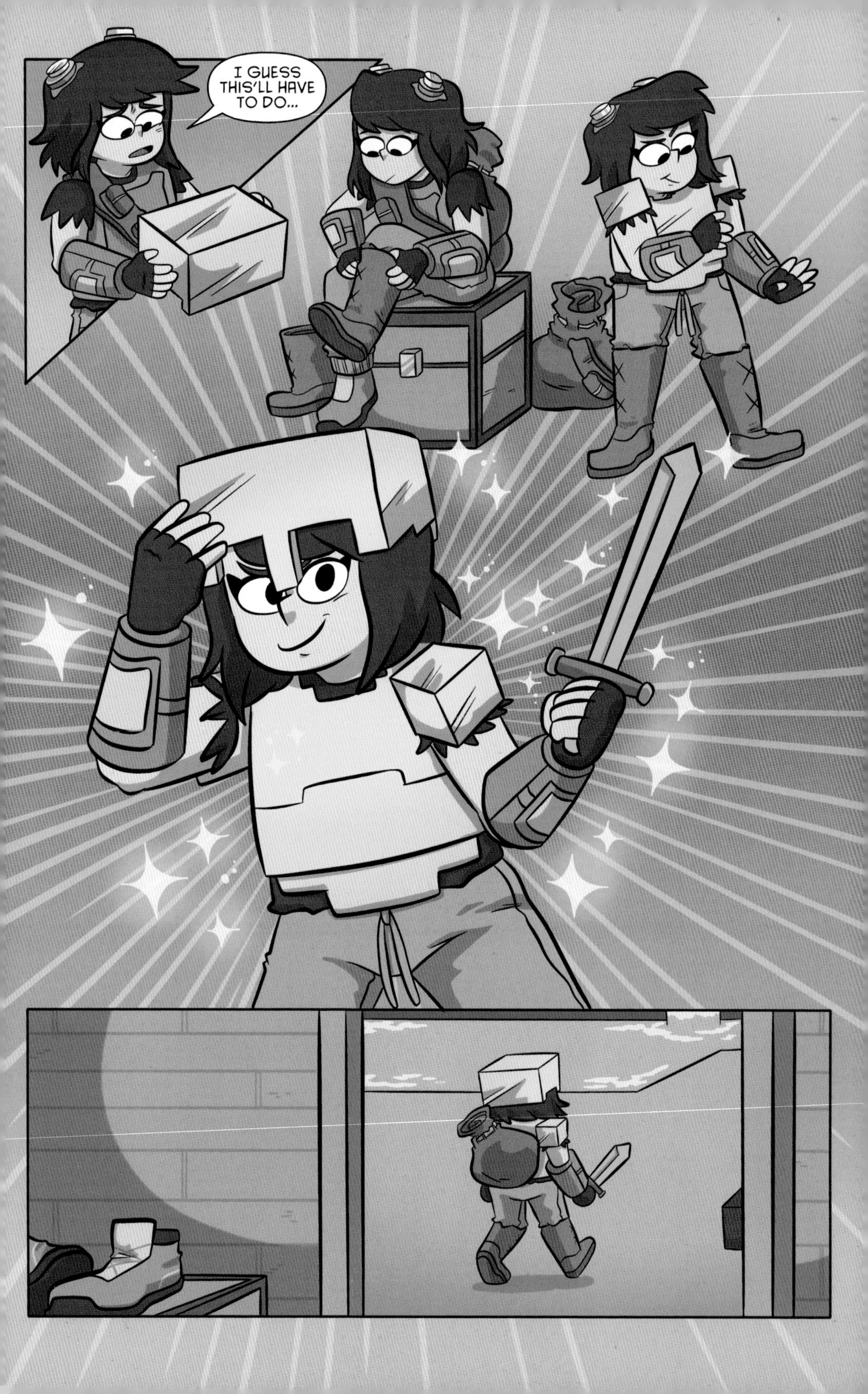
I GUESS THIS'LL HAVE TO DO...

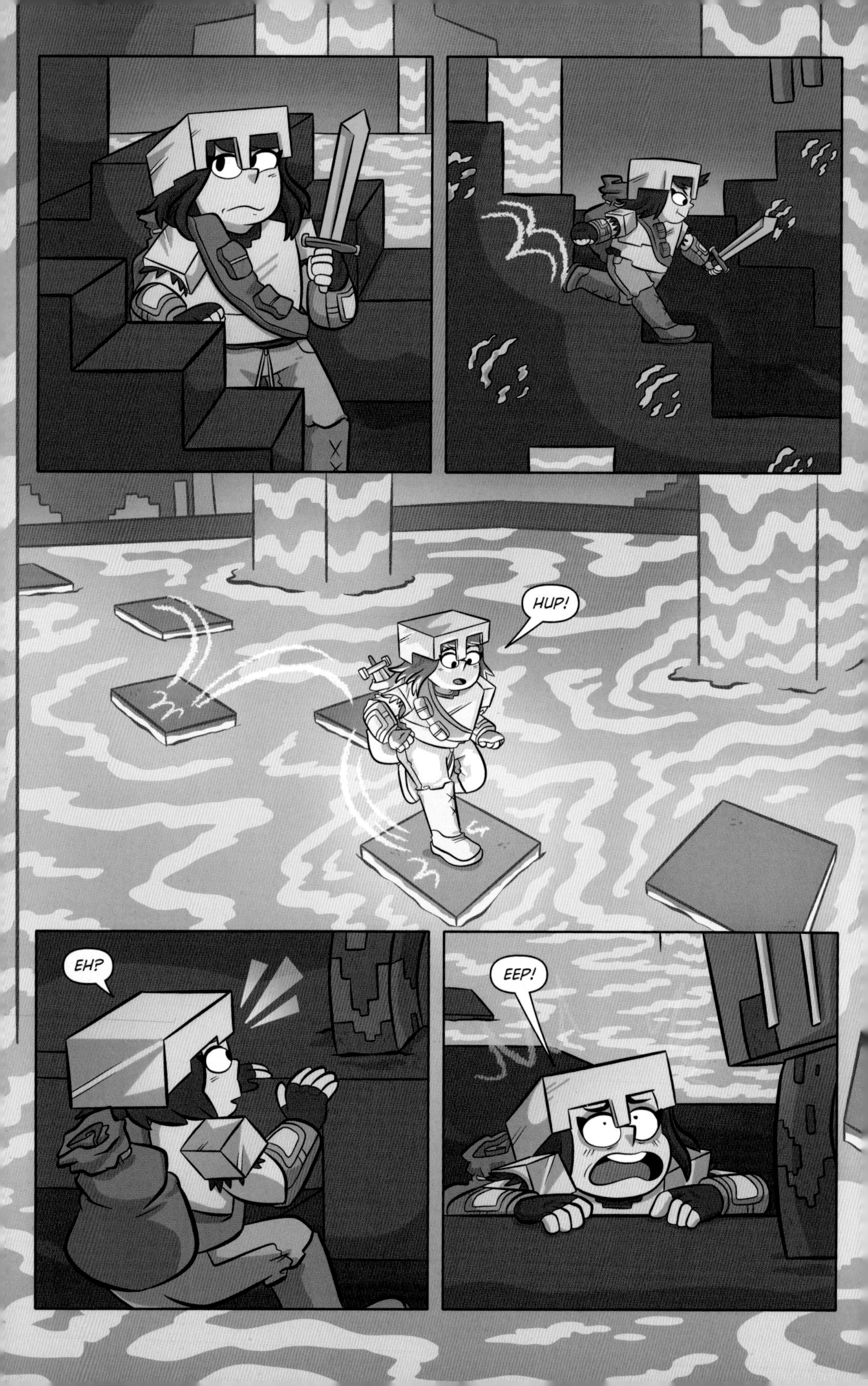
HUP!
EH?
EEP!

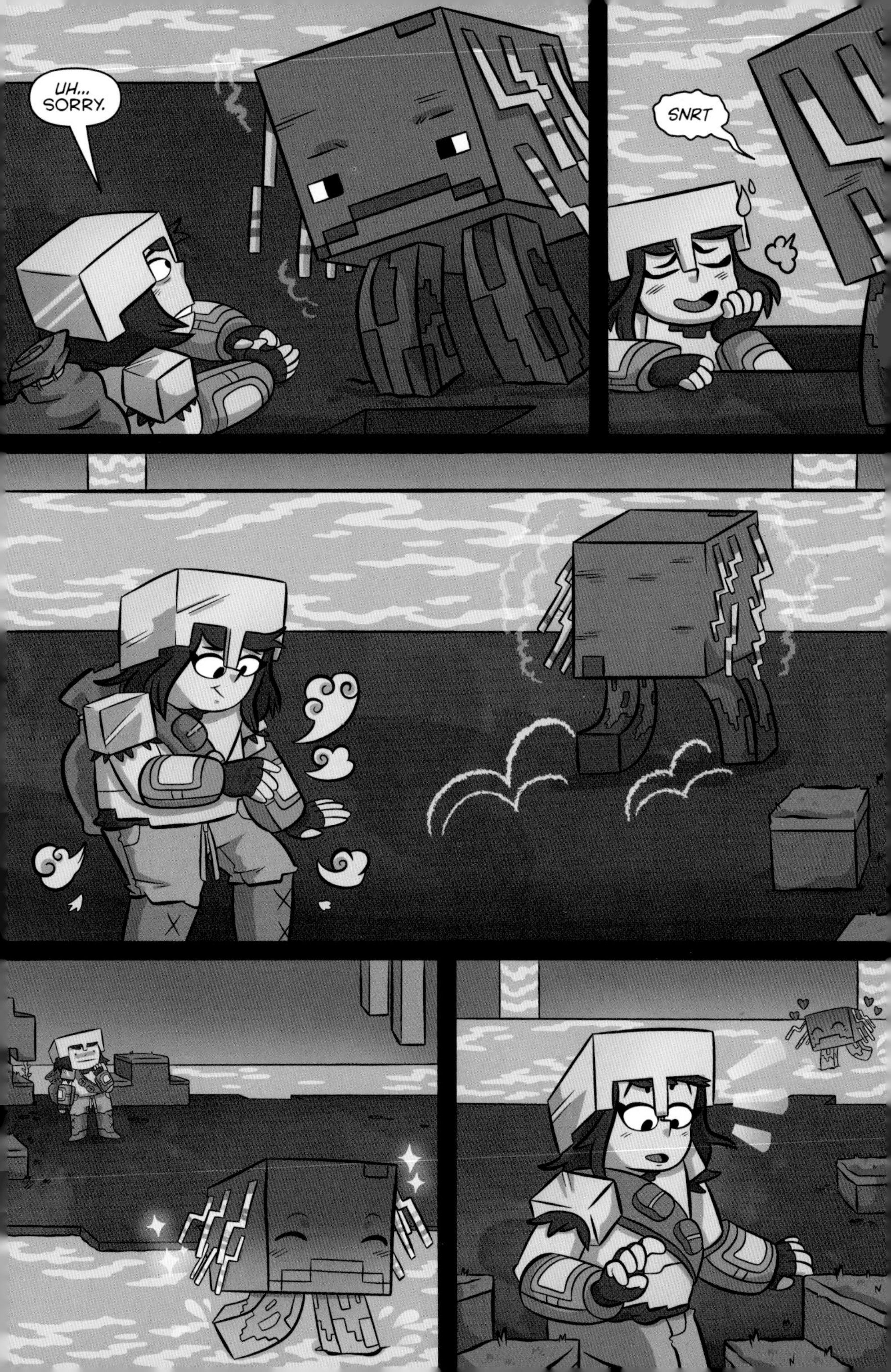
UH... SORRY.
SNRT

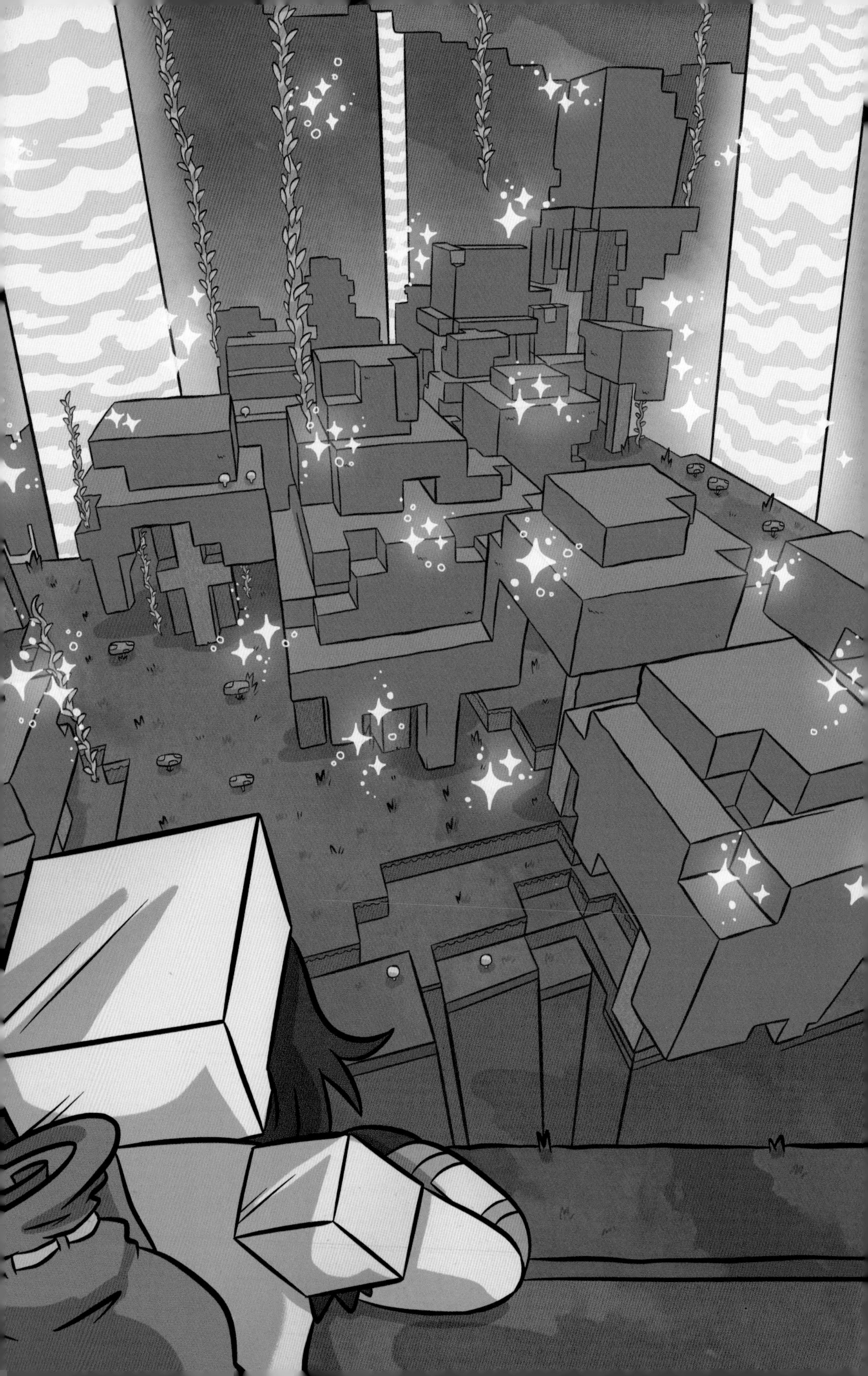

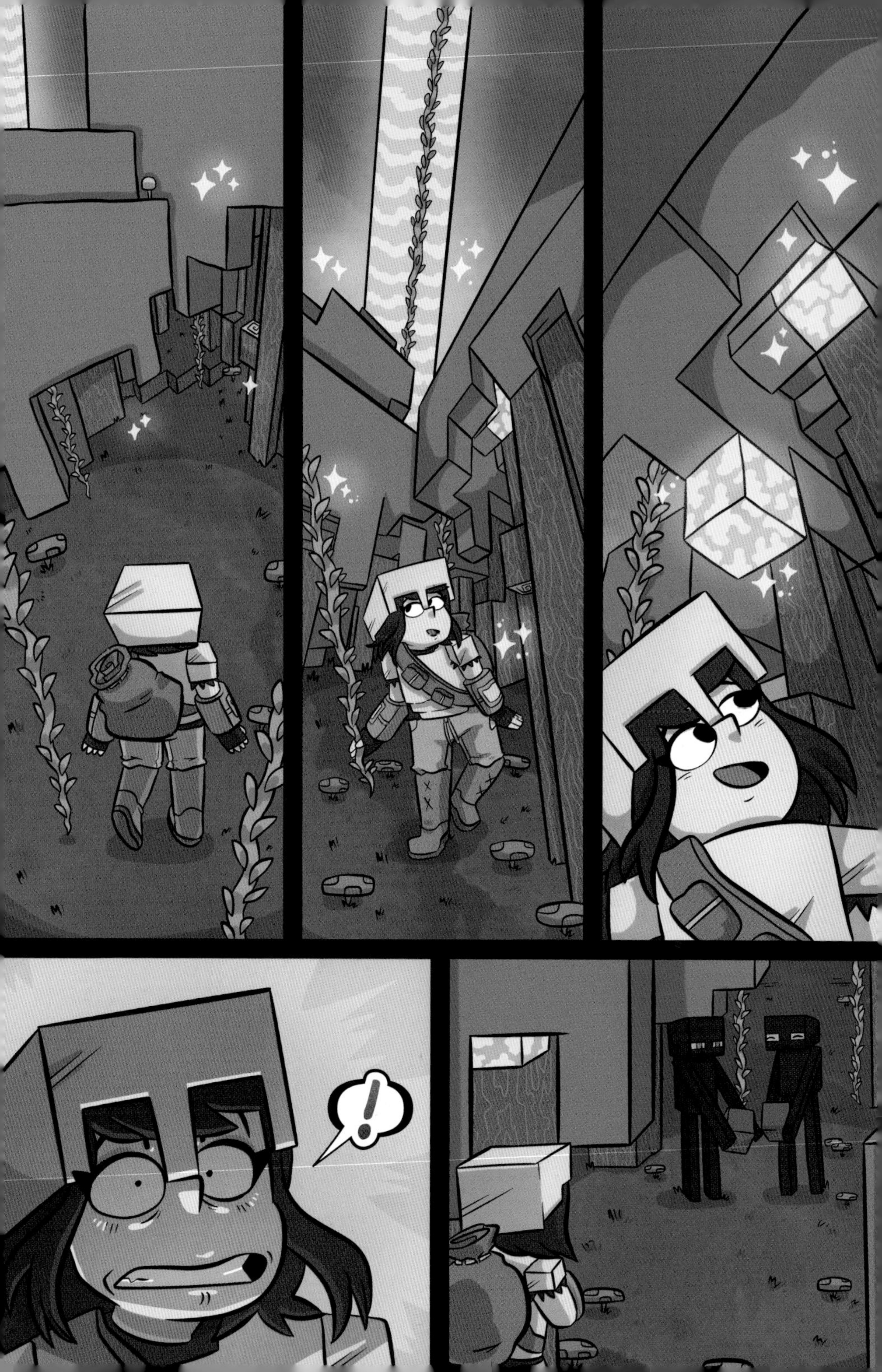
!

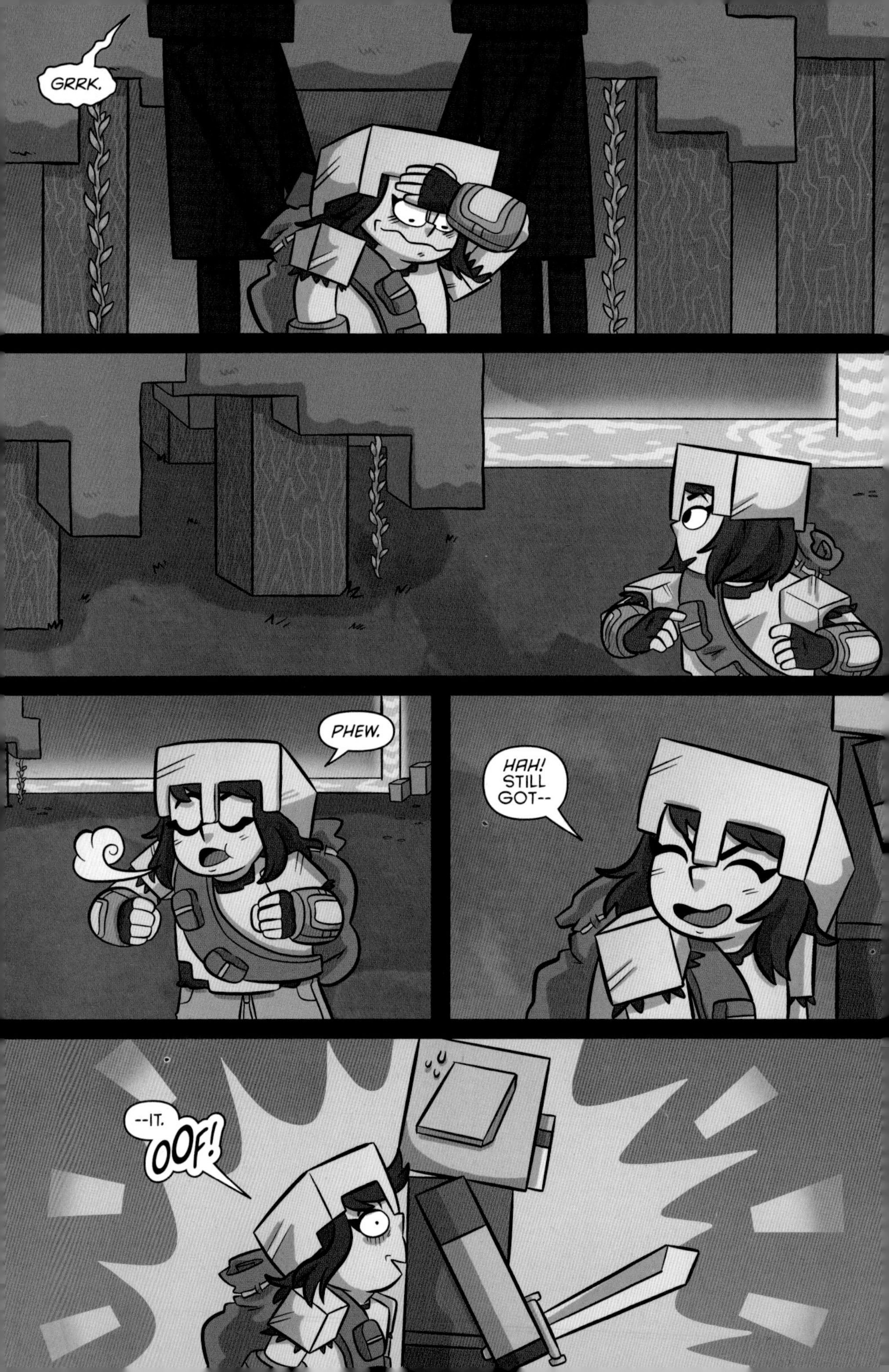
GRRK.
PHEW.
HAH! STILL GOT--
--IT.
OOF!

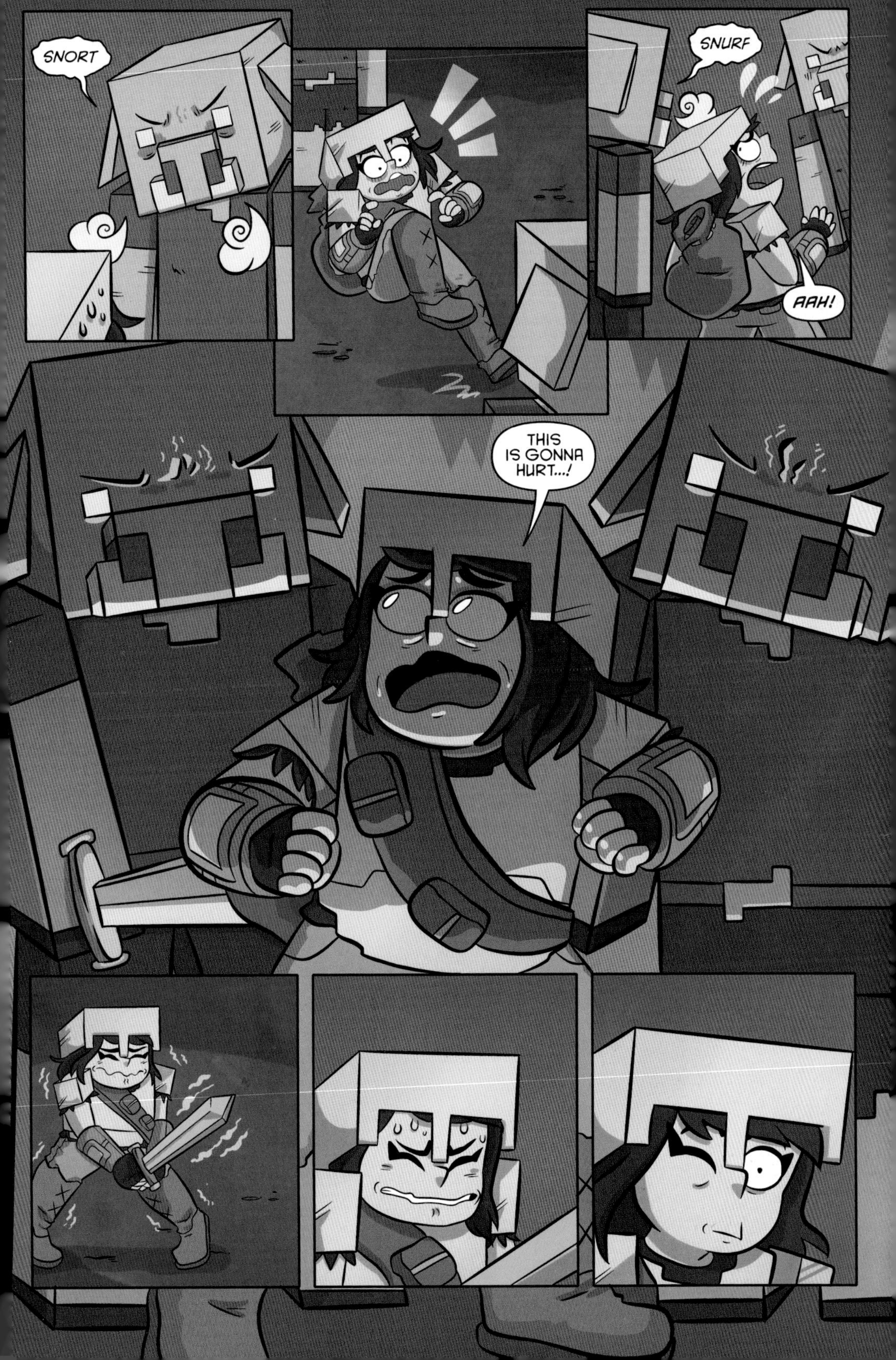
SNORT
SNURF
AAH!
THIS IS GONNA HURT...!

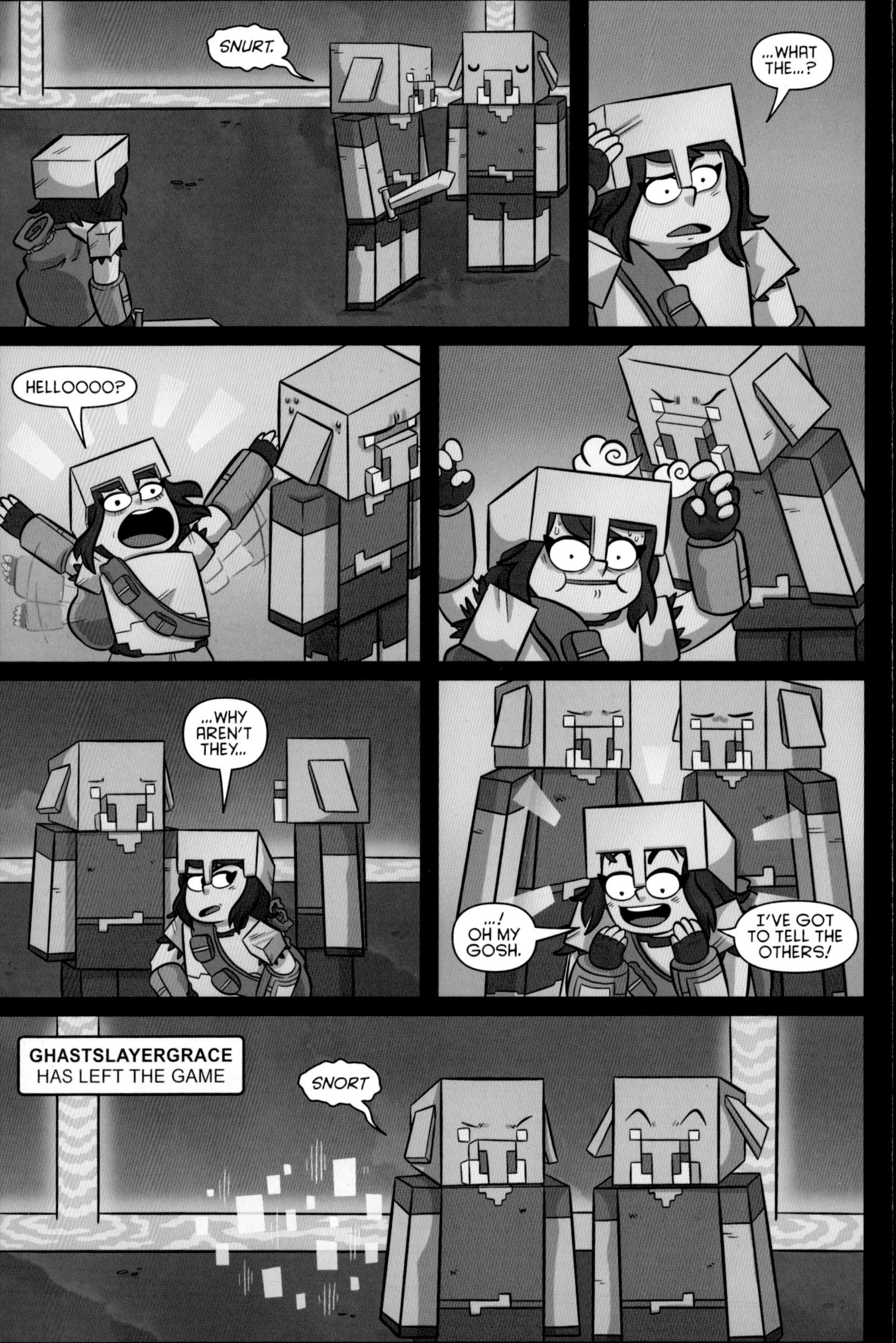
SNURT.
...WHAT THE...?
HELLOOOO?
...WHY AREN'T THEY...
...! OH MY GOSH.
I'VE GOT TO TELL THE OTHERS!
GHASTSLAYERGRACE HAS LEFT THE GAME
SNORT

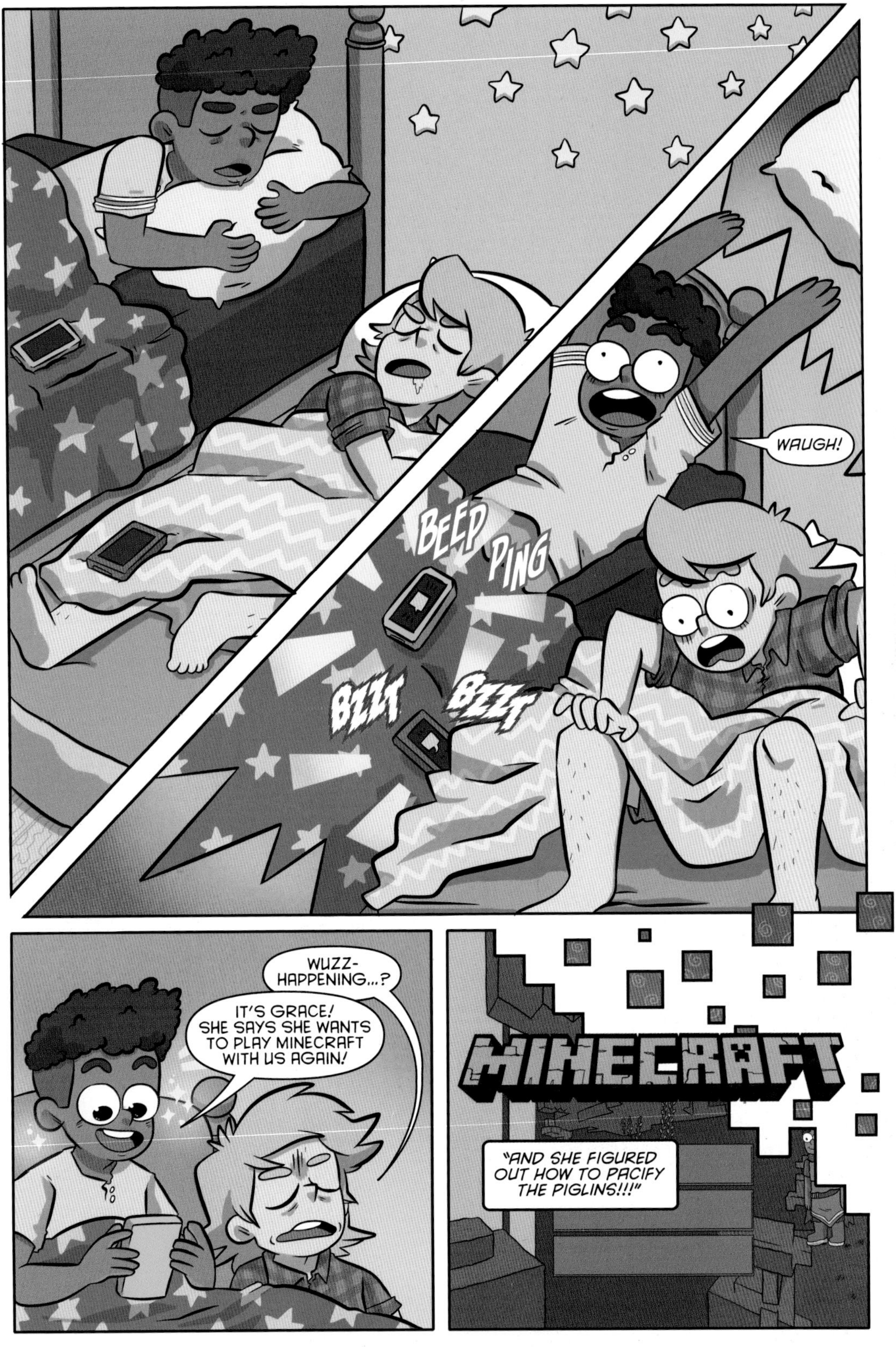
WAUGH!
BEEP
PING
BZZT
BZZT
WUZZ-HAPPENING...?
IT'S GRACE! SHE SAYS SHE WANTS TO PLAY MINECRAFT WITH US AGAIN!
MINECRAFT
"AND SHE FIGURED OUT HOW TO PACIFY THE PIGLINS!!!"

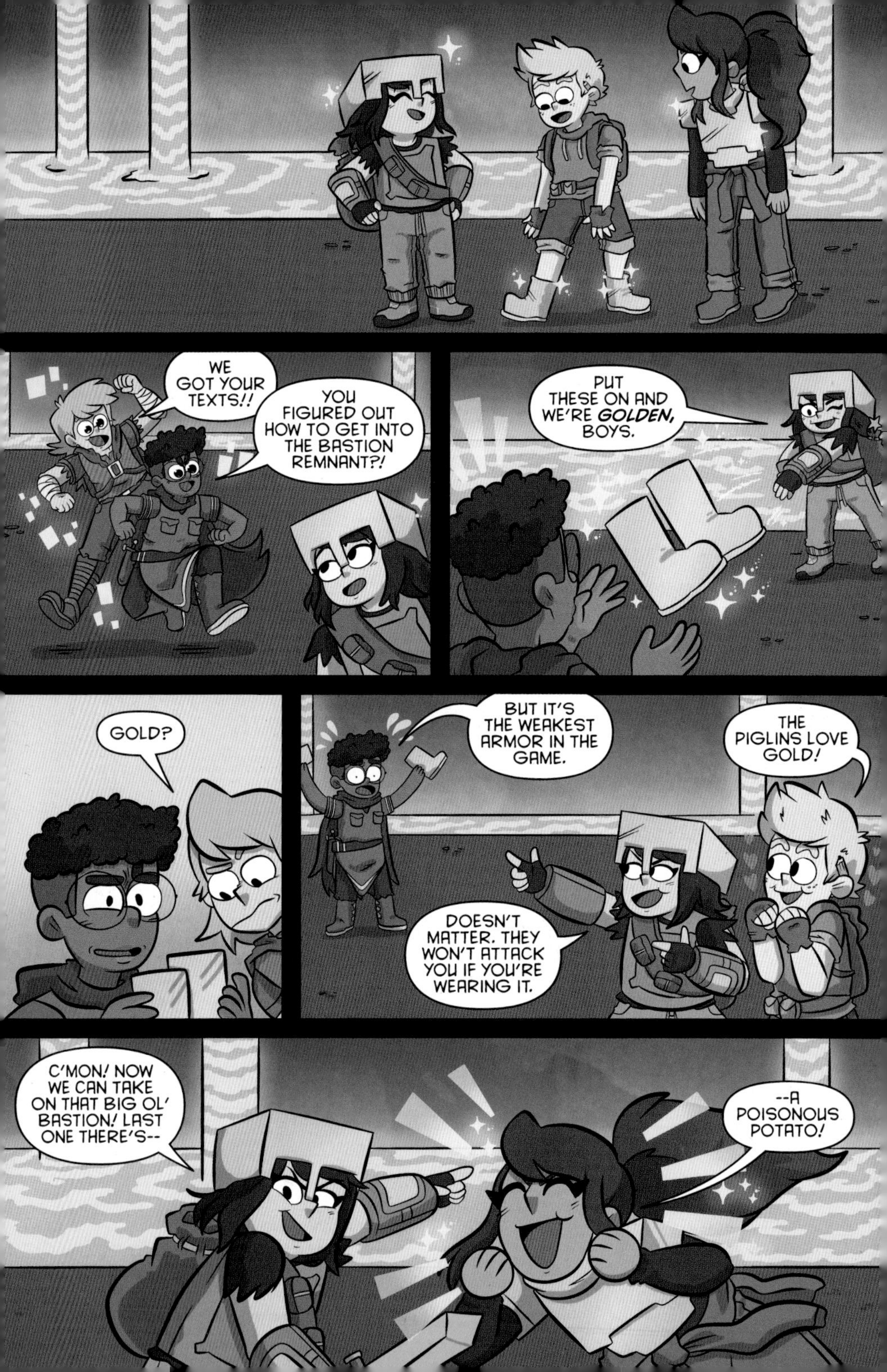
WE GOT YOUR TEXTS!!
YOU FIGURED OUT HOW TO GET INTO THE BASTION REMNANT?!
PUT THESE ON AND WE'RE *GOLDEN,* BOYS.
GOLD?
BUT IT'S THE WEAKEST ARMOR IN THE GAME.
THE PIGLINS LOVE GOLD!
DOESN'T MATTER. THEY WON'T ATTACK YOU IF YOU'RE WEARING IT.
C'MON! NOW WE CAN TAKE ON THAT BIG OL' BASTION! LAST ONE THERE'S--
--A POISONOUS POTATO!

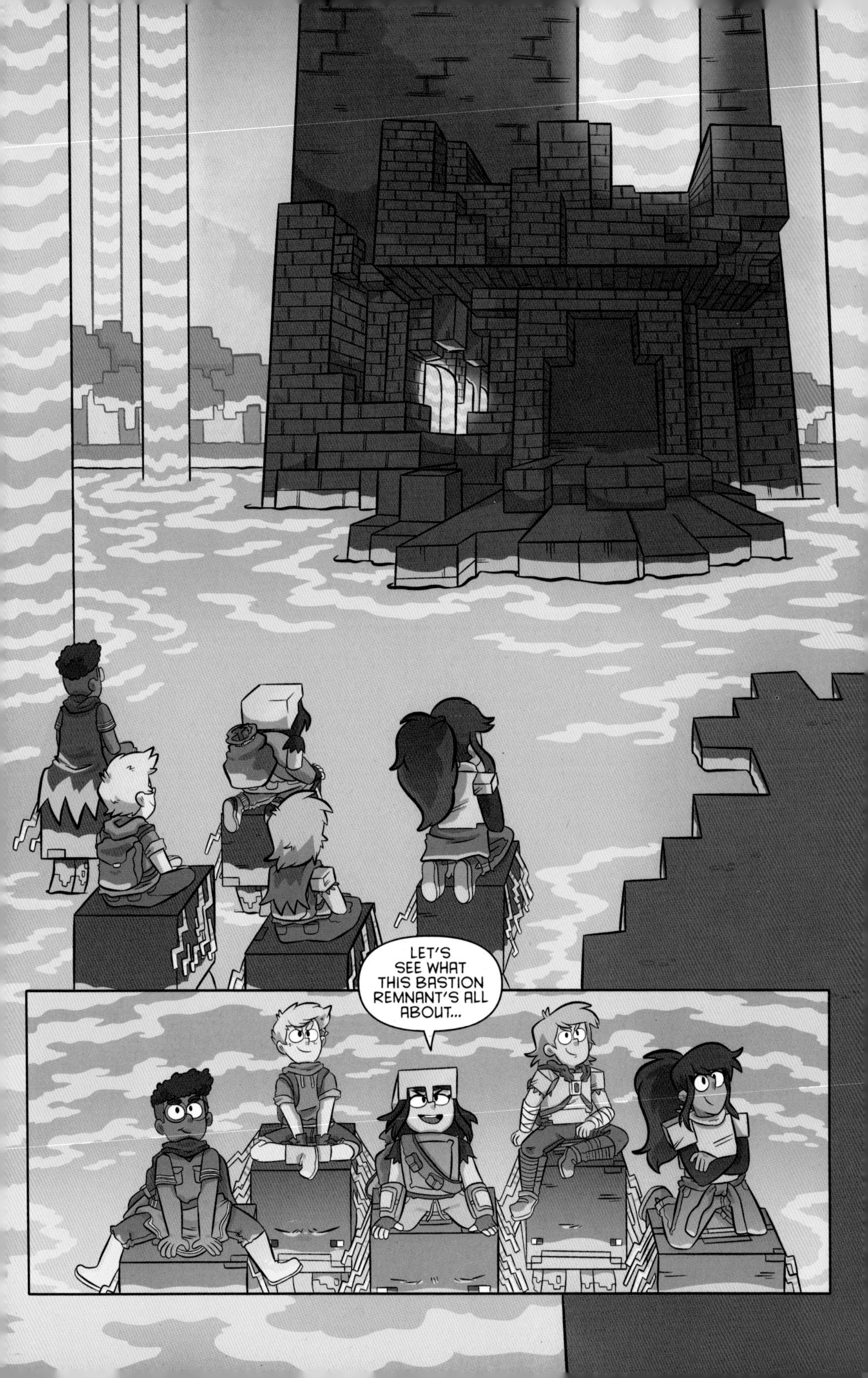
LET'S SEE WHAT THIS BASTION REMNANT'S ALL ABOUT...

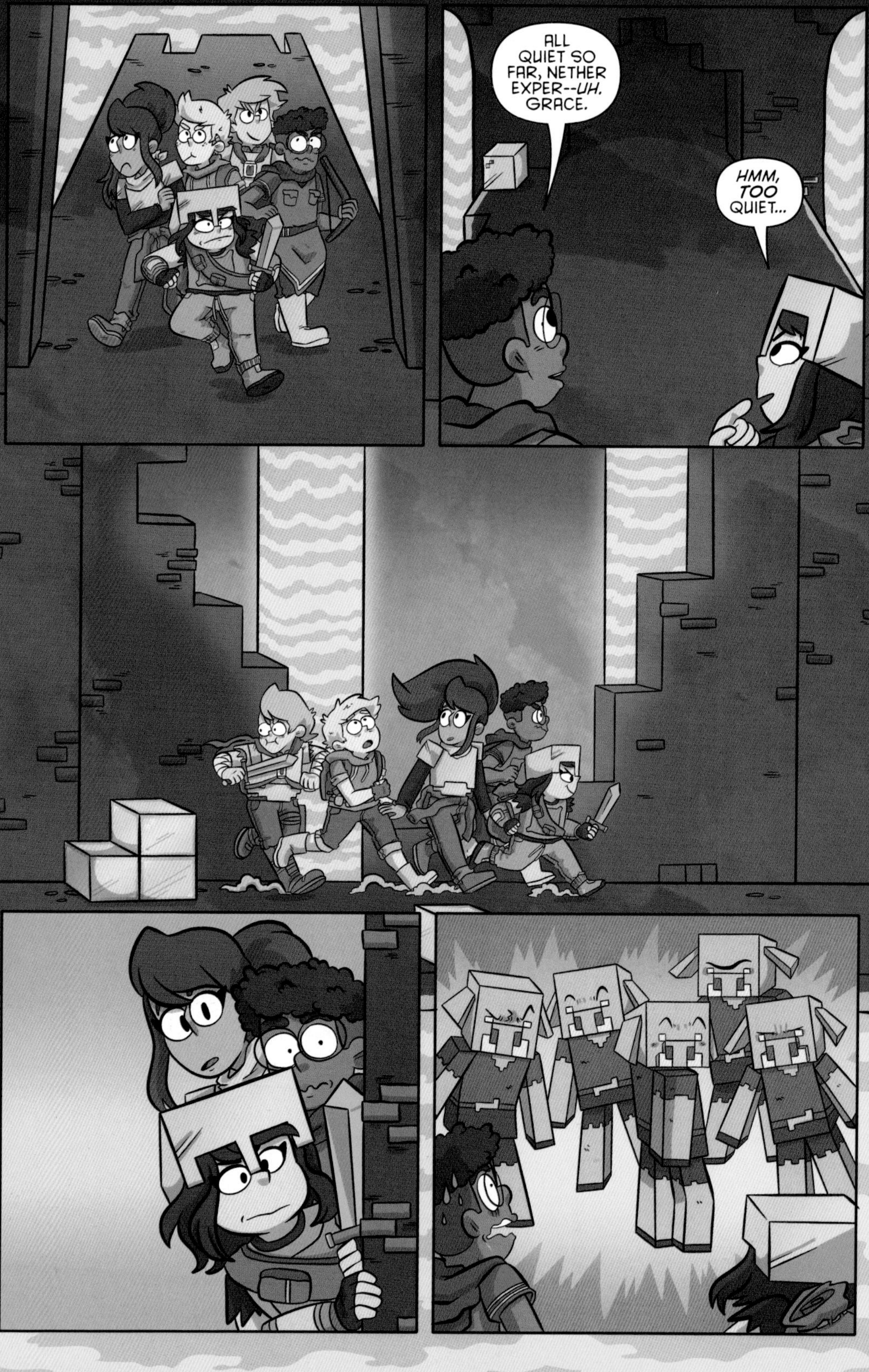
ALL QUIET SO FAR, NETHER EXPER--*UH*, GRACE.
HMM, TOO QUIET...

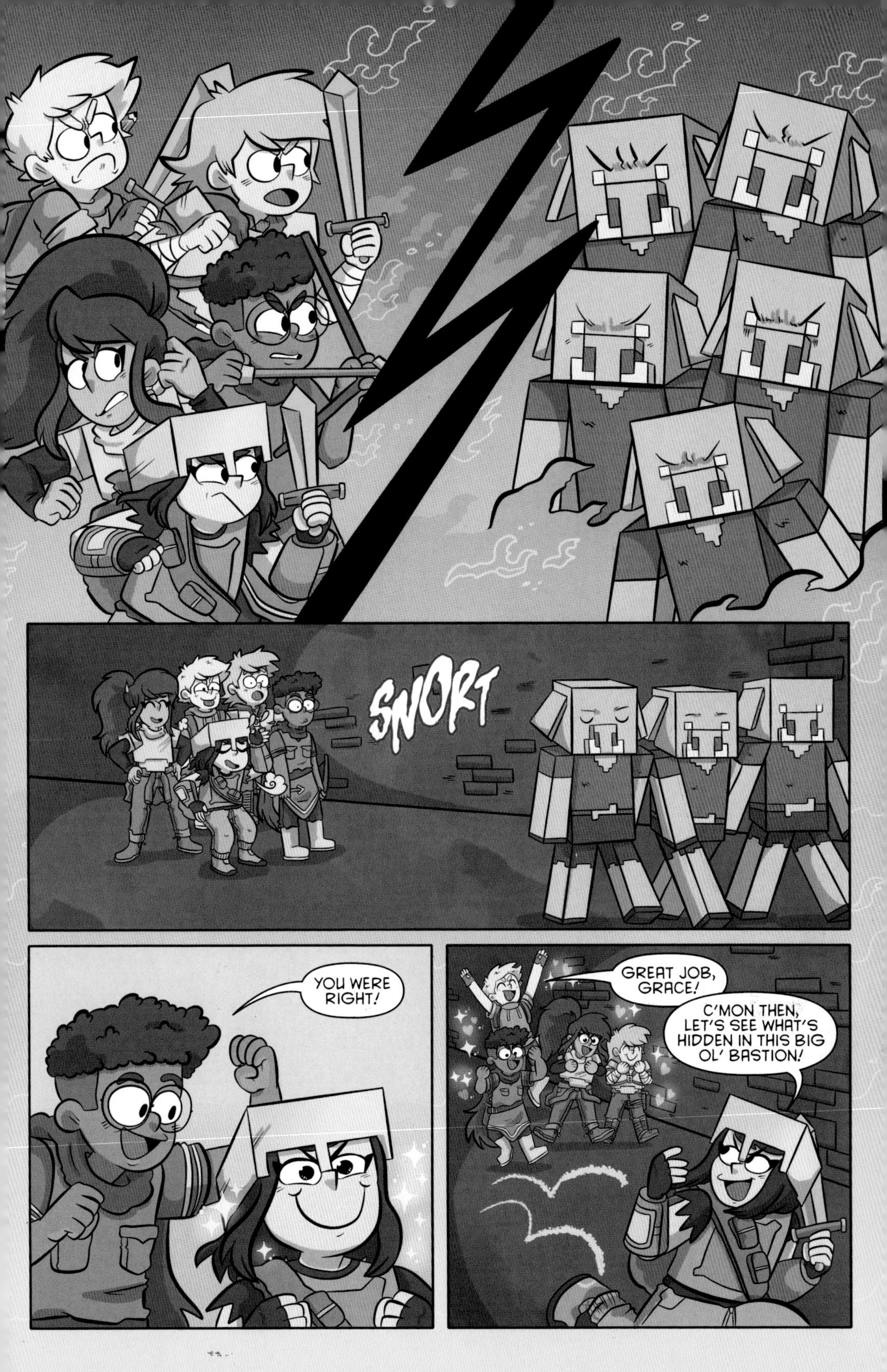
SNORT
YOU WERE RIGHT!
GREAT JOB, GRACE!
C'MON THEN, LET'S SEE WHAT'S HIDDEN IN THIS BIG OL' BASTION!

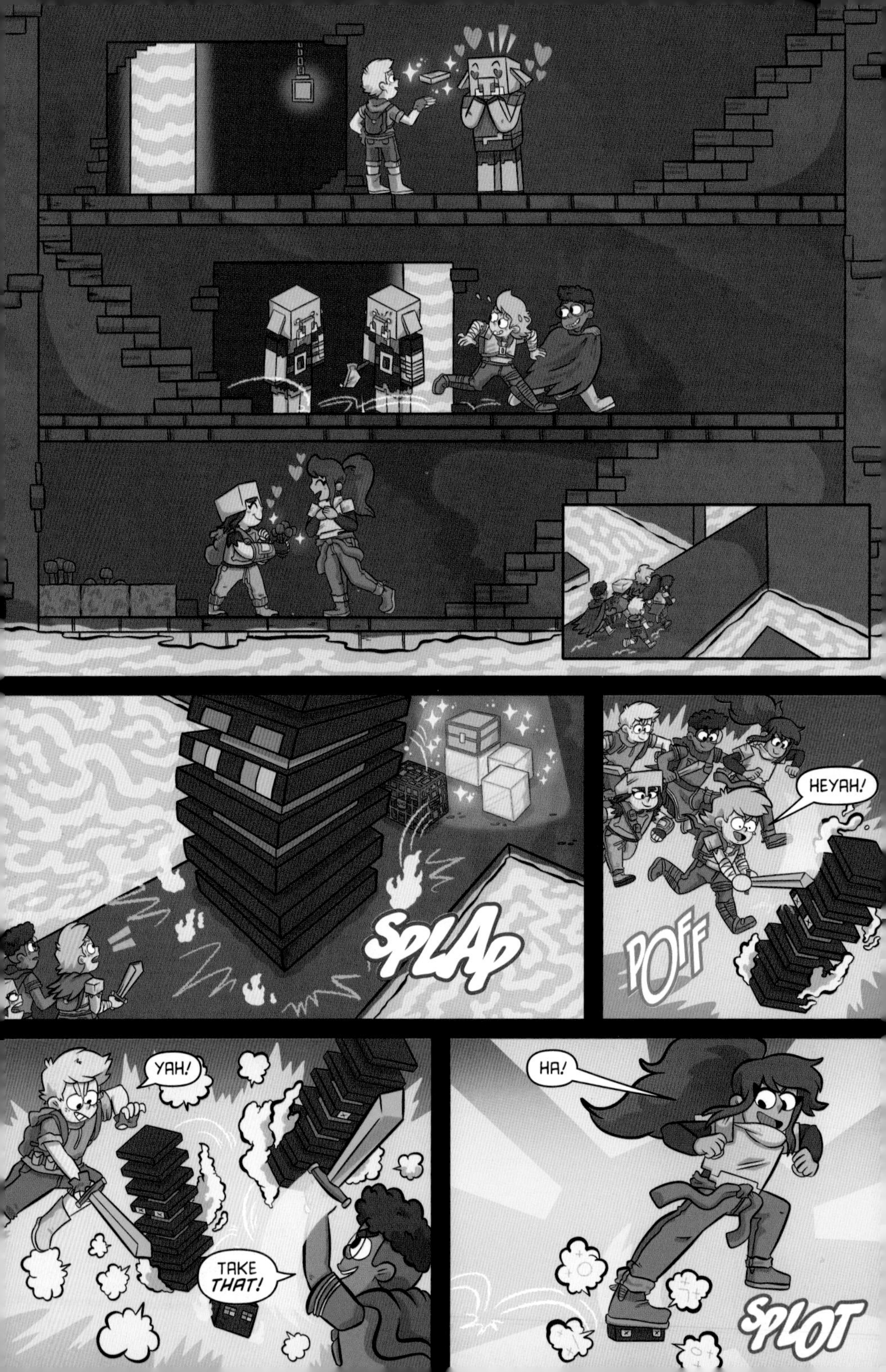
SPLAP
HEYAH!
POFF
YAH!
TAKE THAT!
HA!
SPLOT

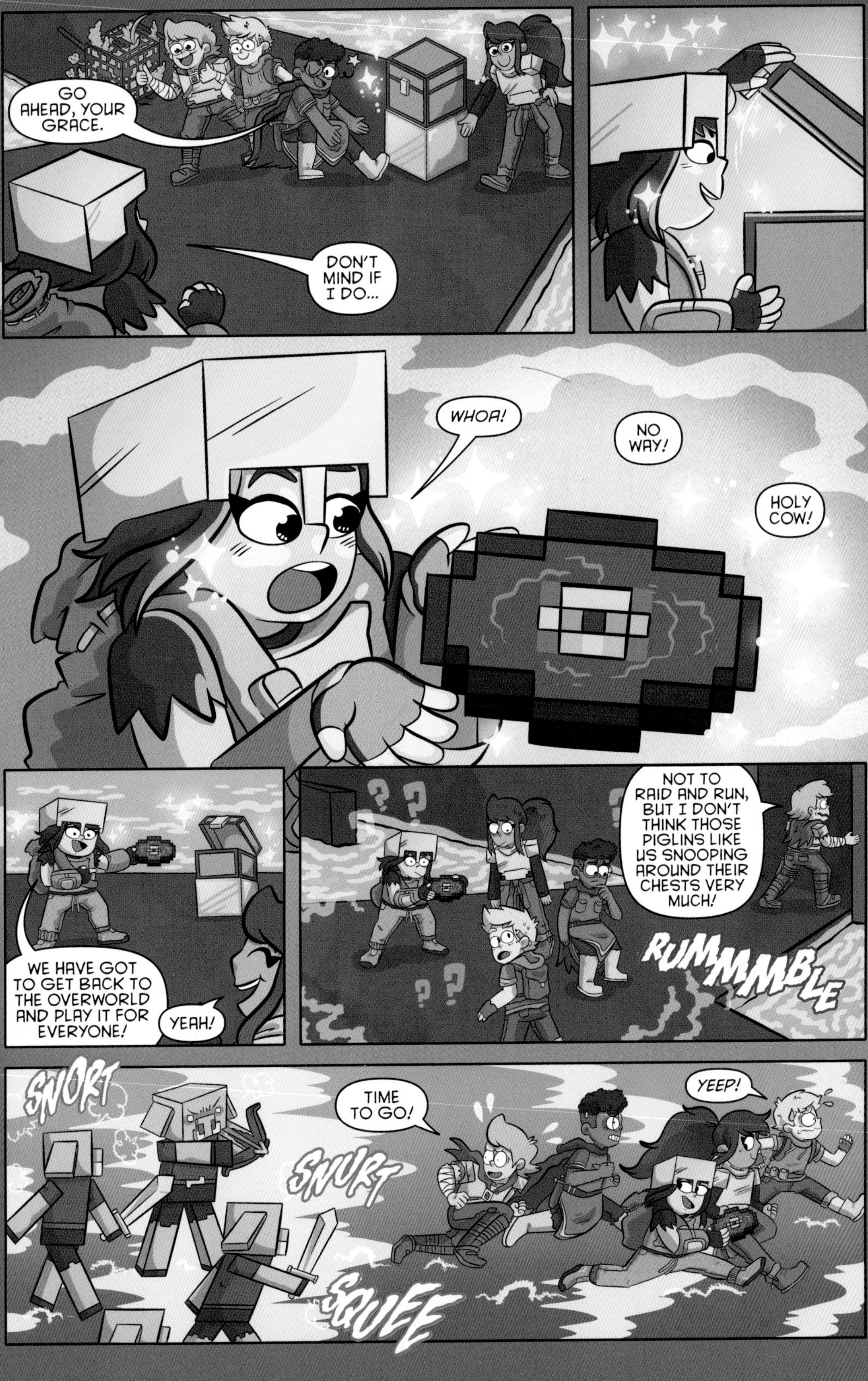
GO AHEAD, YOUR GRACE.
DON'T MIND IF I DO...
WHOA!
NO WAY!
HOLY COW!
WE HAVE GOT TO GET BACK TO THE OVERWORLD AND PLAY IT FOR EVERYONE!
YEAH!
NOT TO RAID AND RUN, BUT I DON'T THINK THOSE PIGLINS LIKE US SNOOPING AROUND THEIR CHESTS VERY MUCH!
RUMMMMBLE
SNORT
TIME TO GO!
YEEP!
SNURT
SQUEE

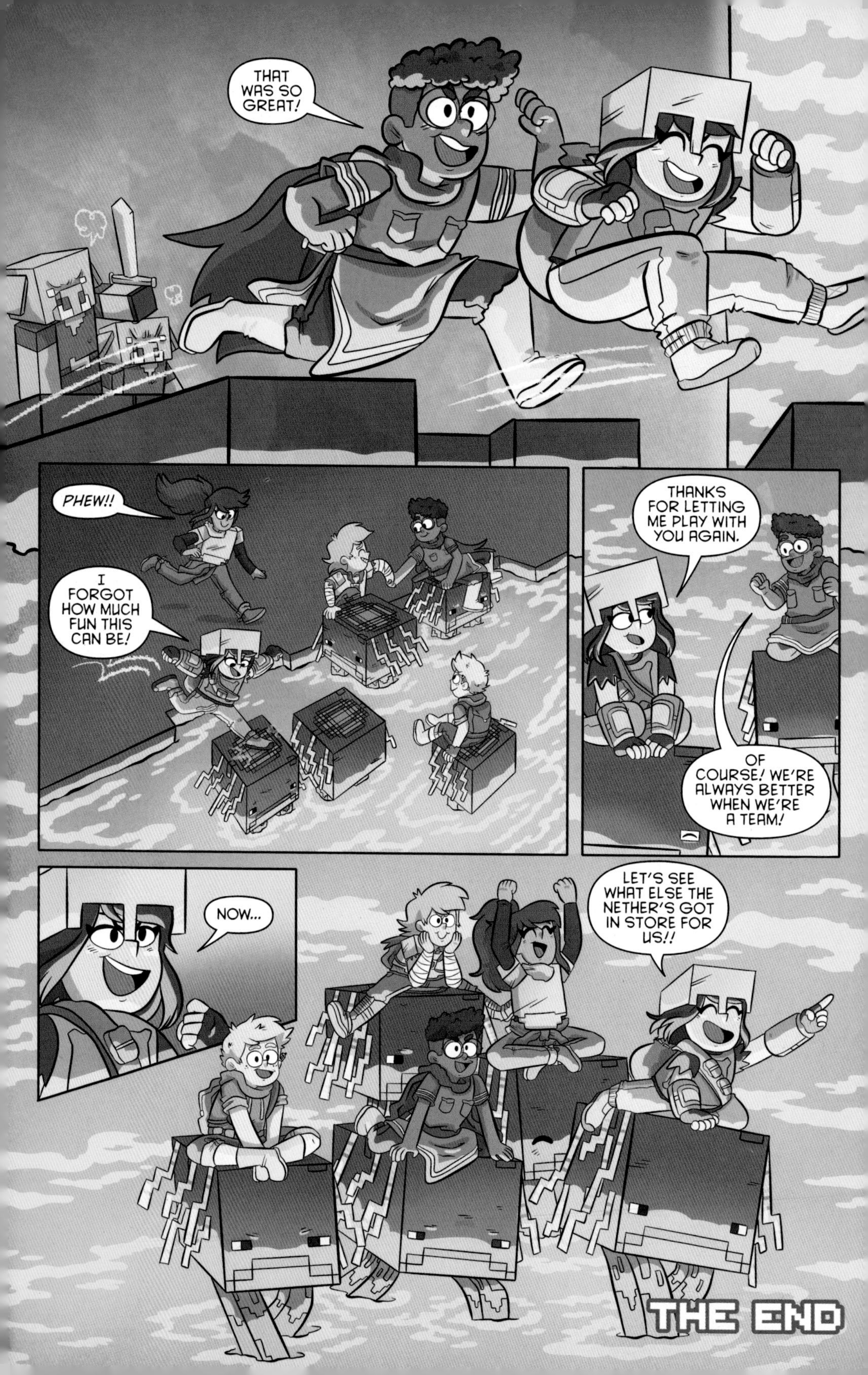
THAT WAS SO GREAT!
PHEW!!
I FORGOT HOW MUCH FUN THIS CAN BE!
THANKS FOR LETTING ME PLAY WITH YOU AGAIN.
OF COURSE! WE'RE ALWAYS BETTER WHEN WE'RE A TEAM!
NOW...
LET'S SEE WHAT ELSE THE NETHER'S GOT IN STORE FOR US!!
THE END

MINECRAFT™

SKETCHBOOK

COMMENTARY BY
SARAH GRALEY

CHARACTER DESIGN

I love designing new outfits for the EverRealm crew! Before starting work on this story I revisited the cast and re-drew them while going through the story and figuring out how many different outfits they would each need.

When coming up with clothes I like to think about what would be practical or make sense for the situation that the character is in...and sometimes I draw clothes that I wish I had, too! (Like the ghosts holding hands t-shirt I gave to Candace! Fashion!!)

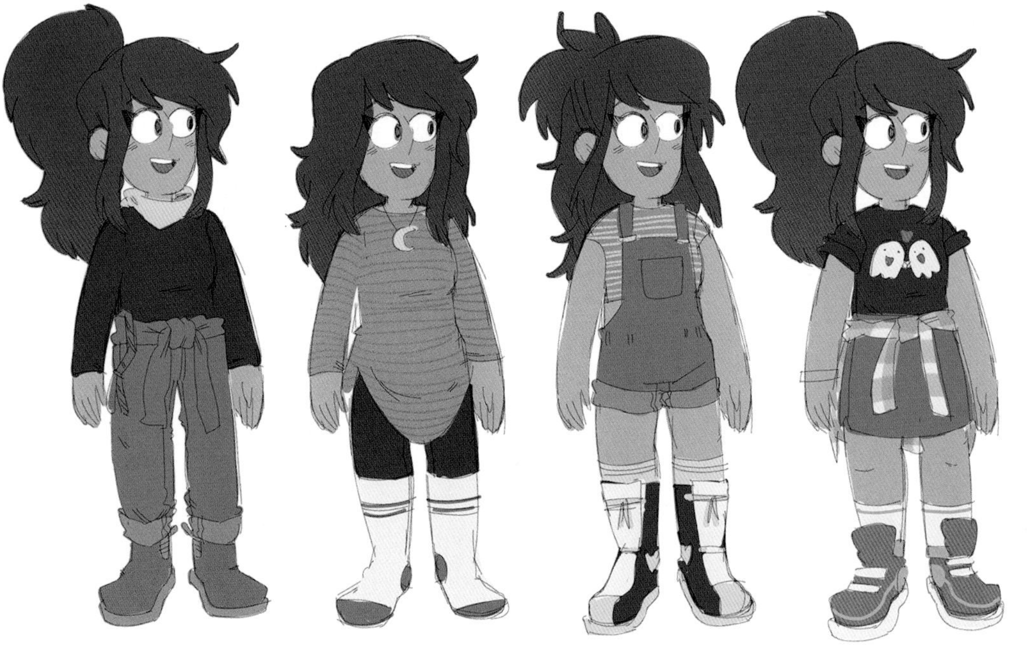

I then print off a huge sheet of paper with all the new character designs and outfits and hang it above my desk before diving into the artwork! If I need to remember what a character looks like, then I just have to look up! Having reference nearby is super helpful—especially when you're drawing the same characters a lot! It helps keep everything consistent and helps me avoid mistakes.

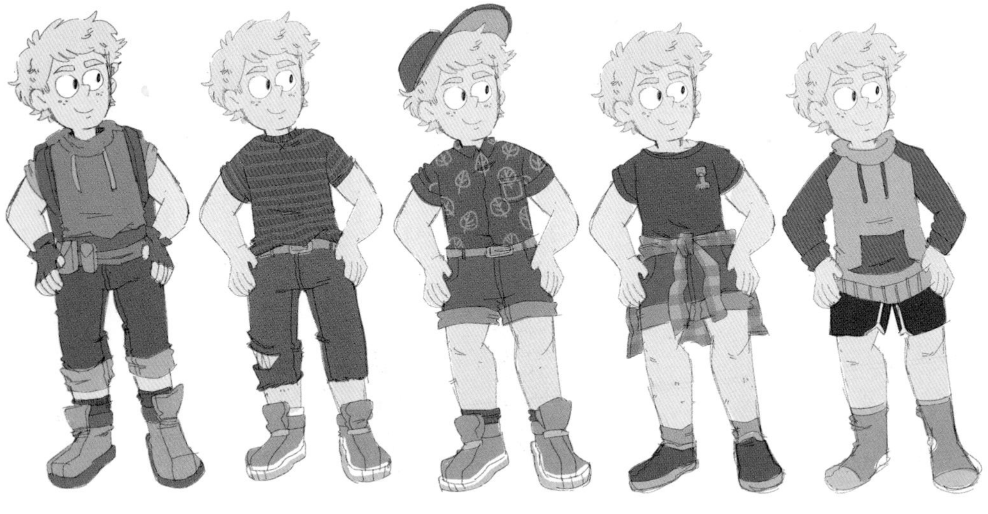

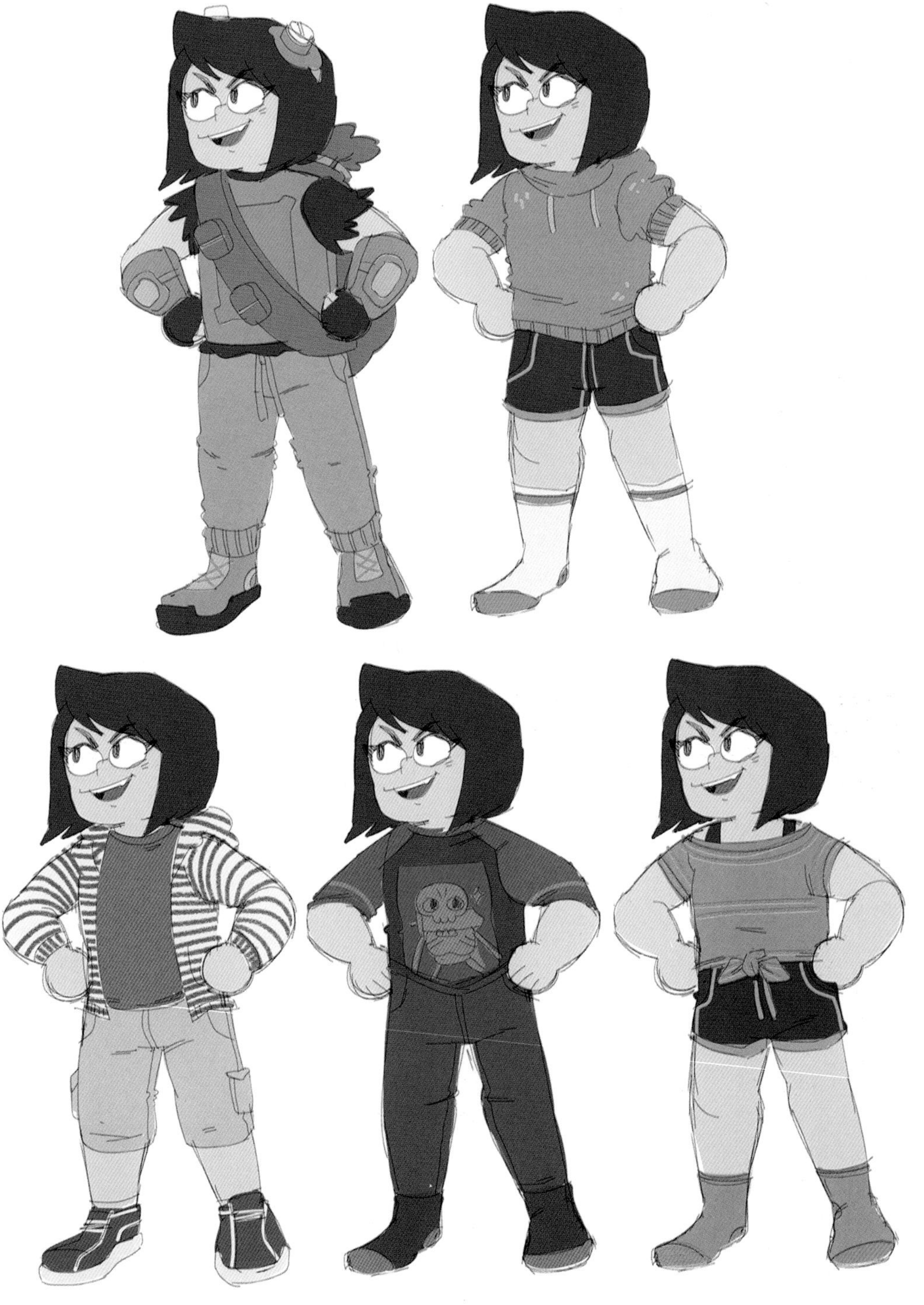

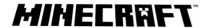

1 Rough cover art and pencils

When designing the book's cover, I always come up with several different ideas based on the main themes and events of the story. I then show them to the teams at Dark Horse and Mojang, and we'll decide which direction is the most fun and exciting—while also showing off best what the book is all about!

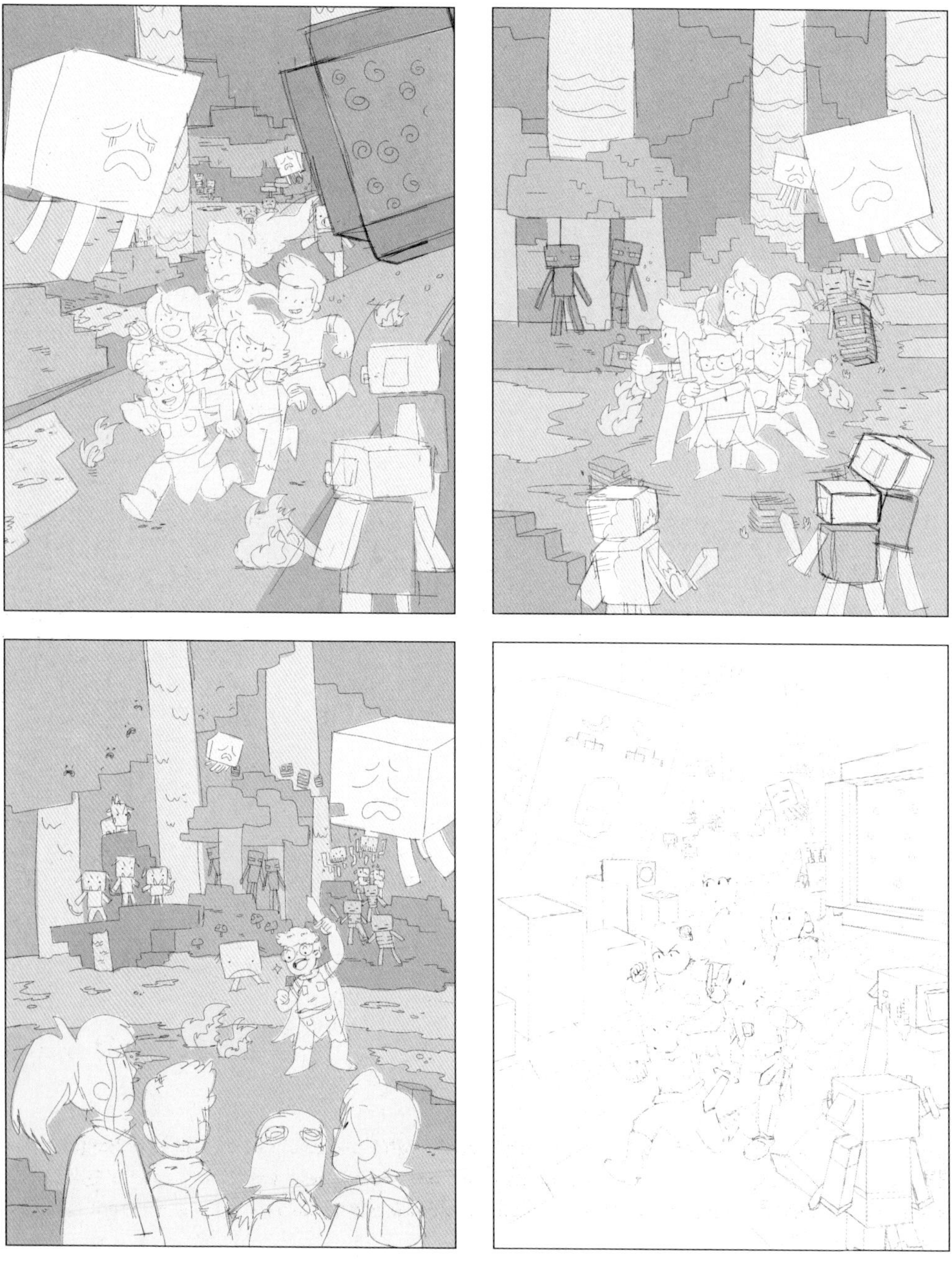

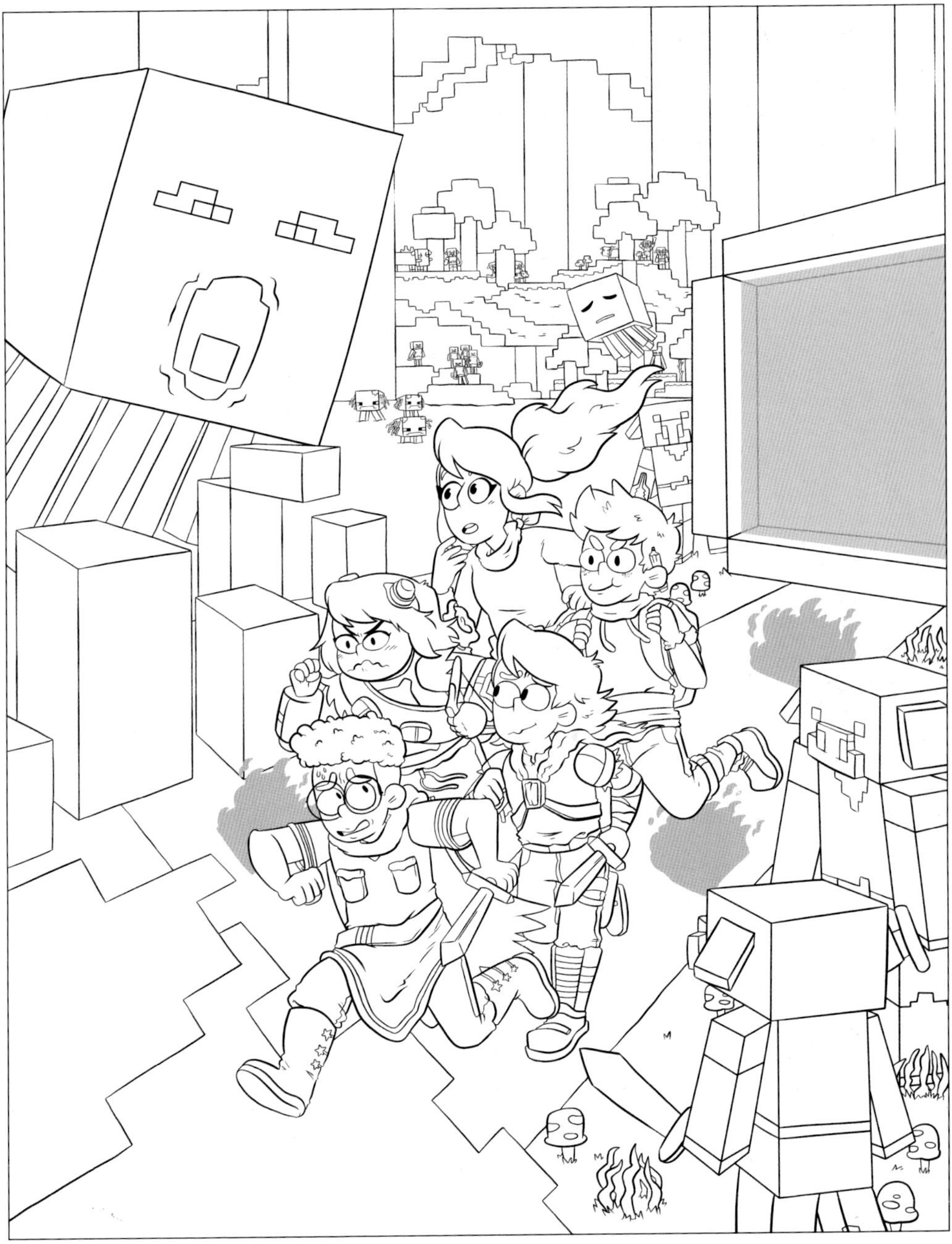

2 Cover inks

I loved coming up with ideas for this book cover! Even though I tend to die A LOT in the Nether (and one time losing my favorite enchanted sword in one of its many lava lakes– R.I.P. "Big Chopper"!), it's such a fun part of Minecraft with lots of different areas to explore, which gave me a lot of different ideas on what to draw!

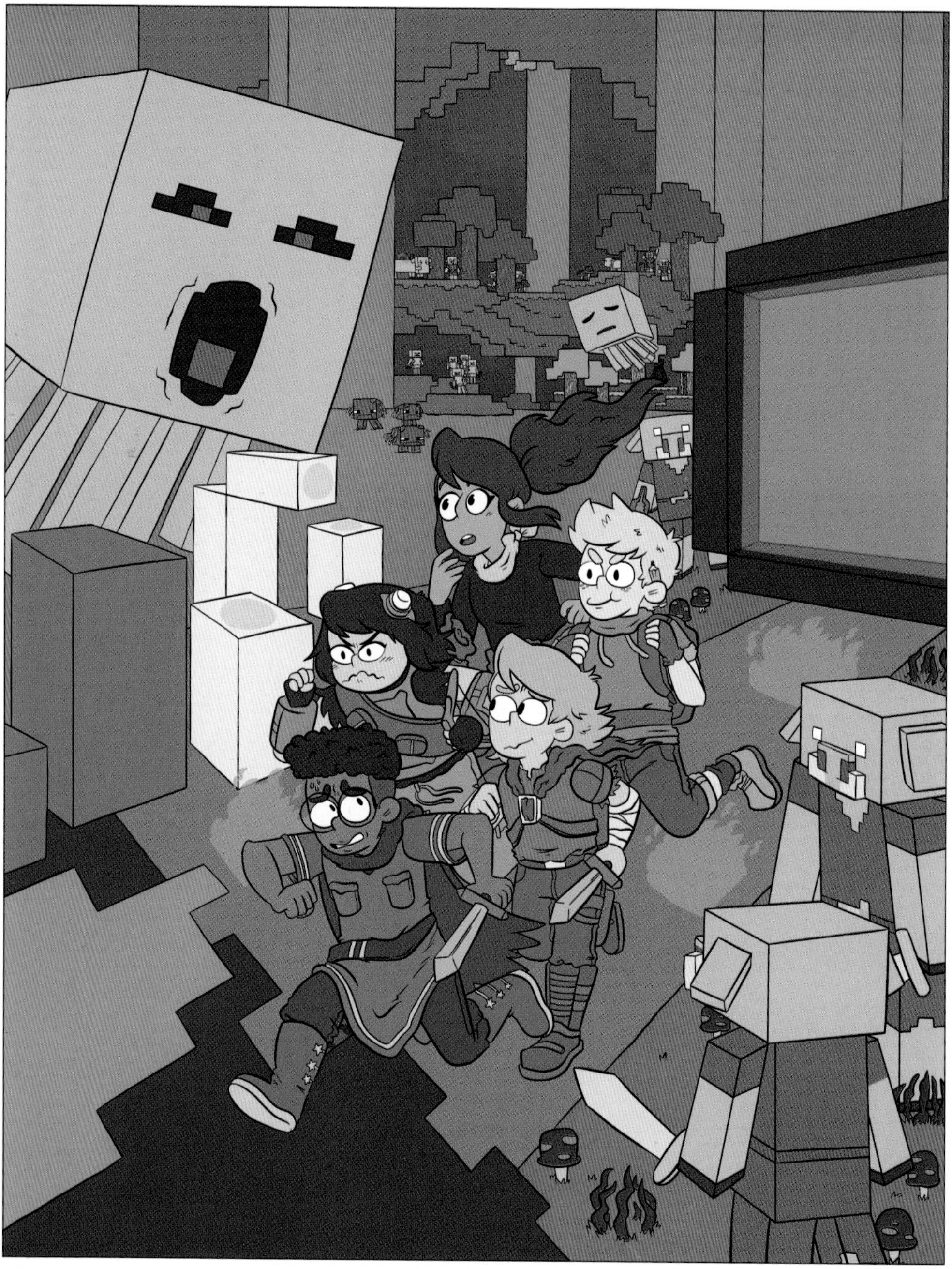

3 Cover with flat color

With the cover I really wanted to highlight all the scary mobs (and the not-so-scary Striders!) and different biomes of the Nether. I'm really happy with the final cover—I think the only main change we had between draft and final was Grace's facial expression.

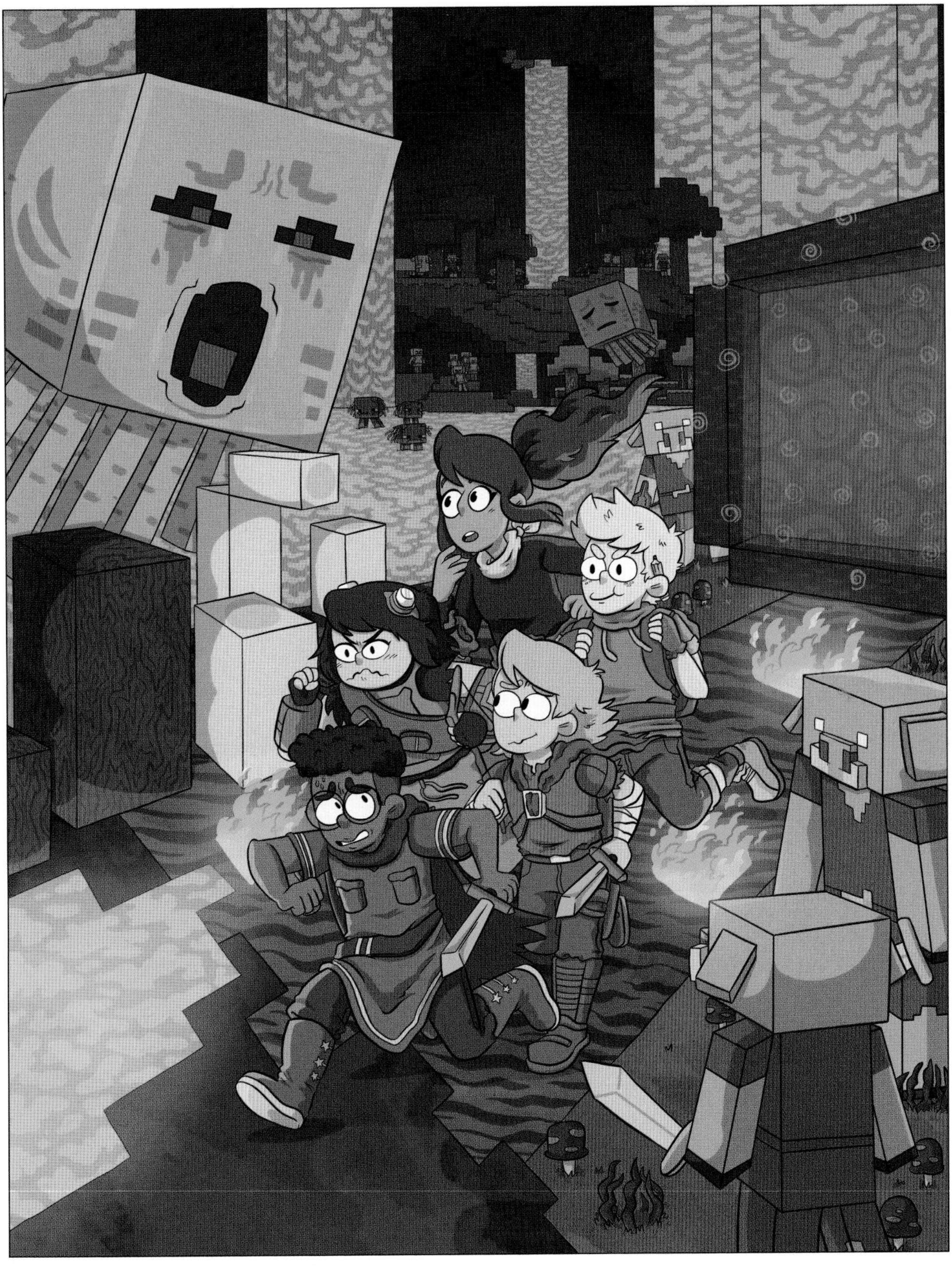

4 Final colored cover

In the original she's really happy—but unless you skipped to this part of the book before reading the story (hey! Go back! Spoilers ahead!) we all know Grace initially has a terrible time in the Nether, so that's now reflected in her expression.

Every page starts off as a scribbly rough version! During this stage—called layouts or thumbnails— I'm reading the script and figuring out where panels need to go, and everything that will go inside them! This will give me a good idea on how to proceed. Sometimes I might scribble a layout down and realize it's not working as I intended and I need to make changes—this is why this stage is so scribbly! It's much easier to adjust things here before I spend a long time drawing everything up as final inked and colored art.

1 **Rough pencil layout**

2 **Pencils**

3 **Inks**

4 **Flat colors**

After I pencil and ink pages, I send them over to my partner Stef, who is the color assistant on this book! He colors in the pages using my character guides—a process called "flatting"—before sending the pages back to me to do more detailed coloring work like shading and lighting and other fancy things! While Stef fills in the pages with color, I'm usually penciling or inking later pages. We work side by side and this teamwork helps us get the book finished quicker! There are a LOT of spaces that need filling in with color, so being able to team up is a huge help! (Thank you, Stef!)

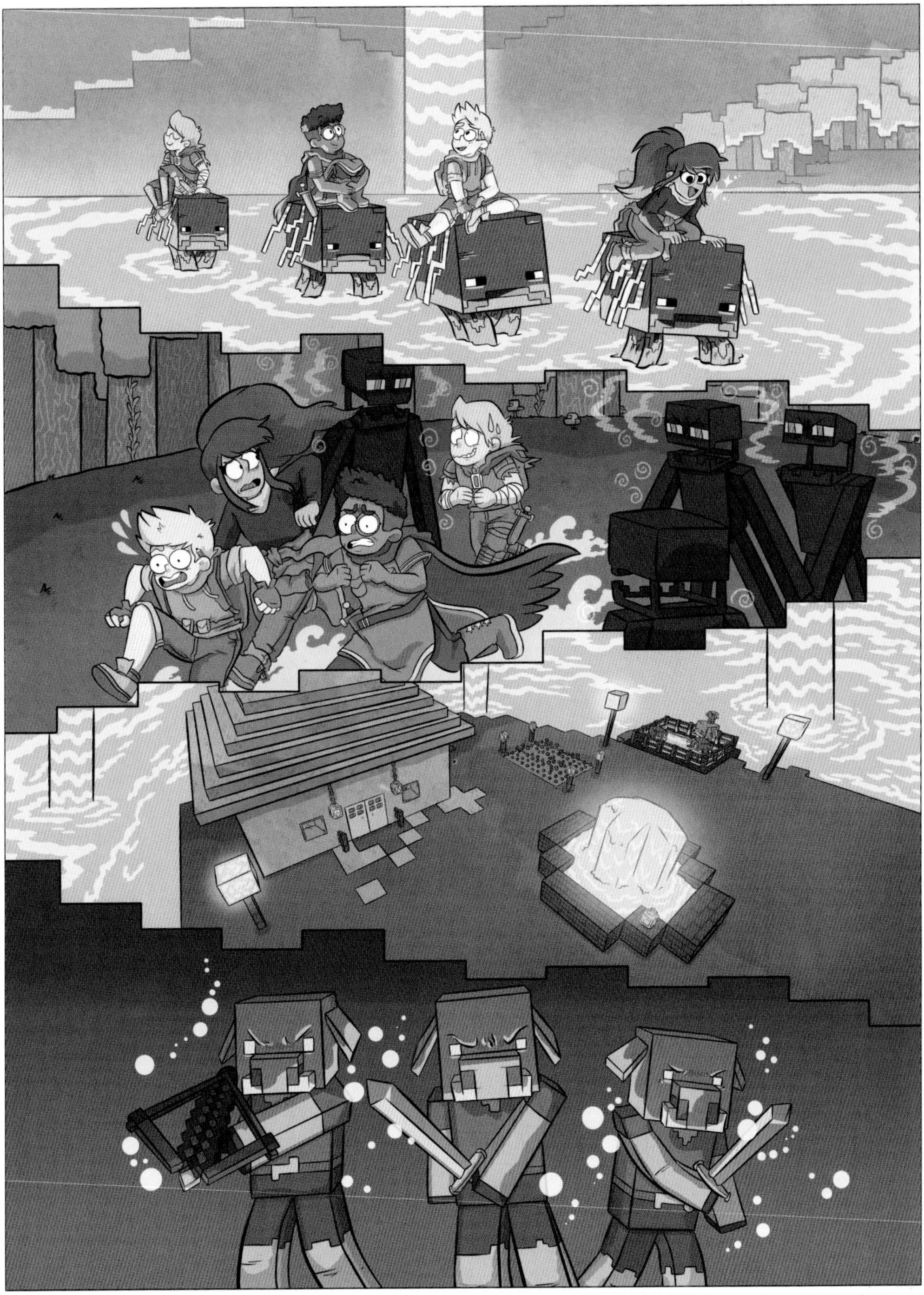

5 Final colored page

When I get the flatted pages back, I'll then add in shading, textures, and detail to the page! This is my favorite part of the process as you see the page really take shape here! It's really fun to look back on these pages and see the scrappy original next to the final polished page!

COMING SOON . . .

MINECRAFT™

WITHER WITHOUT YOU 3

Jump into the Overworld with the conclusion of the *Wither Without You* adventure series from the world's best-selling videogame **MINECRAFT!** ↗

After surviving the horrors of a zombie villager outbreak, the adventurers begin to make their way to Atria's hometown of Woodhaven. But the journey is far from a smooth one, and dangers lurk around every corner, as our heroes witness more evidence of the Wither's path of destruction across the Overworld.

With new allies at their side and an arsenal of magic at their disposal, Senan, Cahira, Orion, Atria, and Wilkie prepare themselves for the final explosive confrontation with the fearsome creature. But are they a match for the mysterious Wither?

AVAILABLE MAY 2022!